A

Gervais Fent... husband—ti... that Rachel as a wife and as a woman could want.

Victor de Lascelles was the most perfect of friends. It was he who had recognized the beauty of Rachel's singing voice and helped train it, giving her a source of strength and solace that stood her in good stead when her stepmother's hatred shadowed her life.

But now Rachel had discovered that her perfect husband was a perfect fraud. At the same time, her perfect friend gave proof positive that he wanted to be far more than that to her.

And Rachel found herself facing a decision that was perfectly impossible. . . .

(For a list of other Signet Regency Romances by Ellen Fitzgerald, please turn page. . . .)

About the Author

Ellen Fitzgerald is a pseudonym for a well-known romance writer. A graduate of the University of Southern California with a B.A. in English and an M.A. in Drama, Ms. Fitzgerald has also attended Yale University and has had numerous plays produced throughout the country. In her spare time, she designs and sells jewelry. Ms. Fitzgerald lives in New York City.

A Streak of Luck

Ellen Fitzgerald

A SIGNET BOOK

NEW AMERICAN LIBRARY

NAL BOOKS ARE AVAILABLE AT QUANTITY DISCOUNTS
WHEN USED TO PROMOTE PRODUCTS OR SERVICES. FOR
INFORMATION PLEASE WRITE TO PREMIUM MARKETING
DIVISION, NEW AMERICAN LIBRARY, 1633 BROADWAY,
NEW YORK, NEW YORK 10019.

SIGNET TRADEMARK REG. U.S. PAT. OFF. AND FOREIGN COUNTRIES
REGISTERED TRADEMARK—MARCA REGISTRADA
HECHO EN CHICAGO, U.S.A.

SIGNET, SIGNET CLASSIC, MENTOR, ONYX, PLUME, MERIDIAN and
NAL BOOKS are published by NAL Penguin Inc.,
1633 Broadway, New York, New York 10019

First Printing, July, 1987

1 2 3 4 5 6 7 8 9

PRINTED IN THE UNITED STATES OF AMERICA

I

1

It was a balmy spring evening, but the hour being late, there were few abroad on London's streets to enjoy the gentle winds or to appreciate a three-quarter moon sailing serenely through a few scattered clouds, an optical illusion, of course, since it was the clouds that were moving.

In the discreet purlieus of Brooks's, the play was still hot and heavy. Servants appeared every so often to replace candles which had burned beyond the halfway mark. They also filled glasses to such good effect that some players were in danger of slipping under the tables. Such libations had been refused, however, by two men who had been playing piquet. They had been hard at the game for three hours and as yet showed no signs of wishing to stop. They appeared to be well-matched, though it seemed that the older player was, perhaps, the better of the two.

That, at least, was the opinion of the Marquess of Dorne, who stood at a respectable distance watching the players. He had just voiced it to Mr. Charles Osmond, recently returned from Paris.

Mr. Osmond, tall, thin, and wearing garments that smacked of French tailoring, visited a look of active dislike upon the younger of the piquet players. "You'll not be telling me that the country bumpkin has bested our Gervais?" he said in acidulous tones.

"He's a canny player." The marquess smiled.

"A match for Gervais?" There was an eagerness to Osmond's speech, edged with a remembered anger. "Surely you will not tell me so?"

"You do not want to hear such news?"

"Does the creature have a name?" Mr. Osmond inquired. "I do not remember having seen him before."

" 'Tis Villiers. Sir Harry Villiers. He has won the last three games—a real streak of luck."

"I thought that our Gervais had cornered all the luck," Mr. Osmond observed. "At least that was my impression. In fact, when I had the misfortune to play with him, I was inclined to credit that old tale about the fortunate Fentons, one born every generation and all that."

"I do not believe that I have heard that bit of apochrypha—or will you tell me it's the truth?" A derisive smile played about the marquess's well-shaped mouth.

"It goes back a few hundred years—to the Dissolution of the Monasteries, when a Fenton, not a papist by the way, saved the life of a Cistercian abbot, hiding him in a secret room and later seeing that he escaped to France. It is said that the grateful cleric, seeing Fenton lose heavily at cards, told him that his son would win back the family fortune. He also said that one in every generation would, er . . . inherit that particular streak of luck."

"Very illuminating." Dorne showed very white teeth in a wider, even more derisive smile. "I put the tale in the same category as St. George's dragon." His gaze was once more on the players. "Judging from young Gervais's expression, he is still going down heavily. However, I am sure that he is under the fatal impression that his luck will turn . . . or, rather, return—a dangerous fallacy, my dear Osmond."

"And one which I hope will persist," Mr. Osmond murmured. "Do you know anything about Sir Harry Villiers?"

"What do you know about him, Osmond?" Dorne countered.

"I've not seen him about London . . . so I expect he is from the provinces."

The marquess nodded. "Chadwick brought him. He said that Sir Harry is rich, respectable, and loathes London. Still, he is here to purchase a house. He is recently remarried and his bride longs for a London address. I have the impression that she is quite young, quite lovely, and a model of rectitude."

Mr. Osmond raised thin eyebrows. "And you say she wishes to live in London?"

"In common with the More named Hannah, she is eager to improve the morals of the working classes or some such thing."

"Not a Methodist!" Mr. Osmond exclaimed in horror.

"Yes, I believe she is of that persuasion." The marquess smiled and signaled to one of the servants, who came to his side immediately. "Ah, Luke, my dear fellow, good evening."

"Good evening, your lordship," the man said with a touch of obsequiousness.

"I noticed that you were near yon table." He indicated the piquet players. "How is our friend Lord Sayre progressing?"

"You know that it is not our policy—" the servant began in a low voice.

"I know it is not"—the marquess opened a closed hand and displayed a sovereign—"but it would do my heart good to have that information, at least I hope it would."

Through some hasty sleight of hand, the sovereign vanished from the marquess's palm. The servant lowered his voice. "Young Lord Sayre has waged his stable and lost."

"Ah, that was worth a sovereign," the marquess murmured as the man moved away. He smiled at his companion and received a brilliant smile in return.

"I think it worth two sovereigns or even three," Mr. Osmond said, "since it has been suggested that it is not the first wager of the evening."

"I believe . . ." The marquess's eyes were on the players again. They were rising. "I believe," he repeated, "that it is the last for our friend Sayre. Is it a trick of the light, do you imagine, that makes him appear so pale?"

"He is quite white," Mr. Osmond observed. "He might even be contemplating the Fleet." His eyes narrowed and there was an ugly look about his mouth. "He has put others there, myself included. Damnable spot, Dorne. I hope he rots in it."

"A most unpleasant notion," Dorne drawled. "However, if he is the favored of Fortune, something might happen to prevent that."

"I would imagine that the abbot is unlikely to rise from his grave," Mr. Osmond murmured as he watched winner and loser move across the room and into another salon.

Though he had drunk nothing stronger than water, Gervais felt oddly light-headed. He did not hesitate to attribute that particular symptom to his losses. He, who had succumbed to the family belief that the Fentons of Sayre, born with that fabled "streak of luck," could not lose, had lost heavily, so heavily that he strongly doubted that he could remain free of Newgate or the Fleet or some other hole. Worse than that, he had lost his horses, his beautiful Samson among them. He could not dwell on the stallion or anything else at this moment—but he would not postpone that time of reckoning any later than the morning. He glanced at the watch at his waist. The morning that commenced at nine was less than five hours away.

"Lord Sayre," Sir Harry Villiers said tentatively. "Might I persuade you to have a drink with me now?"

Meeting his late opponent's eyes, Gervais found them full of a sympathy that surprised him as it annoyed him. He had not expected such an emotion from a man who had just won a hundred thousand pounds from him and his stable to boot. Yet, a drink would be welcome, and, it occurred to him, he would like to know more about Sir Harry's luck. He said, "I thank you, sir, I would be delighted." They sat down at a table near the windows and, a few minutes later, sipping an excellent French wine, Gervais, forcing a smile, said, "You are an uncommonly fine player, Sir Harry."

"The cards were running my way." Sir Harry studied his companion's face.

"I would not attribute it all to luck," Gervais said.

"I hope"—Sir Harry gave him a piercing look—"that you have not relied too heavily upon your luck."

Gervais stared at him in surprise. "You have heard the tale, I see."

"It was told me immediately I asked your identity earlier this evening."

"You were doubly fortunate, then"—Gervais managed another smile—"in not refusing my invitation and in winning."

"I am inclined to discount old wives' tales. But enough. I fear you lost very heavily."

Gervais stiffened. "That is hardly your concern, sir. My debts will be paid. You have but to call upon me tomorrow. I will give you my direction."

Sir Harry said gently, "I am not concerned about that, sir. There is something else that weighs heavily upon me, something I wish to tell you and which I must beg you not to regard as an insult. I must add that I like and respect you. If I cannot approve the lack of caution that led you to plunge so deeply, I do understand that heretofore you have been extremely fortunate."

"I have been," Gervais admitted wryly. "But," he added acerbically, "I do not need to be read homilies upon my wicked ways."

"Your ways are not wicked, my lord, I am quite convinced of that. But we digress. I pray you will let me tell you about my daughter."

"Your . . . daughter, sir?" Gervais responded confusedly. "I am not sure I understand—"

"You must let me explain," Sir Harry interrupted.

"I, er . . . find this rather more awkward than I would have wished, but I pray you will bear with me."

It was more the anxiety that he read in the older man's eyes than his strange words about his daughter that kept Gervais in his chair and listening rather than returning to his house and making a list of the assets he must needs sell to satisfy this horrendous debt. Until this fateful evening he had had little congress with the word "debt." Now it stood fair to haunt him for the rest of a life that promised to be far less comfortable than the first twenty-six years of his existence.

"My daughter," Sir Harry began, "is beautiful and damned."

Gervais sat straighter in his chair and the servant Luke, who at Sir Harry's bidding had filled their glasses again, came near to dropping his tray.

"Your, er . . . daughter—" Gervais began.

Sir Harry held up his hand. "Bear with me," he begged. "I was being facetious, or sarcastic, if you will. But be that as it may, I am partially to blame for her current state of . . . damnation, if you will. Her position grieves me and such is my own that I can do very little to help her. The condition I have mentioned has little to do with her character, which, in my estimation, is admirable." He took another sip of wine. "You see, I am wed a second time—after many years of being a widower. My wife is young." He flushed. "She can give my daugher two years only and consequently is hardly of an age or inclination to be a stepmother." He paused and frowned, saying more to himself than to his now interested if confused listener, "I had not taken that into account when we wed. Also I had not taken into account her very firm religious convictions. She had the pleasure of meeting Hannah More . . . I do not know if you are acquainted with the lady?"

"I know her by reputation, of course. She is a power among the Methodists," Gervais said.

"A power, yes," Sir Harry sighed. "And my wife follows her teaching to the letter. I sometimes feel that were she not presently breeding, she would want to convert the world!''

"How uncomfortable," Gervais observed. He reddened. "I beg your pardon," he said hastily.

"I pray you will not," Sir Harry returned wryly. "It can be a most uncomfortable situation for those of us whose beliefs are not er . . . ironclad. Rachel, my daughter, is of their number, as I am myself. Consequently, my wife is unhappy with her. She, being, as she fondly imagines, of the chosen, has little sympathy with those she honestly imagines to be among the 'fallen.' ''

"She believes your daughter to be fallen, sir?"

"And damned.'' Sir Harry grimaced. "Rachel is strong-willed and impatient with what she chooses to term 'cant.' She has made the error of laughing at some of the opinions of Samantha, my wife. This attitude has naturally widened the gap between them—though Rachel, on my account, I am sure, did make a determined effort not to antagonize her. Yet, I fear that from the first, her very presence antagonized Samantha, given those strict fundamentalist views I have mentioned."

"She . . . did not want to be a stepmother, possibly?" Gervais hazarded.

"I imagine that that was part of it, but mainly there is Rachel's heritage which my wife cannot stomach. As a Christian, she has a marked antipathy to those she terms 'Israelites.' '' Sir Harry paused and sighed.

"Israelites, sir?" Gervais repeated in some confusion. "Your daughter . . ."

"Her mother, my Miriam, was the daughter of Esdras Medina, a banker to whom I was forced to go after a loss at the tables comparable with your own. She happened to be present when I arrived, and though you may not believe in love at first sight, I can only tell you that we saw each other and loved to the point that the barriers raised against us by her parents and mine were as nothing."

Sir Harry was looking at him but Gervais had the distinct impression that his companion was gazing into a well-remembered and much-mourned past. He said gently, "I can imagine there must have been difficulties, given the prejudice on both sides."

Sir Harry's gaze narrowed and fastened on Gervias's face. "You know about such prejudices, my lord?"

"I have heard that the Jews are very clannish, sir."

"Very," Sir Harry agreed ruefully. "Miriam and I used to liken each other to Romeo and Juliet. I will not trouble you with a recounting of our courtship. Suffice to say that our parents were both adamant. Ours was a runaway marriage at Gretna Green. She tried to see her father afterward, but was told that some manner of funeral service had taken place and she was mourned as dead." Another sigh escaped him. "It was a terrible blow. She had been very fond of him and he had been devoted to her. She even tried to call upon Medina at his bank, but was ordered from the premises. Her brothers and sisters were equally adamant—to their minds she was dead."

Gervais shivered. "I had no idea they could be so cruel."

"I have called them cruel and raged against them," Sir Harry said, "but of recent date I have found myself wondering if that cruelty were not based upon worse cruelties suffered in the name of prejudice. Undoubtedly they were only too aware of the problems awaiting Miriam." Again he paused, looking grimly now into a space filled with memories. He continued, "My marriage was not well-received by my parents. My father died shortly afterward and my mother and older sister insisted on attributing his death from overeating and overdrinking to the shock occasioned by my choice of bride. My mother aired her feelings to all who would listen, and Miriam was cut by some of her friends. My friends, however, took to her immediately and called me damned lucky. In spite of the circumstances attendant on our marriage, we were very happy for two years.

Then Miriam conceived. She was a slender, small girl
and her pregnancy was not easy. Rachel proved to be a
large baby and Miriam never quite recovered from her
birth. I took her to the country and a year later she
died." His face darkened. "It took me a long time to
recover from that blow. I traveled whenever it was
possible and left my daughter to the care of nurses.

"She was seven when I came back to stay at Villiers
Court, my country house. I found that she had been
cruelly treated by a nurse who had, alas, the same strict
Christian persuasions as my wife. She was shy and wild.
A groom had taught her to ride, and she loved it. She
also loved to sing."

"To sing?" Gervais questioned. "At that early age?"

"Yes, she had a high, sweet little voice, and a
neighbor, who had been Miriam's best friend before she
died—the Countess de Lascelles, the widow of a nobleman killed in the French Revolution—told me that
Rachel already had a love for music and ought to study
the harp or the pianoforte. By one of those happy
chances, she had a young cousin, Victor de Lascelles,
who was supporting himself by teaching music. She
diffidently suggested that Rachel study with him, and I
agreed." Another sigh shook him. "Until recently, sir,
her singing was one of the joys of my life. But my
wife . . ."

"She does not like music?"

"She likes church music—hymns, only. It . . . is hell,
my lord. I must separate the two of them—for my peace
of mind and for that of my wife and my daughter." He
fixed tortured eyes on Gervais's face. "I must rescue
Rachel . . . that is why I have told you her story. I am
afraid that if she is not soon removed from my household, she will do something desperate."

Gervais's gaze had narrowed. He had an uncomfortable feeling that Sir Harry's reason for recounting
this unhappy history had more than a little to do with
his losses that night. Was the man suggesting. . . ? He
forbore to dwell on what he might possibly be

suggesting. He had an impulse to rise and bid him a cold farewell, but in spite of himself he was moved by his companion's evident anguish. He said, "You do not think she would put an end—"

"No," Sir Harry said quickly, "but she might run away and be lost to me. I never dreamed that when I wed . . . I was not aware of Samantha's beliefs. I was worried only because of the difference in our ages. Yet she seemed honestly fond of me and eager . . . Enough of that, sir. Her feelings toward Rachel are not unknown and she has managed to drop remarks that have alienated some of the families that received us before my marriage. There is prejudice still . . . and was even before I married again. There was, however, a young man who did want to marry Rachel. I do not think she loved him—but Samantha formed a friendship with his sister, and rather recently his family sent him on the Grand Tour.

"I am aware, my lord, that what I am telling you is in the worst possible taste, but it is very near my heart. I would very much like you to meet my daughter, sir. As for your losses tonight—"

"Damn!" Gervais exclaimed explosively. "Are you suggesting. . . ?" He rose.

"Sit down, lad." Sir Harry caught at his sleeve. "I know I am expressing myself very badly, but I pray you will listen to me."

Angry as Gervais was, he was not proof against the anguish in Sir Harry's tones. He resumed his seat but he said determinedly, "I will not consider—"

"My lord," Sir Harry interrupted, "I must tell you that I want only for you to meet my daughter. I ask nothing more than that. You are a man of address. You are also sympathetic. I feel that a person of your caliber would appreciate Rachel, even given her so-called despised heritage. However, I would never expect you to settle your debts in so unorthodox a manner. I know that it would war against your integrity.

"I appeal to you, my lord, because I have been virtually cut off from polite society—save for the country families in my corner of Devonshire—and while I would not count myself an outcast, I have had little congress with many there. I am a bookish sort of a fellow and I let my steward see to the farms and so forth. In the decade before my second marriage, I was perfectly happy in my daughter's company. We were very close. However, the situation has now become untenable and I am at my wits' end trying to find a solution to my liking. I ask you only to meet Rachel, and perhaps you, who have so wide an acquaintance here in London, might be able to suggest some young man . . . Sir, I am quite desperate. I do not want to lose my daughter and Rachel is at the tag end of her patience.'' There were actual tears in Sir Harry's eyes and there was no doubting either his anguish or his sincerity.

Gervais regarded him with a mixture of pity, anger, and confusion. His whole self warred against the excusing of a debt of honor in exchange for his possible offer of marriage. On any other tongue, it would have amounted to an unpardonable insult, one that might easily have merited a challenge. However, in the face of his companion's misery, he could excuse that insult. Furthermore, the situation did not differ greatly from that attendant upon an ordinary marriage. Many a groom proposed because of the size of the dowry rather than the bride's attractions. He had never needed to think along those lines and, he told himself angrily, not even his present circumstances warranted a decision inimical to his every principle! Yet he had found himself much intrigued as well as moved by Sir Harry's situation or, rather, that of the beautiful Rachel. He himself had little tolerance for cant. His own beliefs acknowledged a superior being and little else. During the course of the narrative, he had found himself entirely in sympathy with the girl. He could imagine how very uncomfortable she must be, especially given the happiness and the freedom she had enjoyed while her father remained single.

It was with a combination of embarrassment and

surprise at his own acquiescence that he nodded and said stiffly, "I find that I would enjoy meeting your daughter, sir. But I must hasten to assure you—"

"I know all that you, as the man of honor you obviously are, must want to tell me, my lord, and I assure you, no pressure will be exerted once we have arrived at Villiers Court. My daughter, I might add, is headstrong and as highly principled as yourself. Were she aware of this conversation, I feel her reactions would be similar to your own. We will merely say that you are the son of one of my old friends, if you will not mind the imposture?"

The commitment was upon him. He could not now offer any response but one of acquiescence. He did say, "As for the debt, Sir Harry, that must have no bearing on this situation. I will speak to my man of business in the morrow, and there is the matter of my stable."

"My lord, I beg you, were it not for Rachel's present misery, I would not insist that you ignore the debt for the nonce and come with me tomorrow—but whether you find her to your liking or not, perhaps you will be favorably impressed enough to make a recommendation such as I have mentioned."

Again, and much to his own surprise, Gervais said, "Very well, tomorrow, Sir Harry."

"I am much in your debt, my lord," the latter said.

Gervais smiled wryly. "I think it may be safely said, sir, that that particular shoe fits my foot far better than yours."

In his present confused state, Gervais was not aware of the Marquess of Dorne, who had stood in the doorway for some little time, and nor had he noticed Luke, who had made himself busy in the section of the room conveniently close to the table Sir Harry had chosen. With something less than his usual buoyant step, Gervais came outside and found himself gazing up at a paling sky. His surprise increased as, on consulting his watch again, he found it close on six in the morning of a day which would end in or near Devonshire.

He must needs send a message to Lord and Lady
Frazier. He had been expected at a rout in their garden.
He grimaced. He had been receiving quite a few
invitations from the Fraziers, neighbors in Norham and
longtime friends of his family. They had a daughter,
Lady Charlotte, whom he had known all of his life, and
he had gone to Cambridge with Lord Anthony Frazier,
their son. The three of them had, in fact, been friends
all through their childhood, riding the five miles that lay
between their estates as often as three times a week. He
had always enjoyed speaking to Lady Charlotte, a calm,
no-nonsense girl who knew as much about fishing and
hunting as her brother or himself.

Of late, he had seen her quite often. They went riding
together in Hyde Park and he had danced with her at
subscription balls in Almack's. Her parents, he knew,
expected that he would offer for her, and he himself,
having never been afflicted by the Grand Passion, had
been more than half-inclined to fulfill these
expectations.

Charlotte, while not precisely beautiful, was pretty,
and her background, of course, was impeccable. She
would make a good wife, a good hostess, and a good
mother—but she was not exciting. His Aunt Lily, a
longtime friend of the Fraziers, had waxed highly
enthusiastic over the possible union. He guessed that she
had discussed her hopes with the Fraziers, mother and
daughter. Thinking of that, he was, as always,
conscious of irritation. He guessed that they were
already planning an announcement for the *Morning
Post* and were debating as to whether the ceremony
should be held at St.-Martin-in-the-Fields or St. James's
Church. Little did they know that at this moment, their
hopes had been robbed of any foundation. He could no
more support a bride than . . .

He forbore to follow that train of thought. Yet those
that came in its place were singularly comfusing. On
thinking of Sir Harry's daughter, he could not help
being curious and he discovered within himself a desire

to see this beleaguered beauty. Yet he hoped he had not given Sir Harry any inkling that he would be willing to ignore a debt of honor. He exhaled a long breath that bore every evidence of being a sigh. He must, he decided wearily, forget it for the nonce—for he had promised he would accompany the man to Villiers Court, and that came under the heading of Honor too.

2

Rachel Villiers ran her hands through her tangled and luxuriant mass of blue-black hair. She glared at Anne-Marie de Lascelles quite as if she were the one causing her offense on this bright spring afternoon. She said vehemently, "I cannot find half my wardrobe, or rather, Phoebe cannot. The creature would not have dared to order it, were it not that Papa is away. And I ask you—how will a mere infant appreciate the view over the lake and the gardens?"

Anne-Marie, as fair as Rachel was dark and with blue eyes several shades lighter than those of her friend, looked equally indignant. "It is too bad—to annex your rooms when she's not even dropped the brat!"

"My love"—the Countess de Lascelles looked up from her embroidery frame—"where do you find these dreadful expressions?" She spoke with the French accent that her daughter, born in Paris but leaving it under the straw of a farm cart at the age of one, did not possess. She continued, "I, too, find it *très fâcheux!*"

"She is more than merely disagreeable, Maman. She is a veritable thorn in the side of poor Rachel." She turned back to Rachel. "It is a marvel she did not put you on the third floor with the servants."

"Or in the kitchen, where I must needs sleep beneath the stove and scrape the ashes from the grate like Cinderella?" Rachel actually grinned. She sobered

21

quickly as her indignation with her stepmother increased. "Mrs. Graves has done her best with the rooms allotted me, but they are dark. I am sure there is method in Samantha's madness. She wants to make me as uncomfortable as possible so that I will run away. I vow, were it not for Papa, I would! Fortunately, these rooms are far away from my stepmother's shell-like ears so that I may practice without giving her the migraine."

"The migraine, indeed," Anne-Marie actually snorted. "Victor insists that you have the voice of a Pasta or a Catalani!"

"He will always exaggerate." Rachel laughed.

"He never exaggerates," Anne-Marie contradicted. "Music is his deity, as well you know, and one of his oft-repeated regrets is that you can never be heard in public."

"It is one of mine, as well," Rachel said frankly. "I am sure I would adore the life of a singer—seeing Rome and Berlin and Naples."

"My love"—the countess shook both head and finger—"you would be ruined. No one would receive you."

"Do you think that I care a fig for that? There are precious few who have received me, and since the advent of my stepmother, that number has lessened considerably. If she were to have her way, not even you would welcome me."

"Rachel!" Anne-Marie leapt to her feet. "How dare you even breathe such a thing! You are my dearest friend."

"Yes, that is too bad of you, Rachel." The countess frowned. "You know in what esteem I held your dear mother."

"I pray you will calm down," Rachel hastened to say. "I said 'if'! Did you not hear me? I know that I can depend on you both." She sighed. "Oh, dear, Anne-Marie, I shall miss you when you are wed and living in London."

"How you talk!" Anne-Marie scoffed. "I have received no offers."

"If the Earl of Stirling does not come up to scratch within a day of his return from Inverness, I shall be extremely surprised," Rachel said bluntly.

Anne-Marie blushed. "Douglas . . . er, the earl will not be back for another six weeks and two days."

"And how many hours, minutes, and seconds?" Rachel teased.

"If I should marry," Anne-Marie said earnestly, "I will see that you are not only my maid of honor but also my frequent guest in London. And . . ." She paused as the clock on the mantelshelf in their small parlor emitted four crystalline peals.

"Oh!" Rachel jumped up. "I had no idea it was so late. The she-dragon will have something to say about this, no doubt." She kissed Anne-Marie and her mother, adding as the latter started to rise from her embroidery frame, "No, no, stay. Anne-Marie may see me out, if she chooses."

"Of course she chooses!" Anne-Marie exclaimed.

"I will have your horse brought around, at least." The countess started to rise again.

"There is no need. I have him tethered to a post outside your door." Rachel blew her another kiss, and with Anne-Marie behind her, hurried down a long hall to the door.

Once outside, Rachel pulled up her skirt and tucked it into the breeches she wore beneath it, winking at Anne-Marie. "I did not wish to scandalize your dear mama."

"Do you think I did not know that?" Anne-Marie giggled. "And I must tell you that she did, too. Your skirt was a mite hiked up, and Mama's sight is excellent."

"Oh, dear," Rachel sighed. She added defensively, "I cannot ride astride in skirts, and it's much more comfortable this way."

"Be sure to pull your skirt down all the way before you go inside your house."

"I will, never fear." Rachel grimaced. "As you know, I used always to ride in breeches before the arrival of sweet Samantha."

"You were sixteen then. You are turned eighteen, and come November, will be nineteen."

"Anne-Marie, if you are going to chastise me too—" Rachel began.

"I am not, I am thinking only of you. She can be so horrid. And to turn you out of the rooms you have had all your life, I declare, I . . . I could bite her." Anne-Marie suddenly looked quite fierce.

Rachel flung her arms around her friend. "Oh, my dearest, I do not know what I would do without you."

Anne-Marie regarded her soberly. "I wish there were someone else to fend for you, Rachel. If only your mother were alive."

Rachel laughed. "If she were, then there would be no Samantha."

"Of course there would not be." Anne-Marie also laughed. "I do talk nonsense, do I not?"

"It is the sort of nonsense I like to hear." Rachel smiled and then sobered. "Do not go away from here too quickly, Anne-Marie."

"It will not be tomorrow," her friend said with an equal seriousness. "And who knows, Rachel, you might be the first of us to be wed."

"And the moon is made from green cheese, my love," Rachel responded dryly. She swung up in her saddle and with a wave of her hand she was off, urging her horse into a canter.

As she came out of the carriageway, Rachel's dark brows drew together. She was visited by a fugitive wish that she might ride to the ends of the earth rather than to the house she had once called home. It no longer bore that designation. It was only a place where she was temporarily residing until . . . Her frown deepened. "I cannot," she muttered. "Where would I go if I chose to run away?" She emitted a wry chuckle. "To the Jews?" Another chuckle escaped her. That door was shut against her as tightly as some of those in and around Barnstaple Bay, the village that lay closest to the Court. She had another, much more exotic suggestion for herself. Vienna. Victor de Lascelles spoke about that city almost as reverently as his native Paris. "It is where music is king," he had told her. "Mozart lived there and now there is Beethoven. It is close to Prague, too. Were you able to take the place for which you were intended by the muses, you would sing on the stages of all three cities, for I count Paris, too—five, I mean, for there are Rome and Naples. Yours is not a voice that should be heard only in a few scattered parlors."

"You grow extravagant, Victor," Rachel muttered, repeating words she had recently addressed to him during one of their lessons. She shook her head. To perform in public for money would, as the countess had contended, close all those doors which yet remained open to her. Women who went on the stage, be it as actresses or singers, were damned by society. They might have noble lovers but never noble husbands, or at least not very often. There were actresses who had become duchesses, and singers might have done so too, for all she knew. They did not, however, come from families which could trace their ancestry back to a Villiers who had ridden across the field of Hastings at the side of William the Conqueror.

"Yet to stay here . . ." Rachel whispered, unwillingly conjuring up an image of Samantha, the stepmother who was only two years and three months her senior.

Their closeness in years had embarrassed her father. She grimaced as she remembered his naive and hopeful words when he had told her of his intentions. "You could be . . . sisters. I hope you will be."

Samantha, golden and glowing, meeting her step-daughter for the first time, had gazed at her out of narrowed eyes, an expression that had warred with her effusive greeting. "Oh, my dear, your papa has told me so very much about you. I have been on pins and needles wanting to meet you."

Subsequently, Rachel thought with a wry grin, Samantha had collected all those "pins and needles" with an idea of puncturing her stepdaughter's confidence as well as her position in the community.

It was really amazing that in a little over two years Samantha had managed to insert wedges between Rachel and many of the people who had once called themselves her good friends. Rachel guessed that she had played upon deep-rooted prejudices, partially forgotten after the death of her mother. This suspicion had been confirmed at a recent hunt when she had heard her stepmother saying to Sir Richard Linley, an old friend of her father's, "Dear Rachel does sit her horse astonishingly well, do you not agree?"

"I think she sits it well, ma'am, but she has been riding most of her life, so I cannot think it astonishing," had been his blunt reply.

"Yes, but *they* are not generally sportsmen, you must agree?"

"The Villiers family?" Sir Richard had not immediately understood her. "I must contradict you, Lady Villiers. Sir Harry's family have been avid hunters and—"

"I was not speaking about his ancestors," Samantha had pursued. "I meant that his late wife's connections have not generally been known for sports—beyond the counting house." She had laughed lightly.

Sir Richard, bless his heart, had stared at her coldly and said in accents that matched his stare, "To my thinking, Rachel's a damned fine girl and I never heard that a seat on a horse was inherited." He had turned away, leaving her stepmother blushing—more in anger than confusion, she was sure.

The fact that these barbed comments did not always fall on such fallow ground had been brought home to her in many ways. It seemed to Rachel that when she attended church of a Sunday, there were now many who regarded her curiously and even askance, as if, indeed, she thought indignantly, she, baptized at that very font, had no right to cross that holy threshold. She thought it very likely that her stepmother would have been only too pleased to see her forced to wear a yellow star as

Jews had in certain medieval communities. Her mother must have loved her father greatly to have braved the disapproval of not only her parents and his living relatives but also his friends and acquaintances on his native heath.

In the years before his second marriage, she had enjoyed so close a communion with her father that she had barely noticed that there were some doors closed against her—but with the arrival of Samantha and her subsequent questions regarding certain of the people who had not presented calling cards, she had become all too aware of that. More fuel had been added to that particular flame because the one person whom Samantha tried desperately to charm remained aloof for quite another reason.

The Countess de Lascelles, among whose ancestors was the Angoulême who had married King John and who was also distantly related to the Capet family, which had been and now was again the ruling clan of France, steadfastly refused the invitations issued by the new Lady Villiers, and nor did she make any effort to meet the bride. Furthermore, when they had met at various functions, the countess's attitude had been gently condescending.

Rachel laughed. Of late, Samantha had been dropping disparaging remarks, some based on neighborhood gossip concerning the fact that the countess seemed in no hurry to return to France in the train of her distant cousin Louis XVIII. However, her main target was Victor de Lascelles, the countess's second cousin.

"I do think it is unwise to allow so handsome a young man to teach the pianoforte and voice to impressionable young girls. There have been many unfortunate incidents arising from such situations."

This comment, addressed to Sir Harry in Rachel's presence, had brought only laughter and the light response that if he did not trust Victor, which he did, he would trust Rachel not to make a cake of herself.

"And," he had added, "I would be extremely surprised if Victor were to make advances to Rachel. His main passion in life is music."

"But," Samantha had continued determinedly, "when they are alone in the music room . . ."

"He is putting her through her vocal exercises, my dear."

"I feel that in her best interests, a third party ought to be present," Samantha had continued insistently.

"There is a third party present, my love." He had still spoken lightly, but with an edge to his voice that ought to have warned her to abandon the argument. "We call her Euterpe."

"Oh, dear, I do wish you would be serious," Samantha had complained.

"I am entirely serious and I think we will have no further discussion on this particular subject."

Samantha had not attempted to prolong the argument but she had not dropped the subject. She had, instead, mentioned it to the friends she had made in the community, with the result that poor Victor had lost two of his pupils. He himself had appeared indifferent to that loss. "They were most prodigiously untalented, my dear. The strain on my ears was immense."

That there had also been a strain on his slender means, he had not mentioned. Rachel's horse suddenly snorted and she realized she had been holding the reins far too tightly. She shook her head, wishing that she need not return home. The thought of conversing with Samantha and pretending that she did not understand her sly digs was irksome. Her father ought to have been home by now. She wondered what was keeping him so long away and prayed it was nothing untoward. It was close to two hundred miles to London and road hazards must not be discounted. Fortunately the weather had been generally fine. Still . . . She came to a stop, as, arriving at the turnoff to Villiers Court, she heard the sound of a carriage. In another second the vehicle had rounded a bend in the road and she saw Jude, their coachman, driving, while Enoch, their postilion, was mounted on one of the four horses. There was another horseman accompanying the carriage. She had an impression of dark auburn hair and a handsome countenance dominated by flashing eyes, the color of which she was not sure, for he had ridden past her very swiftly. Then the post chaise drew to a stop and and the horseman, wheeling around, came back, as, at that same moment, her father thrust open the coach door.

"Rachel!" he exclaimed.

"Oh, Papa." She rode up to the open door. "Oh, I am so glad you are home!" There was a wealth of love in her tone, and behind it, unspoken confidences which, from the instant comprehension in his eyes, she knew he understood.

He said gently, "I am glad to be home, and as I wrote, here is Lord Sayre come to visit us."

"As you wrote?" she questioned with a slight frown, just as the man on horseback rode up. "I did not know you were returning today or that you intended to bring anyone with you."

"You did not know?" He frowned. "But I sent messages to your stepmother . . ." His frown deepened. Then, looking up at his guest, he added, "I would like you to meet my daughter, Gervais. This is Rachel."

"I thought it must be, sir," the horseman said. His eyes, which were gray-green, lingered on Rachel's face. "I am delighted to make your acquaintance, Miss Villiers."

Meeting that candid gaze, Rachel blushed, aware now of her breeches and her tangled locks, neither of which would have been in evidence had she known they were expected today. "I have been riding," she murmured. "And I . . ." she brought up a hand to thrust her hair back, "I am glad to know you, my lord."

Sir Harry said quickly, "My messages must not have arrived. My daughter did not know we were expected. Gervais, my dear, is the son of my old friend, the

Marquess of Sayre, unhappily deceased since last I was in London. We had fallen out of touch, which was why, I expect, that I was not informed.''

"That is the way of it, Sir Harry," Gervais said easily, "It was a very sudden thing."

"I am sorry," Rachel said quickly. "It must have been very hard for you, if 'twas unexpected."

"Very," he agreed.

She noted a slight flush on his face and wondered if it were a new grief. In that same instance she thought of offering more sympathy and decided against it. He might want to put that recent sorrow behind him.

Sir Harry said, "Shall we continue on to the house? I am sure that Gervais might like to rest. We left the inn at seven."

Gervais was still looking at Rachel. "It was an easy ride, though. I find this very pleasant country."

"It is beautiful, is it not?" she agreed. "You are not familiar with Devonshire, my lord?"

"No, my roots are deep in the soil of Northumberland."

"Ah, a Border lord." She smiled.

"Quite, though I reject the pillage, the burnings, and the sheep thefts that the name implies," he said gravely.

"I am sure that Rachel was not implying—" Sir Harry began.

"No, I was not, and I suspect that his lordship is teasing me," Rachel interrupted, and then blushed. "At least I hope so."

"You are quite right," Gervais responded, his gravity gone and his eyes alight with mischief.

"There, Papa!" she said triumphantly.

Sir Harry gave her a fond glance. "Then we are all right and tight and, again, I suggest that we conclude our journey." His eyes lingered on Rachel. "However, my love, I think it would be more to the point if you were to precede us."

There was a grave look in his eyes now, one she had no trouble interpreting. Her face changed and her eyes grew somber. "Yes, of course, I do understand." She urged her horse forward and in a few seconds was lost to view.

"May I catch up with her?" Gervais inquired eagerly.

"No," Sir Harry said quickly. "My wife would have much to say about her attire, especially if she were to learn that we had met en route."

"Oh, I do understand." There was an edge to Gervais's tone. He added, "You did not exaggerate, Sir Harry. She is quite the most beautiful girl that I have ever had the pleasure of meeting or seeing."

"Do you really believe that, Gervais?" Sir Harry said with an excitement he could not quell. He tried to temper it, as he added, "She was not really at her best. I am afraid that it was I who first allowed her to ride astride and in breeches."

"It is a pity that all females do not follow her example," Gervais said. "They would be much more comfortable. I would hate to ride sidesaddle myself."

"That is exactly my point. However, I fear I only added to the existing onus . . ." He loosed a long sigh and then said abruptly, "Shall we go now?"

"Please," Gervais assented.

Rachel, coming from the stable, hurried into the house through the kitchen. With a smiling greeting to Mrs. Blake, the cook, and her helpers, she ran hastily into a passageway and up the back stairs. She had almost reached her chamber when she remembered that she had been relocated. She was starting down the hall when she was arrested by a slight shriek.

"What are you wearing?" Lady Villiers demanded in accents of horror.

Rachel came to a stop. She visited an annoyed look on her stepmother's shocked countenance. That annoyance was evenly divided between the lady and her own failure to remember the warnings issued by the countess and Anne-Marie. In the excitement attendant upon her father's return and her meeting with his

extremely handsome young companion, she had not
pulled her gown out of her breeches! Consequently she
had now to face a wearisome homily on her reprehen-
sible conduct. She said, "This is the way I used always
to ride with Papa. It was at his suggestion that I donned
this sort of attire."

"I am sure that poor dear Harry never said anything
of the sort." Lady Villiers glared at her. "I am
sure . . ." She paused as Silas, one of the footmen,
came up the stairs. "Well, Silas?"

"Beggin' yer pardon, milady, but Sir 'Arry's back."

"Oh, yes, and he is bringing a guest, I believe?"

"Yes, ma'am."

"Thank you, Silas, you may go."

"You did not tell me that Papa was expected today,"
Rachel commented coldly.

"Did I not? I daresay it slipped my mind," Lady
Villiers said with equal coldness. She added, "It is a
marvel you did not encounter them, and in that dis-
gusting attire. You will change at once and do not let me
see you in such dreadful garments ever again." She
turned on her heel and hurried to a mirror that hung at
the head of the stairs. Examining her reflection, she
pushed a stray lock of hair away from her face and
smilingly descended the stairs.

Gervais, coming into a larger house than he had
expected, and Palladian in design, was impressed by a
hall rising two stories, decorated with Grecian intaglios
and the requisite marble busts set in various niches. A
sweeping marble staircase led to the upper floors and a
patterned marble floor was half-hidden by a
magnificent Oriental rug. His host, as he had already
half-suspected, was a man of considerable substance,
and two days spent in his company had engendered a
respect and a liking for him that made him wish heartily
that they had met under less constricting circumstances.
Those feelings had risen to an even higher peak once he
had met one who, as he had not hesitated to tell her

father, was incredibly beautiful. He could have enlarged
upon that particular statement, could have waxed absolutely rhapsodic over eyes as blue as sapphires and a
mouth with lips that invited kisses. Her nose was
beautifully shaped, and her hair, untidy though it had
been, a perfect frame for that incredibly lovely oval.
Her body was equally beautiful, even in the small
glimpse that had been vouchsafed him. Her legs, in their
tight breeches, were slender, tapering to ankles he could
span with one hand. He had hated to see her ride away,
had wanted to follow her, had wanted much, much
more, and was amazed and embarrassed at the thoughts
which had formed in his head and still lurked there.

" 'Whoever loved that loved not at first sight?' " The
line ran through his mind. He had read it . . . where? In
Shakespeare? No, he had not read it in Shakespeare, for
once. It came from *Hero and Leander*, by Marlowe,
which he had read in school. He had not fully
appreciated the poet until this moment, when he agreed
with him wholly. Had he? Had he actually fallen in love
at first sight?

"*Gervais*," Sir Harry said in tones which suggested
he might have spoken before.

Gervais visited a bemused stare upon his host's face.
"I beg your pardon, sir," he said. "I was thinking," he
explained, and wondered embarrassedly if such an
explanation were necessary.

"I imagine you were lost in thought," Sir Harry said
in a low voice. "I beg you will not allow the situation to
interfere with your visit. As far as I am concerned, it
does not exist. You are my guest and I am delighted that
you could spare the time away from your busy life to
come."

"I am delighted to be here, Sir Harry. And . . ." He
paused as he heard a voice trill from a spot somewhere
above them, "Harry, my love, you are home so
swiftly!"

Both gentlemen looked up to see Lady Villiers
descending the stairs with the care one in a delicate

condition must needs observe. Sir Harry looked surprised. "But you must have received my messages, my love."

"Oh, I did," she responded, "but still I insist you must have traveled fast." She reached the foot of the stairs and turned a brilliant smile on Gervais. "And you must be Lord Sayre."

"I am, you, ladyship." He bowed over her outstretched hand and could agree with his host that in spite of the fact that she was quite obviously breeding, she was very lovely, even though she lacked the distinctiveness of her stepdaughter—the distinctiveness and the distinction, he decided. One could meet a dozen golden-haired pink-and-white females on any Wednesday night at Almack's Assembly Rooms. The chances of finding a dark beauty with sapphire eyes were few, a dark beauty with creamy skin, he added mentally, and wondered if Rachel were actually as beautiful as his brief glimpse of her had informed him. Perhaps a lively imagination was improving the image in his mind's eye. He must see her again . . . and where was she?

Sir Harry said, "Where is Rachel?"

As he waited for her ladyship's response, Gervais mentally approved Sir Harry's suggestion that the girl ride on ahead of them. He was quite positive that his hostess would not have appreciated the attire he had found so provocative. In fact, given Sir Harry's attitude, which had been even more revealing than his words, he was quite positive that nothing about the girl would have pleased her youthful stepmother.

Lady Villiers frowned. "She is changing her garments," she said. She looked as if she would have preferred to say more, much more. She added, "But Lord Sayre will want to be shown to his room. I have given him the southwest chamber."

Sir Harry looked surprised. "But Rachel—"

"Oh, dear," Lady Villiers murmured. "I quite forgot. Dearest Rachel, so thoughtful always, said it

would be better for our . . . little one if she removed to
the Yellow Room. The breeze from the lake, you understand . . . so refreshing in the warmer weather. She has
such a generous nature. I was really quite touched. But
meanwhile, I thought that Lord Sayre might enjoy the
view. It is one of the most agreeable in the house.''

"Yes, indeed it is." Sir Harry visited a narrow,
searching glance upon his wife. "It was very generous of
Rachel to give up chambers she had occupied since
childhood—and her mother before her," he said coolly.
"I am sure that you will find them pleasant, Gervais."

"I am sure I will, Sir Harry," Gervais responded
politely, the while feeling extremely uncomfortable.

"I will have Thomas show you the way, Lord Sayre,"
Lady Villiers said.

The rooms in question were beautiful. They were
done in Chinese Chippendale, and Gervais, appre-
ciatively noting such luxuries as hand-painted Oriental
wallpaper, a pale green japanned wardrobe chest, and
exquisite carving over the mantelshelf, guessed that it
must have been with considerable reluctance that Rachel
had relinquished rooms which were certainly not
suitable for a nursery and, unless he missed his guess,
would never be utilized for such purposes.

Sir Harry's description of the unhappy relations
between his wife and her stepdaughter had been all too
accurate. That Lady Villiers actively disliked Rachel was
apparent even in the brief time they had spoken. This
change of apartments was only one more exchange of
fire in what he feared must be a most uneven combat.
Even if he had not been so favorably impressed by
Rachel, he would have wanted to take up cudgels in her
behalf, given the petty cruelty of her stepmother. As he
moved around the rooms, looking at a bed bedecked
with dragons and a marvelous screen decorated with
mother-of-pearl birds and flowers, he decided that the
cruelty was not quite so petty. A child would have
adored these premises, and the girl she had become must
have had a very special affection for them.

"She must not stay under this roof much longer," he muttered, and then he said, "I must take her away." It was an entirely logical progression of thought, given his prior knowledge of the circumstances. He could well understand why Sir Harry longed to separate his daughter and her stepmother. Money would be no object. He could easily afford to ignore the debt!

Gervais grimaced. Sir Harry must not be permitted to ignore that debt, no matter what the cost to himself! He did not want to pursue Rachel with such an agreement or, rather, bargain, hanging over his head. Yet, were he to settle in full, as he *must* (and that as soon as he returned to London), he could not afford to pursue Rachel, had no right to pursue her, given his reduced circumstances!

Gervais groaned aloud. In all his twenty-six years, five months, and three days, he had never been perched on the horns of such a dilemma—and horns they were, sharp and hurtful, piercing his tender self-esteem if not his flesh! It also occurred to him that never before had he been so drawn to a female. It was peculiarly ironic that the two situations should occur at precisely the same time. Yet, if the one had not taken place, the other could not have followed in its wake. He could almost wish that he had never set foot in Brooks's that night, or, if he had set foot there in, he might have played with a less worthy opponent—Osmond, for instance.

His lip curled. He never would have played with that creature, or rather, that creature would never have played again. Once had sufficed for them both. He could still hear Osmond's sniveling, "You have ruined me, my lord."

Implicit in that statement had been a plea to forget the debt. He had not heeded that plea—despite a certain pity for Osmond. He had thought that the man must be taught a lesson, an arrogant conclusion, he now realized. He had been younger then, a year younger, only, but looking back on his twenty-fifth year, he could wish it were now. His winning streak had been at its height. He had even won considerable money from the Marquess of Dorne, much to that gentleman's subsequent and barely concealed annoyance. However, he had not caviled at paying the thousands of pounds he had lost. He was not Charles Osmond, and if he, Gervais Fenton, were to accept Sir Harry's offer, he would be no better than the man he had despised.

A tap on the door startled him out of his gloomy reflections. "Yes?" he called, almost expecting to see his host come with further persuasions. However, it was only a manservant with hot-water cans and asking if he might valet him. He accepted the first but refused the latter service. He, almost alone out of his friends and acquaintances, had no use for a valet. He was capable of bathing himself, shaving himself, arranging a cravat to his liking, and brushing his own suits. Gloom descended once more as he realized that this particular aversion to the race of valets, whose acendancy and intimate knowledge of their masters' secrets had always put him off, would eventually serve him well in the Fleet or Newgate. Meanwhile, however, he would shove these reflections into the back of his head and dress for a dinner which must afford him another opportunity to converse with the beautiful, the enchanting Rachel Villiers!

Rachel gazed into her mirror. "My hair," she said anxiously. "Do you think it has grown too long, Phoebe?"

"It is just right, Miss Rachel." Phoebe, her abigail since both were a tender twelve, spoke bracingly. She had been bracing ever since the regretted arrival of the second Lady Villiers. She added darkly, "I've told my granny about the change in yer rooms, Miss Rachel, 'n she's a-workin' on it, she be."

Rachel said a shade anxiously, "I hope she's not casting her spells at this precise moment, Phoebe. I quite like Papa's friend Lord Sayre."

"Oh, no, Miss Rachel," her handmaiden hastened to

assure her. " 'Tis only 'er wot'll rue the day she put ye
out." She added wistfully, " 'Tis a great shame ye'll not
allow me to collect 'er 'air. Granny says it be most
effective when ye mix it with 'enbane'n a peppercorn'n
say:

> "I do not boil the 'air alone,
> But all these things together thrown
> Wi' 'er 'eart'n soul that she
> May perish'n foever be
> Only in witches' company."

It was on the tip of Rachel's tongue to say that she
would not wish Samantha on the witches—but that
would sugest she credited the witchery, something she
considered arrant nonsense! She contented herself with
telling Phoebe gently, "Even if I approved your
granny's magic, which I do not, I would not want to
wish ill on another. As Shakespeare says, 'Evil
intentions being taught, return to plague the inventor.' I
am not implying, mind you, that your granny is evil."

"Oh, she 'as been from time to time," Phoebe
allowed. "But only to wrong'uns such as 'er ladyship."

Again, though it was immensely pleasurable to hear
Samantha described in those terms, particularly when
she looked out of her window and failed to see the lake,
Rachel said firmly, "She is the female that Papa
married, Phoebe."

Phoebe tossed her head. "I wouldn't be surprised if
she'd used spells to trap 'im, I wouldn't. My granny
knew yer mama'n she says that compared to 'er,
Samantha's grisly gudgeon, whatever that be."

Rachel could offer no enlightenment. "I always
thought a gudgeon was a sort of fish," she said vaguely.
"But it does not matter." She stared into her mirror and
found herself full of doubts. Phoebe had dressed her
hair becomingly enough, but it had never looked so very
dark. Samantha had spoken disaparagingly about her
un-English looks, adding that there was a yellow cast to

her skin which she herself thought a pity. She had made that observation immediately after Rachel had appeared in her new yellow lutestring, a gown that Phoebe and subsequently Anne-Marie had praised most highly, saying separately but agreeing that they had never seen her in such looks.

Samantha, seemingly full of concern for her unfortunate stepdaughter, had suggested bleaches.

Rachel had not worn the gown again.

Did her skin look yellow? Rachel wondered nervously. Certainly it was not the pink and white possessed by her stepmother and also by Anne-Marie and her mother. In the summer sunshine, she did not freckle. Her skin only took on a deeper hue, becoming almost golden. She had had a touch of sun this day. Her dark brows drew together. She ought to have worn a hat. Yet, she hated hats, loved to feel the wind in her hair as she rode—*astride*.

She had been riding astride when she had met *him*. Had *he* been shocked? He had not appeared shocked, and if he had been, what difference would it make? He was not a member of the community, would not join in the gossip that circulated throughout the district. His stay would be brief. A sigh escaped her. She did not like to look ahead to the moment when he would no longer be a guest in their house.

Rachel chuckled. This was his first night at the Court and she was already mourning his departure, the departure of someone she did not know very well and who, on further acquaintance, might not attract her at all—no, she did not anticipate any such happening! He would grow more attractive, she was sure of that, and was truly surprised at herself. It was not often that she had been . . . She paused, realizing that she had never been so attracted to anyone—and furthermore, she had a feeling that he had liked *her*, too, breeches and all!

Immediately that thought crossed her mind, she made a little face at her mirror image. He was her father's guest. Her father would have spoken well of her and naturally he would be well-disposed toward her. Whether he remained in that state of mind depended on herself. No, that was not precisely true. There was Samantha! Samantha would be lying in wait hoping for an opportunity to disparage her.

"Oh, dear," Rachel murmured, her pleasure in the thought of her father's guest diminishing. Samantha would not miss an opportunity to put her down. She would do it sweetly but tellingly. If there were no such opportunity, she would invent one and then lose one of her tiny but well-aimed darts. Enough of these darts and one could resemble a rather battered pincushion. Rachel had a futile moment of wishing that she had been the son her father had needed to carry on the title—but if she had been the son, she would not now be anticipating the moment when, despite the aforementioned obstacle, she would be seeing her father's guest again. And what would she wear?

"What shall I wear?" she said a little despairingly to Phoebe as she mentally sorted through her wardrobe.

"The yellow lutestring, Miss Rachel," Phoebe said with a certain measure of defiance. "And yer mama's topazes."

"Very well," Rachel said. "The yellow lutestring it will be, Phoebe."

3

Directed to the drawing room by a passing servant, Gervais, on entering, paused just beyond the doorway, admiring another beautifully appointed chamber. Long windows to his left afforded him another view of the darkening gardens and the shimmering lake. He appreciated the paneled walls, another fine Oriental carpet, and furniture which, again, bore the stamp of Chippendale. Advancing farther into the room, he saw a marble mantelpiece held up by two beautifully sculptured caryatids. Etched into the middle was an intricate pattern which held his attention until he happened to glance up and see the portrait of a young woman with her hair piled high over a cushion. She had a sweet face and he thought he glimpsed a look of Rachel in the blue eyes and the winged brows, even though these were fair.

"That is my husband's mother. Do you not think her lovely?"

Gervais turned quickly, to find Lady Villiers standing behind him. She was in a blue gown, cut full and very flattering to her coloring. If she were a bit puffy about the face, she was still beautiful. Yet, her lips were thin, he noted. Her mouth was actually her least beautiful feature. Her hair, however, was a glorious shade of gold and dressed most becomingly. Her blue eyes, though paler than he liked, were well-shaped, as was her nose.

41

Her complexion was flawless. He bowed over her hand, murmured a few pleasantries concerning his delight at meeting her. Then, recalling that she had asked him a question, he added, "I do find the lady beautiful. I also detect a slight resemblance to Miss Villiers."

Lady Villiers raised her eyebrows. "You have met my stepdaughter?"

Gervais was conscious of embarrassment and annoyance. He should never have mentioned that earlier encounter. "I glimpsed her upstairs—at least I believe it must have been she," he said quickly. "Her father has described her to me."

"I see . . . and you think she resembles her grandmother?"

"It is there in the eyes and the brows, I think."

"Really?" Lady Villiers was silent a moment, scanning the portrait. "I must disagree," she said finally. "I would say that she inherited her looks and, of course, her dark coloring from her mother. Everyone who remembers the late Lady Villiers agrees, though I understand Rachel is taller. *They* are not usually very tall."

"They?" he inquired.

Lady Villiers appeared surprised and rather pleased. "Did not my husband tell you about her . . . mother? A regrettable and, I think I am safe in saying, a regretted *mésalliance*, contracted when he was a very young man. Oh, dear," she sighed, and looked up at him pleadingly. "I should not have said that. I pray you will not betray me. Dearest Harry is, understandably, a mite touchy on the subject."

Gervais's fists clenched. Even though he had been warned, he found himself quite amazingly angry with his hostess, the more so since courtesy precluded the comment or, rather, string of comments he wished he might direct at her. She was regarding him expectantly, he noted. Quite obviously she was anxious for the query which would result in the revelation she longed to provide. He declined to give her that opening. He said merely, "I understand she died young."

"Yes, before her twenty-third year. She was a very slight little person, I am given to understand, and Rachel was an immense baby. Her mother became quite ill after her birth and died, a blessing, given her . . . uh, precarious state of health."

Despite his anger, Gervais had to admire the subtle way in which Lady Villiers, repeating much of what his host had already told him, managed to disparage her stepdaughter, elliptically blaming her for the death of the woman whose memory she obviously despised. Furthermore, he guessed that she was bursting to reveal Rachel's maternal heritage. Her gaze, fixed on his face, seemed actually to demand further questions. Fortunately, he was saved from these by the arrival of his host, looking well in a plum-colored coat and white breeches.

Following a polite exchange of greetings, Lady Villiers said, "We were just commenting on the Reynolds portrait of your mother, Harry dear."

"Oh, yes, she was a great beauty in her day." Sir Harry nodded. "Is not Rachel down yet?"

"You know she has a tendency to dawdle over her dressing," Lady Villiers said lightly.

"No, Samantha, I do not know that," Sir Harry said frankly. "I do not know that at all. Generally my daughter is extremely prompt." He looked at Gervais.

"According to my husband, Rachel can do no wrong." Lady Villiers smiled provocatively up at Gervais. "I hope he will be as fond of our son."

"Whether the child is son or daughter, I will welcome his arrival, my dear." Sir Harry was smiling, but, Gervais noted, his eyes held no accompanying gleam.

"Oh, I know he will be a boy," Lady Villiers said confidently. "I have five brothers."

"Good evening, Papa . . . er, Stepmama, and Lord Sayre." Rachel, wearing a gown of rose-colored silk, came toward them.

"My dear"—her father looked at her fondly—"well-met by candlelight."

"Really, Rachel, we were beginning to despair of you," Lady Villiers said with a little laugh.

Rachel turned swiftly. "I am sorry for that," she said coolly, "but it was a matter of trying to find where your Susan put my gowns. I had intended to wear the yellow lutestring, but though Phoebe searched most diligently for it, she could not find the gown anywhere."

"I remember that gown," Sir Harry said. "It was new, was it not?"

"Yes, Mrs. Martin just finished it," Rachel said. "I had worn it but once."

"I will have to take the blame for its disappearance, my dear," Lady Villiers said with a smile. "Since I stand in for your dear mama, I feel it my duty to help you in every way possible—and the yellow lutestring was, I think I have already told you, not becoming. I gave it to Susan. I was sure that after our discussion, you would not mind."

Gervais, looking from one to the other, saw a flash of fury in Rachel's eyes. It was gone in a second as she said merely, "No, of course not, but I do wish I might have been consulted. It would have saved Phoebe considerable time in searching for it."

"My dear, you were from home and the servants primed to complete the change in apartments and, at the same time, render your new quarters habitable—they having been closed for some little time. Consequently, I took it upon myself to make that decision. If you wish to have the gown again, I am sure that Susan will gladly return it."

"No, I expect you are right." Rachel turned to Gervais. "I do hope you will pardon this discussion of . . . wardrobe, Lord Sayre."

Gervais said gently, "I can well understand your confusion, Miss Villiers, but I must say that I can only applaud the happy result. I am quite sure that the yellow could not have been as becoming as the rose."

"My belief exactly." Sir Harry nodded.

"Then I am vindicated," Lady Villiers responded

coolly, visiting a small smile on her husband. Before anyone could comment further, she added, "I do think we must go in to dinner now that dear Rachel has finally joined us."

Gervais, moving to Rachel's side, found to his embarrassment that his teeth and fists were both clenched. To his added confusion, he discovered within himself a totally unfamiliar and, needless to say, ungallant desire to shove both fists into his hostess's blue eyes!

Dinner, beautifully served in a banquet hall of a size that might have seemed small only for Beowulf and his roistering followers, was preceded by a lengthy grace spoken by her ladyship, during which not only the immediate family and guest received blessings but also the Methodist church, Hannah More, a Reverend Mr. Jameson, and the souls of several deceased relatives— not excluding her ladyship's uncle and Sir Harry's parents. Her predecessor went unblessed.

As the soup, necessarily a trifle cool, was served, Gervais read annoyance written large upon Sir Henry's countenance. Since Rachel was seated beside him, he could not look full into her face, something he regretted, but he was sure he had heard a sigh from her directly upon the final "Amen." He himself found that he had been again gritting his teeth—this time against words of comfort for Rachel and rebuke for her ladyship. He could understand Sir Harry's deep concern for his daughter. He was well on the way to sharing it.

Conversation at dinner was desultory and strained, particularly since Lady Villiers addressed either her husband or their guest. Between moutfuls of soup, fish, and neat's tongue, she mainly spoke about London and her desire to visit the city once she was more herself.

Gervais, beyond the monosyllables with which she found he could answer most of her questions, gazed at walls hung with magnificent paintings. Several of these were by artists he recognized—Murillo, Raphael, and El Greco. There was one landscape he could not place.

Upon asking the name of the artist, he was pleased to
learn that it had been painted by Joseph Turner, a man
for whom he had profound respect. He was surprised
and interested when, following Sir Harry's identifi-
cation, Lady Villiers said, "Ah, yes, I believe he visited
here—before my time, of course."

"He did," Sir Harry said enthusiastically. "I met him
at his exhibition in the Royal Academy three years ago.
He was with his father, who, I discovered, was a Devonshire man like myself. We fell to talking and I invited
them both to visit the Court. However, only the artist
came. He made a sketch of the house. It is in the library.
You must see it."

"I should like to see it," Gervais responded. "You
are indeed fortunate in your acquaintance, Sir Harry.
He is already a master and I can only think that in
future years he will grow even greater. Did he remain
here long?"

"No, unfortunately, he did not. He had been asked to
visit a friend in Scotland, but he wanted to see my
particular corner of the district. I like to pride myself on
the fact that I helped renew his interest in this part of the
country. As you probably know, his *Crossing the
Brook*, which appeared in the Royal Academy last year,
was a view of the river Tamar."

"I saw it," Gervais said excitedly. "A friend, more
knowledgeable than myself, tells me that it is a mile-
stone!"

"My opinion exactly," Sir Harry responded enthusiastically. "The coloring alone is splendid. I do wish
he might have remained with us a little longer. I should
like to count such a man among my friends. However,
he has declined my subsequent invitations."

"I imagine that he must have felt very uncomfortable
here, my dear, which is one of the reasons for his
refusals," Lady Villiers remarked.

"I remember him," Rachel commented. "He did not
seem in the least uncomfortable."

"You were younger then. A child would not notice,

but he is rather uncouth, I have heard. The son of a barber, is he not?''

"That is true." Sir Harry looked surprised and embarrassed. He added, ''But Christ was a carpenter's son and I cannot think that anyone would have protested his presence at table.''

Lady Villiers' eyes widened and she turned red, then white. ''Harry, that . . . that is hardly an apt comparison. To . . . to liken a journeyman painter to . . . to the Son of the Creator!''

"Come, my dear, I was but teasing." Sir Harry smiled.

Lady Villiers raised blue eyes suffused with tears. "I . . . One does not jest on such a subject. I cannot imagine what our guest must be thinking!''

Gervais, meeting the lady's anguished stare, said gently, ''I took the observation as it was meant, Lady Villiers. I am quite sure that no comparisons were intended.''

"Lord Sayre has put it most succinctly, Samantha, my dear. Certainly no comparisons *were* intended," Sir Harry assured her.

Much to Gervais's relief, Lady Villiers regained her composure and a short time later, upon the sweet being served, she and Rachel quitted the room, leaving the gentlemen to their brandy.

Finding his host's eyes upon him, Gervais was sorely tempted to take refuge in banalities. Though he would have liked to praise his beautiful and, he thought resentfully, truly beleaguered daughter, he did not want to raise hopes that must needs be vain, given his own sense of honor. Yet, having met her ladyship, he could certainly understand his concern for the poor girl. Indeed, he wondered why Sir Harry had ever formed a liking for the female. Even if he, Gervais Fenton, had not been given some inkling as to her intrinsic nature, he would have divined the pettiness and the insincerity beneath that beautiful facade. Had Sir Harry been so besotted by that same facade that he had not seen her dislike for his daughter?

It was more than mere dislike, he was sure. Lady Villiers was consumed with jealousy, and was determined, at all costs, to put a wedge between father and daughter. Her arbitrary decision to thrust the girl from her rooms was proof of that, and she, he guessed, was quite sure her husband would not protest the move. In view of the child she was expecting, he would feel the need to humor her. Gervais wondered angrily how much more humoring Sir Harry must needs do before the advent of his possible heir. He found himself hoping against hope that the infant proved to be female. It would serve them both right. Immediately upon this thought he remembered the anguish of the man on the night of their meeting—was that only two days since?—and his sympathy returned.

He could imagine that upon a first encounter with the beautiful Samantha—even he had to admit that she *was* beautiful—one could be totally beguiled by her spurious sweetness. Sir Harry had undoubtedly believed that he was bringing home a pleasant companion for his daughter. And what was he, Gervais, to say to him, given feelings that were swiftly approaching the chaotic? Despite his awakening passion—he was loath to dub it "awakened" so soon—despite his pity for Rachel and his active dislike for Lady Villiers, he could not allow himself to become interested in her—not under these circumstances. Indeed, it was utterly unthinkable. When the time came to speak frankly, he must needs explain his feelings to her father and then leave, but that, of course, was not necessary upon his first evening at Villiers Court.

He forced a smile, which died immediately as he saw the misery in his host's eyes. Sir Harry said, "The animosity between them is increasing. This matter of ousting Rachel from her rooms . . . I could, of course, countermand my wife's order, but nominally she is in charge of the house. I little thought that she would take her position so seriously—nor would she, were she not determined to assert her authority." He grimaced.

"You will pardon me for being so frank. I feel I can talk to you, who stand on the outside of this situation."

"I must agree that it is unfortunate," Gervais said carefully. "It is obvious that there is little sympathy between them. Of course, I expect we must allow for Lady Villiers' delicate condition."

"Yes, that is quite true. Though from the outset . . . But I have aleady taxed your patience enough. Indeed, I think it were better if we joined the ladies."

"I agree," Gervais responded with alacrity. Despite his many cavils, he was finding himself eager—indeed, impatient—to see Rachel again. Even if he dared not entertain a hope of possessing her, it would afford him considerable pleasure just to be in her presence and to watch the play of expression on her lovely face. Indeed, he thought with a rare surge of jealousy, he was almost glad that her heritage had made of her a partial outcast. In any other circumstances, she must have been bespoken and comfortably settled into matrimony by now. It was an idea that he hurried to dismiss from his mind.

Rachel, seated in the drawing room with her stepmother, wished strongly that custom had not demanded a separation from her father and his guest. It was not only that she wished to see one to whom she had been immediately attracted; she was weary of her stepmother's oft-repeated reasons for the changing of the rooms. Were it not for the aforementioned guest, she would have been quite unable to refrain from inviting another quarrel, first because of Samantha's arbitrary decision and second because of her ridiculous statement, "Once Lord Sayre has left us, I intend to redecorate them. Chippendale is all very well, but not for a child, and those horrid dragons would strike fear into him and—"

"Ah, my dear." Sir Harry and Lord Sayre, entering, created the diversion for which Rachel had been longing.

Meeting Lord Sayre's smile, Rachel smiled back, experiencing a feeling of pleasure that was entirely too heightened for the occasion. She had felt, indeed, as if they had been separated even longer than the half-hour that had passed since she and Samantha had quitted the dining room.

Her father continued, "Should we not go into the music room? Gervais has told me that he has a great fondness for the opera, and I have told him that he shares that fondness with you, my love."

"I would like to hear you sing, Miss Villiers," Gervais amplified.

"Yes, do sing for his lordship, my dear." Lady Villiers produced a half-smile. She added, "Rachel does have a very nice little voice."

Hearing the patronizing tone in the lady's voice, Gervais found that his fists were once more clenched. He said, "I am particularly fond of Mozart. Are you familiar with his works, Miss Villiers?"

"Yes." She nodded. "I, too, am fond of his music."

"And I," Sir Harry said. "Come, my dear." He smiled at his wife.

The music room, bathed in the glow from several candelabra, was, to Gervais's mind, one of the most beautiful of its kind that he had ever had the pleasure of viewing. The walls were a pale green and the Aubusson carpet picked up the color. A huge square mirror framed in gold reflected the pianoforte, a harp, and, across the room, a glass case containing a violin. There was a music stand near the piano, and in the center of the room a round table was surrounded by four chairs of French design with petit-point seat covers in pale green and gold scrolls to match the design of the rug. The ceiling, a fantasy of garlands, was centered by a magnificent crystal chandelier. It was, he thought, a worthy frame for the jewel that was Rachel Villiers.

Invited to sit down, Gervais settled himself in an armchair, while Lady Villiers chose a chaise longue covered in green damask. To Gervais's surprise, Sir Harry seated himself at the piano, and with Rachel standing in the curve of the instrument, ran his hands over the keys. "What will it be, my dear?" he inquired. Before she could respond, he added, " '*Dove Sono*'?"

Rachel smiled down at her father. "If you wish."

Gervais, catching the look that passed between them, was aware of a closeness which, he guessed, must irk her ladyship. He was sure of it when, glancing at her, he found a frown between her eyes. She said, "Oh, dear, I do find Gluck tedious."

"Then you will like '*Dove Sono*,' my dear, since it was written by Gervais's favorite composer, Mozart," Sir Harry responded. Before she could comment, he had run his fingers over the keys and, a second later, struck the opening chords.

Gervais had had only her father's word for Rachel's musical ability, and as a man who also had a passion for music, particularly opera, he realized that he had been half-afraid to hear her, lest he be disappointed. However, from her opening notes onward, he sat as one entranced. It was not only the quality of her sound, it was the expression that she put into the Countess Almaviva's yearning, bittersweet aria. Replete in its cadences was the sadness of a lost love, of disillusionment and betrayal, emotions that she, a girl of eighteen, could hardly be expected to understand. His eyes sought the chaise longue where Lady Villiers lay, and then he was not so sure. There had been an inadvertent betrayal here—it was apparent in the beautiful Samantha's petulant gaze and turned-down mouth. Rachel's magnificent voice had not pierced the shield of her dislike, her jealousy, and even, he feared, her hatred of her stepdaughter. His pity for Rachel's situation increased. It must be damnably hard to be continually confronted with an animosity that showed no signs of abating and which, indeed, could only increase, given Lady Villiers' obviously limited intelligence and deep resentment of the bond between father and daughter.

Remembering Sir Harry's anguish on that night of equal anguish for himself, Gervais could well understand the reasons behind his offer. As a young lad, he had dreamed of performing knightly quests—among them, the rescue of a princess from a tower—and surely no princess was more in need of rescue than poor Rachel Villiers!

Her song ended, Gervais leapt to his feet, crying loudly, "Bravo!"

Rachel, blushing, murmured a thank-you and was briefly held in her father's arms.

"I vow, my dearest child," he said, "I think you are better each time I hear you!" Turning to his wife, he continued, "I'm sure you must agree, my dear?"

"Indeed, I do." Lady Villiers nodded. "She does have a very pleasant voice. I might add that Mr. Soames, our minister, has asked me more than once why Rachel will not come to sing in our choir. We often have visiting singers, but she has steadfastly refused. I understand that she does not even sing in her own church."

"I think, my love," Sir Harry responded, "that were Rachel to raise her voice in song, she must discourage the participation of everyone else."

"Papa," Rachel laughed, "you do exaggerate."

"Indeed, he does," her stepmother agreed. "It is a large congregation and I doubt that even Rachel's voice would carry that well."

"I am of the opinion, Lady Villiers, that were I a member of that congregation, I would stop singing just to hear her," Gervais said. "It is a pity, Sir Harry, that you are not living in London. You might join one of the music societies, and Rachel could give others a chance to hear her."

"She could not sing in public!" Lady Villiers exclaimed in horror.

"A music society is no more public than a church choir," Gervais said gently. "Indeed, it is less so, for it has a much smaller attendance."

"I cannot believe it proper," Lady Villiers said stubbornly, "that a young woman of gentle birth appear before strangers. In fact, she should not even wish to put herself forward to that degree."

"I have not said that I did wish it, Samantha," Rachel said coolly.

"But I hope that you will sing again tonight," Gervais said. "Please?"

"Of course she will." Sir Harry smiled at his daughter. "Would you care to make the selection yourself, my dear?" He pointed to a pile of music near the pianoforte.

"I think that it would be very pleasant if my husband were to play. Whatever talent his daughter possesses was, I am sure, inherited from him," Lady Villiers said pointedly. She added, "I do enjoy his playing."

Sir Harry reddened. "Oh, my dear, I am far better as an accompanist than on my own—besides being sadly out of practice."

"You do dissemble far too much, my dear," Lady Villiers said loyally.

"You do indeed, Papa," Rachel said. "I beg you will play Beethoven's 'Pathétique' sonata."

"I will play if you will sing," he said insistently.

"Surely she cannot sing a sonata!" Lady Villiers exclaimed.

"You did not give me an opportunity to finish what I was saying, my love." There was a definite edge to Sir Harry's tone. "I would have Rachel sing a ballad."

"A ballad for a Border lord." Gervais smiled at her.

"We will see. However, first you must hear Papa."

"The first movement only," Sir Harry said firmly.

He played well. It was obvious that he was a gifted amateur, and hearing him, Gervais was inclined to agree with Lady Villiers that Rachel must have inherited her talent—her great talent—from him.

As he struck the final chord, Lady Villiers rose. "That was splendid, my dear. But I do find myself entirely weary, and so must you, after so many hours on the road. I fear I have not the strength to remain down here another moment. I am sure that you must be weary too, Lord Sayre.''

"I am not too weary to hear Miss Villiers sing a Border ballad,'' he responded.

"Nor am I too weary to accompany her,'' Sir Harry said firmly.

Lady Villiers' gaze was icy. "You may do as you choose, but . . . Oh, dear . . .'' She passed a hand over her eyes. "I . . . I . . .'' She swayed and swooned, falling carefully on the chaise longue.

"My dear Samantha . . .'' Sir Harry hurried to her side. He cast a concerned glance at his daughter. "Do we have a vinaigrette?''

"There is one in the drawing room. I will fetch it,'' Rachel said, moving toward the door.

"Ohhhhh,'' Lady Villiers moaned. She opened her eyes. "What happened? I do feel most unwell.''

"You swooned, my love,'' Sir Harry said concernedly. He glanced at Rachel, who had just opened the door to the hall. "We do not need the vinaigrette after all. Samantha is better, as you see.''

"Oh, Harry, dearest, do take me upstairs,'' Lady Villiers moaned. "I am still so very dizzy.''

"Of course, my love.'' He lifted her in his arms and with a murmured apology to his guest bore her out of the room.

Gervais looked toward Rachel but, to his surprise, found that she was no longer there. He wondered if she shared his anger at her stepmother's shoddy little stratagem. He wished he might speak to her, and better yet, accompany her while she sang her ballad. He himself was a fair pianist. With that in mind, he came into the hall, but he did not see her and nor was she in the drawing room. With a sigh, he went to his chamber.

Rachel had gone outside. The house, huge though it was, had seemed small and confining this night. She needed air. She needed a view of the lake and the old trees rising on either side of it and the moon reflected in its pellucid waters. That sight had given wings to the imagination of the child she had been and it had served to calm her turbulent spirit. She had always been a creature of moods, happy one moment, despairing the next. In the years of her childhood, these had been kept in check by her father. She adored him and she had been very happy with him until two years ago. Then he had brought home his beautiful bride, but beauty is as beauty does—and this particular beauty hated her for her heritage and because she resented anyone with a prior claim to her husband's love.

The whole miserable situation had reached a climax tonight. It had started with the incident of the yellow dress, had continued with her father's easy acceptance of the change in rooms, something Rachel had hoped, had indeed expected he must challenge—and then there had been that spurious swoon! Her father had looked actually anxious—as if he did not know she had been feigning the swoon, had been, indeed, determined on preventing her, Rachel, from enjoying a pleasant interlude with a young man who seemed interested in her. On the morrow, Samantha would spin her webs and entangle him in their meshes. He would hear, as had others in the community, the details concerning her father's first marriage, and would soon turn away, as had many acquaintances and even a few so-called friends, not excluding Sir Robert Palmer, who had told her many times that he intended to offer for her. That he had not fulfilled those intentions, that he was now in Italy, did not matter. She would not have accepted him. Lord Sayre was another matter. She paused in her thinking. Why was he another matter?

"Because," she whispered, "he seemed interested in me."

"So did Robert," her other self whispered back. "And you knew him well . . . you have only just met this man. It is too soon to erect airy castles."

She essayed a laugh but it did not penetrate the

barrier of her lips. Disappointment was large in her mind, and accompanying it was a sensation very close to despair. She had hoped . . . But she could not bear to consider those foolish hopes. Lord Sayre might have seemed interested in her, but that in itself meant very little.

She had neared the lake, which looked particularly beautiful this night. The moon, high, small, and full, was very white. Its light gilded the treetops and its face silvered the water. "Oh . . ." Rachel stretched out her arms to it. Tears filled her eyes. "Oh, I will miss you," she mourned, and sank down in the high grass. Generally she did not cry, but tonight she could not blink away tears of hurt, of betrayal, of disappointment. There were far too many of them.

"No, no, you must not weep!" a gentle voice came to her ears.

Tensing, Rachel sat up. She would have risen, but a hand on her shoulder prevented that. She gazed up at Lord Sayre's moon-gilded countenance. "I . . . You . . ." she stuttered, her confusion preventing any intelligent or, indeed, intelligible response.

"Do you mind if I sit beside you?" he asked.

"No, p-please," she said, still amazed by his sudden appearance.

He did not sit close to her. He placed himself at least a foot away, a courtesy she appreciated, being tardily aware that the rules of proper conduct had been breached. Had her stepmother known of his proximity, she must have thrown up her hands in horror at an encounter that she would have called "clandestine." And how had he happened to come here?"

Quite as though she had voiced that question aloud, he said, "I saw you from the window. I had wanted to talk to you. I had thought you must be as distressed as myself by the abrupt conclusion of the evening. Do you mind if I speak frankly?"

"N-no, of . . . of course not," Rachel stuttered.

"I can see that you and your stepmother are not in sympathy. I must tell you that I have met other young women in her condition, and quite often they are guilty of the most contrary behavior. When she has delivered the infant—"

"When she has delivered the infant," Rachel broke in, "it will be no different. I pray you will not mind if I emulate your frankness and tell you the truth of the matter."

"Of course I do not mind," he assured her.

"Very well, you must know that we have never been in sympathy. Papa, you see, made the mistake of marrying my mother and fathering me. I would not mention this, but you will hear it tomorrow or the next day from my stepmother. It is a constant source of surprise to her that this regrettable *mésalliance* was perpetrated by the man she calls husband and whom she appears to respect in all matters save this one. My mother's name before she wed was Miriam Medina. The Medina family numbers among its members several prestigious bankers who, however, are known less as bankers than by another term which is not quite so felicitous. When one or another young man is fleeced at a gaming table, he goes to the banking house of Medina—but he calls it 'the Jews.' Have I shocked you?" She stared at him half-defiantly.

"Yes, you have shocked me. Indeed, I am not only shocked but also angered to learn that your stepmother would hold you in contempt for . . ."

"For my father's error?"

"I was not going to say that. I was going to say that for one who counts herself a good Christian, your stepmother must be singularly lacking in knowledge, since Christ himself was a Jew."

"You must know the fallacy of that argument," Rachel said. "I will not tax you with its oft-repeated rebuttal. My stepmother was raised by an Evangelical nurse and later came under the influence of Hannah More, whom she is pleased to call friend. Naturally, being so extremely pious, she is grieved by my connections."

"It is you who ought to have the grievance. And I

must tell you that lip service is not piety. That is a truth
that many self-proclaimed Christians fail to take into
account. If your stepmother adhered to the true
meaning of Christianity, she would let her stones lie on
the ground rather than casting them at those who
cannot defend themselves."

"Oh," Rachel said softly. "You sound like Victor."

"Victor?" he repeated.

"Victor de Lascelles. He is my teacher and the cousin
of my best friend, Anne-Marie de Lascelles. They are
French émigrés. Victor is most incensed because
Samantha is, in his terms, a bigot of the worst description. Oh, dear . . ." She broke off. "You must
forgive me."

"Forgive you for what?"

"I have no right to burden you with my problems."

"They are no burden," he assured her. "And you
should share them. It is far better than keeping them
bottled up inside you."

"I do not precisely bottle them," she said frankly.
"My best friends, again the de Lascelles, have become
quite weary of my plaints, I can assure you."

"I am sure you exaggerate," he said. "And a young
woman of your beauty and talent should not need to
suffer fools gladly."

"Now I know you are funning me," she protested.

"And I swear to you that I am not," he said
seriously. He added, "I have two requests I must make.
I hope you will agree to them."

"That depends, sir," she said lightly now, "on what
they might be."

"You'll not buy a pig in a poke, I see," he teased.

"Had you intended to sell me one, my lord?"

"No, I had intended to tell you what they are, and I
will. I would like to see some of the countryside and I
hope that you will go riding with your father and myself
and help show it to me."

"That can easily be arranged, sir. I would be
delighted to accompany you and Papa. And your
second request?"

"I would like to hear you sing a Border ballad and also I would like to hear anything else you might choose to sing. Your voice is one of the most beautiful that I have ever heard. And I might tell you that I am passionately fond of opera and have heard all the great artists who have come to London anytime in the past fifteen years."

"Oh," she breathed. In a voice that was not quite steady, she said, "S-surely you exaggerate, my lord."

"Not in the least, Miss Villiers. Were it possible for you to perform in public, I do not hesitate to tell you that there would be managers from many of the great houses clamoring for you. Indeed, it is a great pity that you cannot share that splendid instrument with the many rather than the few."

"I still cannot believe that you are serious, Lord Sayre."

"I am entirely serious," he assured her. "And when you know me better, you will understand that I am not in the habit of giving empty compliments."

"Then I thank you, my lord."

"Rather let me thank you for that aria tonight and for the others that you will sing for me. And now, I think we had best go in, do you not agree?"

"I do . . . but I think we must not go together. The servants . . ."

"Oh, of course. Then I will accompany you to within a short distance of whatever door you choose to enter. Then I shall wait a discreet time before I return. Is that satisfactory?"

"Eminently so, my lord."

"My name is Gervais," he said. "Would you object to using it?"

There was a pause before she answered. "I would not object," she said finally. "But there would be objections."

He sighed. "There are far too many Mrs. Grundys in our world, Miss-Villiers-whom-I-may-not-address-as-Rachel. Or may I?"

"I am afraid that our Mrs. Grundy would complain a

great deal, given the fact that she knows we have only just met.''

"I feel that I have known you much longer," he said seriously. "I expect that is because your father has spoken of you so often to me—in the last few days. No," he continued before she could comment, "listen to me. There are certain Indian religions that insist that we visit the world in many guises throughout many centuries. I have been inclined to dismiss that belief as mere wishful thinking, until now. Is it not possible that we have met before . . . somewhere?''

Rachel pressed her hand against her bosom. She felt breathless and excited. His words had struck a chord. She thought of dreams she had had, of strange places, of fragmented images, familiar yet unfamiliar, and she thought, too, of their meeting—had it been only a few hours ago? Had there been a sense of familiarity, of two people greeting each other after a long separation . . . an unhappy separation, she suddenly thought. She was not sure. She said slowly, "I . . . have never thought about it before, but . . . but . . ." She paused and then found words on her tongue that demanded utterance. "I . . . do feel as if I know or have known you," she whispered, and was suddenly positive that she spoke the truth. Unthinkingly, she put out her hand.

He seized it, pressing it to his lips. Releasing it, he said huskily, urgently, "You must go in now. And I beg you will hurry, please."

She nodded, and turning, actually fled across the moon-touched grass.

Gervais, watching her go, groaned aloud. Rather than kissing her hand, he had longed to embrace her. His halfhearted interest in Lady Charlotte Frazier might never have existed; that lady herself might never have existed. He had, he realized, never known what it was to love passionately, with his whole being!

Heretofore his only passion had been music and, unfortunately, gambling. Was the latter to rob him of this girl? But she was not really a girl, she was already a woman, a beautiful, passionate woman who could be his for the taking!

He now understood the emotions of an Adam in the Garden of Paradise—not even the wrath of the Lord had driven him from Eve. Was his own debt—rather, his honor—worth such a sacrifice? He threw himself facedown in the grass. All his being cried out against the thought of losing her. Turning over on his back, he stared up at the moon. Moonlight could be deceptive. In the moonlight she had seemed a creature from another world. In the morning light, on horseback, she might prove considerably less desirable. He could only pray that she would—else honor must needs be sacrificed!

4

Gervais's sleep was troubled with dreams. At one point he was dancing with Lady Charlotte, but when he looked at her, her face changed and it was Rachel who was in his arms. At another point he was at Brooks's and playing with the Marquess of Dorne, who was winning. The marquess faded away and it was Sir Harry, and then it was Rachel once more, lying beside him. That last dream was so real and so exciting that it was with something akin to amazement that he awoke to find himself alone in the huge carved four-poster that, he thought with another surge of excitement, she had occupied until very recently. He could wish . . . But to give reins to those wishes in his mind was to experience an overwhelming sense of frustration.

He propped himself up against his pillows and buried his face in his hands. "How can I dare to think of accepting. . . ?" he muttered, and rising, paced back and forth across the room, noticing, as he did, its luxurious appointments. The debt was something Sir Harry could easily ignore—but with it would go honor. He could, of course, refuse the dowry, but that would give rise to speculation within the ranks of his family. Though his living relatives consisted only of his father's elder sister Aunt Lily and her son, who would be his heir were he to die intestate, there would be questions—since his man of business also handled his aunt's estate. He emitted a short, harsh laugh. He was way ahead of himself—thinking of marriage when he had met Rachel only yesterday.

Again, the sense of having known her long before that meeting was with him. If that were true, it would have explained much, not excluding his reluctance to make a commitment to Lady Charlotte. If he were to wed Rachel, he might lose Tony Frazier's friendship. He would be very sorry about that—but he had never so much as hinted that he wanted to marry Lady Charlotte. Yet, had his actions spoken louder than words? No, they were friends only. Did she understand that? She must, and if she did not . . . He could not dwell on pleasant, unexciting Charlotte. Rachel's lovely face, her obvious intelligence, and her voice, a speaking voice as melodious as her singing voice, blotted Charlotte out of existence. She became a name without even a remembered face.

He moved toward the window. The sun was rising and the sky was a grayish pink, reflected on the surface of the lake. It was a lovely sight, one that until very recently had been viewed by poor Rachel. His dislike of Sir Harry's wife rose another notch. He was torn by pity for his host and surprise at his choice. Lady Villiers was a type he himself could never have stomached. How could the man not have seen through her from the start? Gervais had an answer for that. Beauty. Beauty could be a trap, and he must needs remember that. He stared into the rosy-hued waters below him. Had he been beguiled by Rachel's beauty last night—her beauty and her misery? Morning and further acquaintance might save him from a possible folly. He found himself hoping that might be true. Otherwise . . . He sighed deeply and forbore to dwell on that problem.

"And here is Queen Anne's Walk," Rachel said. "Papa said I must show you this colonnade. It's a pleasant sight . . . so close to the river, do you not agree?"

"Very," Gervais agreed, his eyes straying to her face.

"It is a pity that Papa could not come with us this morning. I do not possess as much historical knowledge."

It was on the tip of Gervais's tongue to tell her that he did not regret Sir Harry's absence. However, caution prompted him to say merely, "Did the queen walk here, or does she 'walk' as Queen Anne Boleyn is reputed to do—on the ramparts of the Tower?"

Rachel laughed. "I have never known Queen Anne to walk, and I doubt very much that poor Anne Boleyn takes the midnight air." Her horse suddenly snorted. "You see? Horatio agrees with me."

Gervais, riding at her side, said, "I take it that neither of you believes in ghosts?"

"Well, I have not sounded him out on the subject— but he is a sensible horse and consequently I am inclined to believe him a doubter."

"Ah, a lady after my own heart!" Gervais exclaimed, and felt his face grow warm. He continued hastily, "My old nurse used always to frighten me with talk about the haunted room at Sayre Hold."

"That is your family home?" she asked interestedly.

He nodded. "It used to be a castle, and that is why it is called the Hold, but in 1661 when my ancestor Christopher Fenton returned from France after the Civil War, he found it largely destroyed save for the keep, where, as was their habit, the Puritans had seen fit to stable their horses."

"Oh, how dreadful!" Rachel exclaimed.

"I cannot say that he spent much time in futile regrets." Gervais grinned. "The castle was ancient, built in 1110. It had very few creature comforts, even with sundry additions from the fourteenth century onward. Consequently, he built another house near the keep, which has also had its additions—some not so felicitous. However, to return to our ghost. She was a Scottish lassie who might have figured in one or another of your Border ballads. You have mentioned the Border wars—the Fentons were involved in some of these, and in the course of one of them they made a point of capturing Red Lizzie MacGowan, who was wont to ride to the fray with her four brothers. She was called Red Lizzie because she had a great mane of red hair. She had been meeting my umpteen-times-great-grandfather on the sly and he thought it was high time they married. Hence her capture, but she, resenting his high-handed ways, leapt from the tower window and was instantly killed. He was brokenhearted, and so, it appears, was she, for she returned to wail and wring her hands at her own foolishness. It is said that whenever the winds are high, one can hear Lizzie's complaining voice."

"Or the wail of the wind?" Rachel grinned.

"For the purposes of my nurse, it was Lizzie." Gervais also grinned. "I believed in her spectral presence implicitly, at least in those years."

"Did she confine her haunting to the tower or did she roam about at will?"

"The tower only—but for the purposes of my nurse, she removed bag and baggage from the tower to the east room facing the tower. It is a bit more comfortable, the tower having deteriorated since Lizzie's day."

"Do you know?" Rachel sniffed, "I do not believe you."

"For all that, it is as true as most ghost stories are. There was a lass named Red Lizzie and, more important, there was a bairn, as she might have called it in her Scotch way." He touched his auburn locks. "My ancestor had him declared legitimate. That proved to be an exceedingly wise decision, for he was killed in his twenty-fifth year and there was none but his by-blow to inherit." He flushed. "I hope you will forgive this questionable slice of family history?"

"I think it is intensely romantic." Rachel laughed and then sobered. "But if she had had a bairn with him, why did she leap from the tower? It does seem as if she were bent on cutting off her nose to spite her face."

"When you come to the Hold, you will have to ask her," he said lightly. Then realizing the implications of that remark, he reddened and his horse moved restively beneath him at a sudden tug of the reins. Meeting Rachel's eyes, he read surprise in them, and something else—which had brought back memories of the previous evening, when he had found her in the grass by the lake.

He had hoped, he remembered, that the bright light of morning would restore his common sense. He had hoped that the resulting common sense would assure him that, after all, it had been the night, the moon-gilded lake and beauty-in-distress, that had captured his imagination and stirred his heart. However, the sun was high in the bright summer sky, and Rachel, riding side-saddle in her decorous habit, was covered with dust. Her hair was damp with perspiration and her face flushed. Yet, in that moment, he was positive that he had been waiting for her all of his life—and possibly through lives before this one! Still, with a wild clutch at common sense, he said, "I would like you and your father to see the Hold. And, of course, your step-mother."

"I would love to see it," she said. "However, I think it will be some little time before my stepmother is able to travel north." She glanced up at the sky. "I do think we ought to be riding back, do you not agree?"

He was caught between regret at their imminent return and relief at that smooth change of subject. He had, he knew, been tempted to actually propose to her at that very minute. "Yes," he agreed with alacrity, and turned his horse around. "I hope," he added, "that your father will not think it odd that we have remained away for so long?"

"I am sure that he will understand that Barnstaple is not to be covered in minutes," she said bracingly. "I do know a shorter way back, though."

"I think we must take it," he said as at that moment the clock in the church steeple struck the hour in eleven silvery chimes.

"Oh, gracious!" Rachel regarded him ruefully. "Have we been gone close onto three hours?"

He was equally surprised. "It did not seem nearly so

long," he said, urging his horse forward. "Show me
your shorter way, please, else your father will think I
have abducted you." He wondered what she would have
said had he told her that he had found their time
together far too fleeting, and that, if he had had his
choice, he would have ridden with her to the world's
end! Amazement filled him once again. He could not
remember a time when he had been a prey to such
extravagant fantasies. They were the more unsettling
because he had known her, he realized, less than a day,
if one counted the hours they had spent together. Yet, if
they were to count lifetimes . . . He shook his head.
That, of course, was also pure fantasy. Still, it had not
seemed so last night, and try as he was earnestly doing,
he could not dismiss it from his mind.

They came back the shorter way, racing each other
except where the road was either too narrow or too
rocky to permit such questionable exercise. Rachel, her
hair a wind-combed tangle, gained the stables first and
slid off her horse, preparing to be triumphant, until one
of the stablehands hurried up to her.

"You be wanted by 'er ladyship, Miss Villiers. Said as
'ow you was to meet 'er in the back parlor soon as ever
you come in."

"Is anything amiss, Jamie?"

He did not meet her questioning stare. "I'd not be
knowin', Miss Villiers."

"You used to call me Miss Rachel," she reminded
him.

"That were afore she come," he said quickly, and
flushed. "I mean . . ."

"I am aware of your meaning, Jamie," she said
dryly, but forced a smile as Lord Sayre—or Gervais, as
she called him in her mind—rode up.

"You won!" He smiled at her as he dismounted
before Jamie had a chance to catch the reins. "You
must be awarded a prize! What may I give you?"

"I will need to think about it, my lord. Meanwhile, I
am told that I must attend my stepmother, so I must ask
that you excuse me."

Concern wiped the smile from his lips and eyes. In a low voice he said, "At least you are not in breeches."

She laughed ruefully. "It might have nothing to do with . . ." she began, and blushed, adding lamely, "anything."

He frowned. "Let me come with you."

"If there is . . . anything, that would only make matters worse," she said frankly. "But I must go. Have you seen our library? I think you would enjoy my father's collection of books."

"I will enjoy it only if you will meet me there once you have conversed with Medusa," he said in a low voice.

Rachel reddened, and since she did not trust herself to answer, merely grinned, waved, and hurried inside.

Lady Villiers was seated in a wing chair in the back parlor, which, Rachel, meeting her angry eyes, mentally compared to the seat of judgment. "You wished to see me, Samantha?" she inquired lightly.

"Where have you been these three hours past?" Lady Villiers demanded.

"We were riding. Papa was quite aware of that."

"Your father has been frantic! He went to search for you. He imagined you must have met with an accident, even though I assured him that I was positive nothing of the sort had occurred!"

"Such omniscience deserves commendation, surely," Rachel responded, well aware that her sarcasm was adding fuel to her stepmother's fires. However, she was quite unable to control her own anger at Samantha's untoward assumption of authority.

Lady Villiers rose. "How dare you answer me back?" she demanded. "You are shameless—going off alone with that young man for three mortal hours! What were you doing?"

All manner of explanations rose to Rachel's lips. They ranged from the angry to the shocking. However, she managed to bite them down. She said, "We were riding. Papa asked me to show him the town, and I did."

"For . . . three . . . hours?" Lady Villiers' lips twisted. "I do not believe you."

"What do you imagine we were doing, Samantha?" Rachel demanded. "Lying in some haystack?"

"I would not be surprised," came the furious response. "And since you choose to be impudent rather than truthful, you may go to your room and stay there until your father returns and decides what must be done with you."

"*Done* with me?" Rachel echoed. "I think you must have gone mad, Samantha." She glared at her step-mother. "And *you* dare to . . . to send me to my room? Can you possibly imagine that I will obey you?"

"Do you presume to question my authority?" her stepmother responded in rising accents.

"Yes, I presume to question it!" Rachel responded. "I might also assure you that I have no intention of recognizing it. You take far too much upon yourself, Samantha."

"I will not be addressed as 'Samantha' by you," Lady Villiers snapped.

"Am I supposed to call you 'Mama'?" Rachel demanded sarcastically.

"You may address me as 'ma'am.' "

"As one might speak to the Queen of England?" Rachel stared at her contemptuously. "I do not place you in such exalted company. Furthermore, though you are nominally one of the heads of this household, I will not be treated as a child. I will do as I choose—when I choose—and you . . . you may go to the devil and be damned!" Turning on her heel, she went out of the room and up to the chamber allotted her.

Reaching it, she slammed her door as hard as she could, realizing a split second later that her action could be considered childish and that in coming to her room she had done exactly as her stepmother had ordered. She was, however, in no state of mind to join Lord Sayre in the library. She paced up and down this chamber she must needs call her own, hating it as much as she hated Samantha.

"How dare she," Rachel muttered. "How dare she expel me from my own apartments and . . . and order me to my room as if I were nine rather than nearly nineteen." That, she realized, was not the thing that had angered her the most. She had expected that Samantha would not look kindly on that lengthy ride. She also guessed that her stepmother had urged her father to go out looking for them. No doubt she wanted him out of the house while she vented her anger on her stepdaughter and did her best to ruin what had been a very pleasant excursion. While she did not have a very high opinion of Samantha's intelligence, she was quite positive that her stepmother did not suspect either of them of questionable behavior. No, she knew she was right. Samantha wanted to spoil the pleasure she had taken in the ride, just as last night she had spoiled that impromptu musicale and, given half the opportunity, would waste no time in dropping poison into Lord Sayre's ears and alienating him as she had alienated Rachel's other friends by reminding them of what many had forgotten—her late non-Christian mother. However, Rachel had already forestalled that particular endeavor, thus cutting sweet Samantha's claws—at least to some extent. Yet, perhaps she ought to join him in the library—to remain here would be, she reminded herself again, to do exactly what Samantha wanted.

She glanced at the mirror that hung over her dressing table and was appalled at the condition of her hair. She rang for Phoebe to help her fix her hair and change her gown.

A few minutes later, sitting at her dressing table, she frowned, wondering why the girl had not responded to her ring. Generally she came immediately. A few seconds after that, there was a knocking at her door. She went to open it, and on trying to turn the knob, found it would not yield. She pulled at it and pulled again.

"It won't do no good, Miss Rachel," Phoebe said from beyond the door. "She 'ad Geroge come'n lock you in."

"She . . . what?" Rachel demanded incredulously.

"She 'ad 'im lock you in, Miss Rachel, 'n yer to stay there until Sir 'Arry returns."

"You tell her . . ." Rachel began in a fury.

"I can't tell 'er nothin', Miss Rachel," Phoebe said apologetically. "She says as 'ow you cursed 'er an she be in 'er room bein' sick."

"May she be damned," Rachel said between gritted teeth, pulling at the door again.

"I wish my granny were 'ere," Phoebe said.

"So do I!" Rachel flashed. "Tell her . . ." She paused. "You'd best watch for my father. Tell him what happened, please."

"I will that, Miss Rachel," Phoebe promised. "And I'll be seein' my granny, come Sunday week. She'll 'ear o' it, too."

A strange little shiver passed through Rachel. Again the phrase "evil intentions" was in her mind. "No, Phoebe," she called, but received no answer. The girl had gone. Rachel moved back into her room. She must remember to tell Phoebe . . . But why was she worrying about such things? They were nothing but old wives' tales. Phoebe's grandmother could curse Samantha all she liked, and nothing would come of it. "And more's the pity for that," Rachel muttered between her teeth.

"Locked in her room!" Sir Harry looked at Rachel's little abigail incredulously. He had just dismounted and, as he had anticipated, he had not found Rachel or Lord Sayre. He had gone only to appease a furious Samantha. That she had taken it upon herself to berate his daughter and lock her in her room as she might a recalcitrant three-year-old amazed and angered him almost as much as it had his daughter. It was well-nigh impossible for him to see the incident from his wife's point of view. "Where is she?" he demanded crossly.

Phoebe stared at him in some surprise. "In 'er room, sir."

"I am talking about my wife."

"She be in 'er bed, sir. She be 'avin' a spell o'

sickness, she be,'' Phoebe explained, her eyes respectfully lowered.

"And Lord Sayre. Where is he?"

"I'd not be knowin', sir."

"Damn!" Sir Harry exclaimed with pardonable vehemence. As he strode across the stableyard and into the house, his first impulse was to free his daughter from durance vile—but unfortunately, second thoughts intervened to tell him that such an action would only make matters worse. Steeling himself for the confrontation, he came into his wife's chamber.

Samantha lay propped on her lace-edged pillows. She was alarmingly pale and her eyes were red with weeping. Despite his interior angers, her husband could not help but be concerned over her.

"My dear"—he hurried to the bedside—"what's this I hear?"

"Oh, my love." Samantha half-raised herself. "I . . . I have tried, I have honestly tried . . . but your daughter"—she pronounced the word with a repugnance she was unable to hide—"I . . . only reproved her because she had given us such a fright, disappearing for three hours with a *stranger*."

"He is hardly a stranger, my love," he felt it incumbent upon himself to remind her. "The young man is a friend of mine—and his father before him."

"He is a stranger to *me*," she emphasized, her fair brows contracting at his interruption. "But I was telling you about your . . . daughter, who . . . who h-hates me."

"No . . ."

"She hates me and . . . she cursed me, damned me to hell. I vow, meeting her eyes, I was terrified. There was something so . . . so virulent in her stare. I became ill the minute she left the room. They . . . they do say that some people possess the evil eye, and though I would be loath to lay such an accusation upon your daughter—"

"My daughter does not have the evil eye," Sir Harry said firmly. "No one has the evil eye, Samantha. That is pure superstition. Indeed, I wonder that you credit such foolishness. Rachel does have a temper and—''

"I tell you, she t-terrified me," Samantha whispered. "Her gaze was mesmerizing. I could see flames in it."

"That is your imagination, Samantha," he said coldly. "Rachel, as I have told you more than once, is impatient of authority. I gave her leave to show our guest the town. That it took longer than was expected—''

"You yourself were concerned."

"*You* were concerned," he corrected. "It was to allay your fears that I went in search of them. I thought it very likely that they would return before me, which, I see, they did." An ire he could not conceal crept into his tone. "I hardly imagined that you would take it upon yourself to have Rachel locked in her chamber."

"I have told you what she said to me," Samantha sobbed.

"Did she say it without any provocation?"

"She said it entirely without provocation. I . . . I only told her that it was wrong of her to worry us both so much and to ride out alone with a young man she does not know. It was inviting trouble."

"Did you imagine that he might ravish her in the saddle?" Sir Harry could not help inquiring.

"Harry!" Samantha gasped. "Your langu   . . . and they could have stopped anywhere. Even if th   did not, the impropriety of their actions—''

"She was showing him the town. They might have stopped at one or another point of interest."

"I see nothing particularly interesting about Barnstaple," Samantha responded. "It is *not* London."

Angry as he was, Sir Harry was hard put not to smile at this all-too-revealing evidence of Samantha's discontent. He said merely, "Be that as it may, I think that this young man takes some pleasure in Rachel's company. Indeed, I have reason to believe that he is uncommonly interested in her."

"Uncommonly interested . . . after only a day, less

than a day?'' Samantha demanded incredulously. ''I
can see where *she* might be interested in him, but he, a
man of good, even noble birth, and . . .''

''And what?'' Sir Harry snapped.

''My dearest''—Samantha put a hand to her
bosom—''I know you were f-fond of her mother, a
young man's folly—''

''Folly!'' He glared at her, ''I adored her mother. It
was the happiest day of my life when she consented to
marry me. I beg you will not visit these unseemly
prejudices upon my first marriage. And as for my
daughter, I feel that you have been jealous and unjust.
For someone who counts herself a 'good Christian
woman,' you have a curious lack of the milk of human
kindness.'' Without waiting for her response, he strode
out of the room.

''Harry!'' Samantha wailed to the closing door.
However, as it was closed with a bang, she did not wail.
She only glared at it, hating her stepdaughter more than
ever. ''She is a witch,'' she muttered. ''She has turned
his head with her lies. They say that the Jews used to
poison wells. I believe it. And certainly she has poisoned
his mind. It is all of a piece!'' She thought of what her
husband had said about Lord Sayre and shook her
head, resenting Rachel even more. ''He is besotted,''
she muttered, ''if he thinks that a marquess would offer
for that thin, dark, gawky creature.''

Sir Harry, going toward Rachel's room, encountered
Gervais, who was coming down the hall. The young
man flushed as he saw his host. ''I feel I owe you an
apology. We were not aware of the passing of
time . . .''

Sir Harry, who had been frowning, smoothed that
expression away. ''I quite understand,'' he assured him.
''My wife . . .'' He paused. ''But I have told you about
the reasons for her attitude. I am very sorry for this
unpleasantness. I am going now to release my
daughter.''

"I know she was locked in her room." Gervais frowned. "Surely, at her age—"

"You need say no more." Sir Harry also frowned. "I am in agreement with you. I am sure, however, that Rachel was lacking in tact during her confrontation with my wife. She is impatient of authority, particularly the authority of one who is but two years her senior. I am sorry that such a contretemps arose at this time."

"Given their dissimilarities, I quite understand that contretemps of their nature must be all too common in your household," Gervais said commiseratingly. He added impulsively, "I must tell you, Sir Harry, that . . . that I find your daughter enchanting. I never expected that at . . . at first sight . . ." He swallowed. "Sir, I think I love her. No, it is more than that, I do love her."

"Do you?" Sir Harry could not keep the eagerness from his tone. "Are you sure? You've but seen her—"

"We talked last night in the garden. She was unhappy, and I, being unable to sleep, met her—quite by accident, I assure you. I found her delightful—more than that, I had a feeling we were fated to meet. I am sure you will not be able to credit this, but it is the truth. Never in my entire life have I ever been so attracted to anyone."

"I do credit what you are saying," Sir Harry told him. "I mentioned my meeting with her mother. Practically, upon first glance, I knew that this was the one woman in the world for me."

"Yes, the one woman in the world," Gervais agreed with an eagerness that matched that of his host.

"Yet," Sir Harry said slowly, "I want you to be sure in your mind that you wish to wed her."

"I have never been more sure of anything in my life and I am not generally an impulsive man," Gervais said softly. "But . . . there is the debt."

"I have told you that I do not recognize the debt."

"And I tell you that as a man of honor, I cannot allow you to ignore it."

"I do ignore it," Sir Harry said. He made a sweeping gesture at the hall. "Can you think that I am in need of the ready? Do I require an extra stable? I had a streak of luck and that luck brought me you, whom I respected from the first. I might also tell you that I had an odd feeling that you and my daughter would suit. Were you to insist on honoring your so-called obligations, I would merely double the dowry—so let us hear no more about it, my lad."

"I do not feel comfortable—" Gervais began.

"I would not feel comfortable accepting it," Sir Harry countered. There was a flush on his cheeks. "You must promise me to put it from your mind, else, much as I desire it, I will not countenance the match."

"I . . . I cannot accept that alternative," Gervais said uncomfortably. "I do love her. I thought last night that it might be a trick of the moonlight. Indeed," he added unhappily, "I hoped it might be, given my situation, but this morning when we rode, I took such joy in her presence, I knew I had not been mistaken. It did not seem as if we'd known each other so brief a time. We are both agreed on that. It is as if we had been separated and come together again after many weary years. I hope that does not sound too foolish to you, Sir Harry."

"It does not," Sir Harry responded quickly. "I have explained how it was with me when I met her mother—we had the same feelings, as if we had met long ago."

"It is an intriguing notion, indeed," Gervais said thoughtfully. "And it is also frightening. I might have gone an entire lifetime without meeting her. Indeed, given her beauty and her character, I cannot see why someone has not come before me."

Sir Harry lowered his voice. "Rachel was sixteen when I married again. As I told you, there were those who were already pursuing her. My wife discouraged them—by the time I perceived what was happening, it had happened."

"I am glad it did," Gervais said fervently. "Yet, Sir Harry, I think it were better that I left today. Your wife has already suggested it."

Sir Harry stared at him in dawning anger. "She has?"

"Yes. She had much to say about the impropriety of keeping Rachel from the house for so extended a time, and since she appeared to be on the fine edge of vapors, I did not argue. You may consider that I have already offered for Rachel, but I will, if you will have me, return in a fortnight and go through the formalities of an offer."

"I will be delighted to have you return, but surely you can reconsider leaving."

"I think that were I to stay, it would be exceedingly uncomfortable for all of us," Gervais said firmly. "However, I would like to see Rachel before I go."

Sir Harry said in a low voice, "Samantha seems determined . . . But enough. I grow repetitive, I fear. If you will wait in the drawing room, I will send my daughter to you."

Rachel had stopped pacing the floor. She was seated in a chair by the window, staring at the less-than-prepossessing view of the topiary garden. The trees were cut into the shape of chess pieces, something she did not appreciate. She preferred untrammeled nature to artifice—however clever it might be. Samantha had spoken as if she were granting her stepdaughter a rare boon in giving her the room overlooking the tortured trees. Rachel was quite sure that had there been a stretch of unplanted earth, she would be currently facing that. She released a quavering breath. Her temper had not cooled down in the forty-two minutes of her incarceration. And how long did—? She tensed as she heard a key turning in the lock. In another moment her father stood framed in the aperture.

Evidently anticipating the spate of words currently forming on Rachel's tongue, he said hastily, "My love, I understand what took place and want you to know

that I am in total disagreement. However, young
Gervais is leaving and has requested that you join him in
the drawing room.''

Rachel's hand flew to her throat. "He is leaving!"
she cried, "Has that creature—?"

"My love, it will do you no good to waste words on
your stepmother. Gervais will return. But I beg you will
join him. He—'' Whatever else he might have said died
on his tongue as his daughter, not even pausing to
straighten her disordered locks, hurried out of the
room. He was not sorry for that—he had wanted some
corroboration from her concerning her feelings about
Gervais, and, he realized, he had just had it.

"You are not leaving!" Rachel said tragically as she
came into the drawing room. "I expect you know—"

"I know everything," Gervais came to her, and
taking her hands, kissed one and then the other. "It is
useless for me to say what I feel about her actions,
useless to waste words. Rachel, there are matters I must
settle in town, and I must also go to my estates in
Northumberland. However, I will come back to you. It
may take a little longer than the fortnight I mentioned
to your father . . . but I will be back. And even though
it is early to say it, I . . . I love you.''

"And I love you," Rachel cried. "With all my
heart.''

"Do you?" he asked eagerly. "I prayed you did. Oh,
my darling, I will hate every hour that I must needs
spend away from you, but once we are wed, we will
never be separated again." He flushed. "I . . . I have
not even offered for you. Will you forgive my impul-
siveness?''

"I think I must be dreaming," Rachel said
ecstatically. "Tell me that I am not dreaming.''

"If you are dreaming, so am I," he said huskily. He
put his arms around her and drew her into his embrace.

5

The summer sun shone through the long windows of the house called by its occupants "The Château de Lascelles," in honor of the ancestral home they had left so hurriedly nearly twenty-one years ago.

Seated at the pianoforte in the small salon called the music room, a slender, dark young man known to his pupils as Monsieur Victor Lascelles and to his fellow émigrés as the Comte de Lascelles struck a note on the ivory keys.

The girl standing beside the small square instrument sang a long and perfectly pitched "Ahhhhh" in the key of High C.

"*Très bien*," Victor said, admiration and gloom mingled in his brown eyes. "I expect," he continued in English which had only the barest flavor of the French that as a four-year-old lad he had spoken when he was spirited out of his native Normandy, "that you will not emit a single note once you are La Belle Marquise."

Rachel regarded him indignantly. "Of course I will practice," she responded. "In his last letter Gervais said he was having the pianos tuned in both houses."

"A plague on both your houses!" Victor snarled, and then grinned. "I do not mean it, Rachel, even though I wish . . ."

She looked down into his rueful face. "Victor," she said gently, "we will still be friends and it will be easier

79

for us to see each other in London—since you are dwelling in Marylebone. Gervais's house—''

"I know where his house is," he reminded her crossly. "It is located on St. James Street, the center of fashionable London. The very trees will sneer at your humble music master from Marylebone. And as for your husband, he will be jealous and suspicious."

"What nonsense you talk! He will not be jealous. We know each other, better each day. His letters—"

"Love letters," he reminded her with a sneer. "Love letters are never truthful. They are fantasies. Wait until you experience the reality of marriage!"

"What do you know about the reality of marriage?" Rachel demanded. "You've never been married either."

"I know how I would feel were I the husband of the so-beautiful Rachel," he sighed. "I would keep you under lock and key."

"It is a good thing that I am not marrying you," she said lightly.

His dark eyes grew gloomy. "You rejoice and I mourn."

"Oh, Victor, I do wish you would stop teasing me," Rachel begged.

"And if I said I was not teasing?" he demanded.

"I would tell you that you were provoking beyond all reason," she retorted. "We have known each other for most of our lives and this is the first time I have heard about your broken heart."

"I did not expect that you would meet and promise to marry anyone within a period of two days. *C'est incroyable*!"

"It is not unbelievable, since it happened, and I have told you that we—"

"Ah, yes, a meeting out of time," he said sarcastically. "Anne-Marie has waxed most sentimental about that. My aunt is less sentimental. You should listen to her."

"I have listened to her," Rachel said resentfully. "However, if my own father does not see anything untoward about the arrangement, I cannot see why you are raising these objections."

"I wish you to be happy."

"I am gloriously happy, deliriously happy."

"I would say merely that you are delirious."

"Victor," Rachel said sharply, "if you do not desist, we will not be friends."

"I am not your friend. I love you," he groaned. "But you must promise me one thing. You must promise me not to stop singing."

"I have told you," she said patiently, "that I have already given that promise to Gervais. It will be lovely to sing to him. He is passionately fond of music, you know."

"I do know," he growled. "I know that he is tall, that he has dark red hair, that he has gray-green eyes, that he is handsome, and I must warn you that those with red hair are often of uncertain temper. You must do nothing to make him jealous."

"I will never give him any reason to be jealous," Rachel said softly. "And what do you want me to sing now? I think we have had enough discussion."

"You must pay heed to what I tell you," he said seriously. "You may think you have known each other for centuries, but in this particular century, it has been less than a week."

"I tell you—"

"Do not tell me. Sing Donna Anna's aria."

Much to her secret indignation, Rachel had heard much the same advice from the countess, though in greater detail. "Despite this remarkable meeting, you will have to keep in mind that you do not know him."

"I do know him." Rachel began.

"You know that you love him and that he loves you. Naturally, this is very important. However, there is more to marriage than mere love. I hate to use an example that you will resent—but your father, I am sure, loved your stepmother before they wed. I am

equally sure he did not have any inkling of her pronounced piety and her true character.''

"He did not," Rachel admitted sulkily, "but Gervais
is definitely not pious."

"You are evading or deliberately misunderstanding
my meaning," the countess chided.

"I do know what you mean," Rachel assured her.

"Courtships, at least among us, are not generally so
swift. We ease into matrimony, we rarely plunge.
Beyond your attraction to him and his for you, you
know very little about each other. There ought to have
been a longer period of courtship."

"A period for sweet Samantha to shoot more of her
poisoned darts, do you mean?" Rachel demanded.

The countess's lip curled. "Samantha is nothing.
From what you have told me, he is not one to be swayed
by her forked tongue. It is you that I think about."

"You need not," Rachel said stubbornly. "I love
him. He loves me."

"Love is only a part of marriage. Some of us never
even see our bridegrooms until our parents have
completed the negotiations attendant upon our
betrothals."

Rachel shuddered. "I hope you are not suggesting
that this is the better way?"

"I am not. That is the other side of the coin. However, you might be surpised to learn that some very
happy marriages have resulted from such situations."

"Our marriage will be happy too," Rachel said stubbornly. "And I wish it to take place as soon as possible,
and I want to leave as soon as possible." Meeting the
countess's wise eyes, she blushed. "I do not mean that I
am marrying him merely to escape. The first moment I
saw him . . . it did not seem like the first time. I have
told you that. And nor did it to him. But I will not tax
you with much that I have told you already. And," she
added, "he has not made a formal offer yet. As
Samantha hints, he may very well cry off."

"Samantha!" Anne-Marie had just come into the

room. "Must she puncture every balloon you send aloft? Judging from her attitude heretofore—and mind you, I mean no offense—I should think she would be glad to see the last of you."

Rachel's expression changed from serious to mischievous. "She wants to see me amongst the cinders, surely you understand that. Never did she anticipate that I would marry the prince!"

"The prince is only what you deserve, my dearest, and may you live happily ever after!" Anne-Marie hugged Rachel.

Despite her brave words to the countess, Anne-Marie, and Victor, Rachel, riding home that afternoon, still felt far from sanguine. Even without her stepmother's oft-repeated doubts, it was difficult to imagine herself wed to Gervais Fenton, Marquess of Sayre. She had no doubt that many would consider his choice of bride a regrettable *mésalliance*. It was fortunate, indeed, that he had few living relatives—they being his aunt and a first cousin, who was his heir. "But through his mother, not his father," Gervais had written in one letter, "I am the last to bear the Fenton name."

Though, of course, he had not added that he hoped the situation would be resolved upon marriage, she thought of her father and the pressure put on him to remarry. She could not help wondering what his aunt and her son would think of his bride—a bride brought, seemingly, from nowhere. And they would be living in London after a honeymoon in the Hold, which was not far from Norham, wherever that might be. Yet, strangely enough, the name sounded familiar to her. And with the name, she had an image of a castle, huge and formidable, less a home than a fortress. Undoubtedly she had seen an illustration of it in one or another book. She had spent a great deal of her childhood reading. It was still a favorite pastime, though often replaced by the vocal scores Victor brought her. Thinking of those scores, she smiled. Not very long ago she had actually dreamed of running away and becoming a professional singer, and now . . . It did seem almost too wonderful to be true! Her singing would be done only for her husband!

Husband.

She savored the term, realizing that she had never actually believed she would be married. Samantha had implanted that thought in her mind almost from the day she had arrived to take over the reins of the household or, rather, wrest them from her stepdaughter's hands. Samantha had evidently believed it her Christian duty to discourage any contenders for the hand of one born of a "regrettable *mésalliance*," as she had not hesitated to term it in her stepdaughter's hearing. Yet, here was Gervais Fenton, Marquess of Sayre, about to become her husband, having fallen in love with her as swiftly as the fictional Romeo!

"You galloped into my life and changed it completely," he had written in one of his letters. She smiled. He was referring to that first meeting when they had met on horseback very near to the spot where she was currently riding. Oddly, Sir Harry had never mentioned his great friendship with the late Marquess of Sayre. Taxed with that omission, he had described a chance meeting at Brooks's.

"I had not seen his father in years. We had fallen out of touch, the way even the best of friends occasionally do. Then I saw Gervais and was amazed. It was as though Sayre had grown young again. I commented on the likeness and he explained the relationship. Fancy, I had not even heard of his death! The son, I am pleased to note, bears a close resemblance to his father, in character as well as appearance, and, I might tell you, my love, that I could not wish a better husband for you had I invented him myself."

"I vow you will beggar us, Harry. Surely that young man is wealthy enough in his own right and does not require so large a dowry."

Rachel winced, remembering Samantha's angry

comment or, rather, comments, since she had referred to the subject of the dowry on several occasions, suggesting none too subtly that Gervais was being well-paid for his proposal, suggesting in fact that without it, he must have remained a bachelor. For her own peace of mind, she obviously preferred to believe that love could not possibly have been a motivating factor in the situation.

Rachel had reached the turnoff to the Court. Seeing the outlines of the mansion through the masking trees, she sighed, wishing that she were not counting the days until she need no longer view that solid facade. It was amazing how, in two short years, Samantha had managed to make it her own to the point that she, Rachel Villiers, felt like a stranger in its familiar rooms, now grown unfamiliar by changes of furniture, changes of the draperies, and by bits of Samantha's fancywork, left here and there—establishing her presence even when she was not present. Though Samantha was no reader, she had even invaded the library, and many of the volumes that Rachel had loved were now on high shelves or locked away as unfit reading for the children Samantha meant to bear in the coming years.

Prominent among the works she had put in their place were Jeremy Taylor's *The Rule and Exercises of Holy Living*, *The Rule and Exercises of Holy Dying* and *Ductor Dubitanium or: The Rule of Conscience*, the latter being a manual of ethics for Christians.

Her father's failure to protest this invasion had seriously annoyed Rachel. Indeed, there were times when she thought that Sir Harry had become as unfamiliar as the house itself. Yet he had protested strongly when Samantha had taken it upon herself to lock her "erring" stepdaughter in her room on the day that had ended in Gervais's departure. Rachel frowned and sighed. He had spoken about being away a fortnight, and this morning her stepmother had pointedly reminded her that two weeks had become three weeks as of this day. She had also suggested that despite his letters, he might have changed his mind. "Absence does not always make the heart grow fonder, you know," she had said meaningfully.

Rachel shivered. She had suddenly recalled that moment when Phoebe had mentioned her grandmother—the witch. She did not, of course, believe in witches—but in her fury, she had not protested Phoebe's hint that her grandmother would be informed of Samantha's injustices. "Evil intentions," she whispered to herself. Had they, indeed, returned to spoil her life because of that tacit permission? She could hear her father's laughter had he been informed of so amorphous a threat.

"Have you learned nothing from your years with me?" he would have demanded, coating his words with a well-deserved sarcasm. "It is unlike you, Rachel, to give credence to such nonsense!"

She shook her head, muttering, "And I do agree, Papa, that it is foolish."

Rounding a bend in the road, she reached the gates of Villiers Court and in another few minutes had gained the stables. She drew to a startled halt that brought a protesting snort from her horse. There, tethered to a post was the huge black stallion that Gervais had ridden to the Court three weeks ago. He *had* arrived, and almost on schedule!

"Oh, God, if I had only known he was coming today!" she muttered, wondering why he had not mentioned that fact in his last letter. Without waiting for any help from the stablehands coming to assist her, Rachel dismounted, and leaving her horse for them, ran toward the house.

A few minutes later, upon being told that Lady Villiers was entertaining his lordship in the drawing room, Rachel came in—to find them drinking tea. Gervais rose, immediately she entered.

"My dearest," he said softly, but she noted a curious look in his eyes, almost as if he were hurt or surprised or both.

"You *are* here," she breathed.

"That can hardly be surprising to *you*," Samantha said pointedly. "I must say, my dear, that given Lord Sayre's letter, your visit to your friends the Lascelles was ill-timed. But young Victor is in residence, is he not?" She glanced at Gervais. "Nothing ever stands in the way of her lessons. Of course, Monsieur de Lascelles comes only twice a month. Still, I thought that having received your letter—"

"What letter?" Rachel demanded.

"My dear"—Samantha regarded her out of wide blue eyes—"I left it in your room myself. I do not see how you could have avoided seeing it."

"You are lying," Rachel said bluntly. "I saw no letter."

Samantha drew herself up. She said coldly, "I am telling the truth—a Christian does not lie. I left the letter on the table." She rose. "I will admit that the room was most untidy. You must instruct Phoebe to do her work more efficiently. I will leave you now." She glanced at Gervais. "I must beg that you excuse me, my lord, but in the circumstances, when I am so defamed by my stepdaughter, I cannot remain." With consummate dignity she stalked out of the room.

Rachel looked pleadingly at Gervais. "I . . . I did not see any letter."

His welcome laughter resounded through the room. "Damn the letter, my own dearest, and damn your blasted stepmother with it, if you will pardon my language." Moving to her, he put his arms around Rachel. "Am I permitted to embrace my bride-to-be?"

With his touch, happiness flowed through her entire body. "You are, sir," she murmured.

The embrace was long and passionate. Rachel, strained against her lover's breast, felt as if she were being drawn out of herself, as if, indeed, they had been united soul-to-soul in a oneness from which they could never be separated again.

The sensation remained to warm her even after he had

released her. Still, she was experiencing a regret she could not stifle. "If I had known you were coming, I would have remained here. I have been counting the days . . ."

He put his arm around her shoulders. "And will not need to count them again, my own beloved." He looked down at her. "You are even more beautiful than I remembered."

"With my hair windblown and my habit awry?" she sighed. "My stepmother—"

He slipped his hand over her mouth. "We'll not need to think of that woman ever again, my love. She is part of your past, but she will have no hand in your future—that belongs to me, my angel."

"Oh, Gervais," she murmured. "How could happiness come so quickly?"

"I thought we were agreed that it did not happen quite so quickly," he said, staring into her eyes, almost as if he were willing her to recognize that fact and accept it.

Meeting that intense gaze, Rachel was once more reminded of some encroaching past, a past which, she suddenly, shudderingly realized, might have held as much sorrow as joy—even more of the former. It was an unwelcome supposition, especially in this moment of great happiness. She said, however, "No, not so quickly."

The next few days passed with the vagueness of a dream. In after years, Rachel remembered that she had gone to the de Lascelles' for fittings of the wedding gown being sewn by Madame Durand, a mantua-maker in the countess's employ. The countess had insisted that she must provide the gown, telling Sir Harry that Miriam would have wanted it. Rachel vaguely remembered being asked to turn this way and that, to stand still while the garments, a pink silk slip and a white lace overdress, were being fitted. Yet she had no firm recollection of anything, and when, on the day before her wedding, she found herself the owner of a startlingly beautiful gown of exquisite lace over pink silk, she barely remembered how she had come by it.

She was and had been lost in happiness so intense that the voices of her friends and of her father and even of the man she was to marry had seemed to come from a great distance. Yet within the cocoon of joy there had been a strange feeling of unease—as if her all-encompassing happiness could, were she not careful, disappear like dew on the summer grass. There were times, indeed, when she awoke from dreams which had frightened her, only to realize that she could not remember them specifically, that only the terror remained. Fortunately, these did not occur very often. They did not occur on her last night as a maiden.

She awoke to a sky that was dimming from dark to light. She rose and went to her window and looked out. In that moment she was aware of movement beneath and saw a man walking near the topiary garden, skirting the king and queen chess pieces that had been carved from the yew leaves. It was her father who, in common with everyone else in the house and out of it, had been part of a sort of formless background of late. However, at this moment he came sharply into her vision and into her mind as well.

"Papa," she called, not very loudly, but he stopped immediately, and looking up, waved. "Papa," she cried impulsively, "I want to speak to you. Will you wait for me?"

He nodded and smiled at her so lovingly that for the moment all else faded from her mind. Once more he was not the lonely widower who had married young Samantha, he was her father, who had never gone away from her.

She flung on an old gown that buttoned up the front and thus did not need Phoebe's assistance. Thrusting her feet into an equally ancient pair of kid slippers, she hurried down the front steps and out a side door into the wet grass. Within minutes she had joined him. "Oh,

Papa," she said softly, breathlessly, "imagine . . . it is my wedding morning."

To her surprise, he looked momentarily stricken. He put his arms around her. "My love"—he stared at her intently—"are you happy?"

She sensed his anxiety. She also sensed that in some odd way he was chagrined, even oddly ashamed, and guessed he must be thinking of Samantha, who had made so determined an effort to come between them and, in a sense, had succeeded. If she had not succeeded, there would not have been this precipitate marriage, and undoubtedly that must be what was irking her father. He should not be irked, he should not be allowed to harbor any regrets, not when she was so happy. And, she recalled, he had asked her a question concerning that happiness.

"Yes," she answered. "I am entirely happy, Papa."

"Are you?" he demanded earnestly. He was looking at her oddly, and again she was aware of shame and still that odd regret.

"How could I not be happy?" she demanded.

"You . . . you've not known each other very long, my dearest."

"We have known each other long enough," she assured him, unable to tell him of the odd fancies they both shared and wondering in that same moment if he had played any part in them long ago, provided that there really had been a "long ago." But there had been, she was sure of it.

"He is a very worthy young man. I have become very fond of him." Sir Harry spoke almost defensively.

"Is he much like his father?" she asked.

"His . . . father?" He stared at her blankly. "Oh, his father, yes. He is very like him. I am glad you approve of him. Years ago, we discussed our children. We even speculated about an eventual marriage."

"Did you?" she asked interestedly. "Yet you have never mentioned his father to me."

"As I told you, we lost touch. He remained in

London," he said quickly. "I expected we would meet again . . . but he is dead." He sighed. "I am sorry for that, but we should not be discussing matters so melancholy upon your wedding morning. You'd best go back to your chamber, lest your bridegroom, rising early, see you. That is counted as bad luck."

"I thought you had no patience with such superstitions," she teased, thinking that he was in a very peculiar mood this morning.

"Nor do I," he asserted, and frowned. "And nor must you," he added hastily, looking beyond her.

Turning, Rachel saw Gervais coming toward them. "I could run," she said lightly, "but I think I must needs stand my ground and tempt the fates."

"Good morning, Rachel." Gervais reached them and looked at her so lovingly that she thought she must yet be dreaming.

"Good morning, Gervais," she managed to whisper.

He put an arm around her as he turned to face his future father-in-law. "Good morning, sir."

Looking at them, Sir Harry, who had begun the morning with a strange feeling of fear, even doom, felt this feeling vanish like dew. They did look happy, and a gamble which none but he himself knew the desperation of had paid off, he thought with relief.

The rest of the day passed with amazing swiftness. To Rachel's bemused mind, it had had a dreamlike quality. She scarcely remembered that Anne-Marie had asked if she might help her dress until her friend arrived. Then, once she, because of the combined efforts of Anne-Marie and Phoebe, was arrayed in her gown, she found herself staring into the mirror and wondering what stranger had invaded her room, until she tardily realized that this reflected vision was herself!

The church was surprisingly full. Rachel, whose acquaintance in the neighborhood had been much curtailed by the arrival of her stepmother, found herself greeting and receiving enthusiastic greetings from people she had not seen in one or two years. Everyone seemed delighted and effusive. Even Samantha, looking surprisingly bulky in a pink satin gown, appeared tremulously happy.

There were two tense moments in the church. One took place when Rachel, joining her bridegroom at the altar, tardily realized that she barely knew him. The other tense moment occurred when she hesitated over that response that must change her from bride to wife—mainly because she had been visited by an odd sensation that she was in a dream from which she must presently awaken.

The minister and Gervais had stared at her, and finally she had murmured her hesitant affirmative. Then there was the gentle kiss that her bridegroom, no longer her bridegroom, of course, but her husband, placed on her lips. Then they were moving swiftly up the aisle and everyone was talking at once. After that and without knowing quite how it had happened, she was back in her chamber while Anne-Marie was assisting her to change from her lacy finery into a gown of pale blue silk which had also been fashioned for her by the talented Madame Durand. There were other gowns, already packed by Phoebe, who had been at the back of the church with a mild-looking old lady whom she had introduced as her granny, was hurrying down the stairs to take her place in a post chaise of the bridegroom's providing and in which she would be riding up front with the coachman for the nonce because they were already bound northward, leaving Villiers Court far, far behind—forever!

They had started early enough in the afternoon to reach the town that lay between them and Bristol, where they would be spending the second night of their wedding journey, that journey that would end in the vast unknown that was Northumberland, and more specifically Gervais's part of Northumberland, which lay, he had explained, a stone's throw from the Scottish border and where, on lands which had been in his family's possession since the eleventh century, rose Sayre Hold.

These plans, discussed for days, had fled from Rachel's mind as, amid congratulations and good wishes from friends and acquaintances, even from Samantha, who had smiled at her this day more often than in the two years and odd months they had known each other, she moved between father and bridegroom and was lifted into the coach. She had half-expected that the man she had not yet learned to address as "husband" must ride beside the coach on horseback. Instead, and much to her surprise, he climbed in beside her, and looking as if he could not quite believe she was there, drew her into his arms. Seemingly unmindful of all the well-wishers at the edge of the road, he caught her in an embrace that almost crushed her, the while it filled her with a mounting excitement unlike anything she had ever experienced before.

Neither of them had much to say as the post chaise bore them along one road and then another. Rachel was drowned in confusion and excitement, and Gervais, his arm around her waist, looked at her every so often as if he could not believe she was actually there. They reached the King's Head at Burnham-on-the-Sea just as the sun was descending over that same sea, glimpsed from the courtyard of the inn. It was strange to hear the innkeeper's respectful "Milady" as Rachel, with her husband, mounted stairs that narrowed at the top and came into a chamber with an uneven ceiling and casement windows facing a sea dyed a deep orange.

In this room there were only a table and chairs—several chairs, some wooden, two leather-covered. A white china clock ticked on one end of the mantelshelf, in the middle were two large shells; and on the other end were candles in brass holders. A rag rug lay on the floor.

The smell of the sea invaded the chamber when the maidservant, who had shown them to the suite, opened the windows. Outside, seagulls wheeled against the dimming sky, uttering their raucous plaints. Her husband stood beside her watching the waves and then he kissed her again, a deep, possessive, possessing embrace similar to that he had given her in the coach—but yet different and more exciting.

Supper was eventually served, but Rachel scarcely tasted the food. She was remembering the countess's hurried words as she had come to help Anne-Marie change her from wedding gown to the ensemble she was wearing now.

"Much will seem strange to you, *mon enfant*, and it has occurred to me that you must yet be ignorant of all that marriage can entail. Your husband seems to be an understanding and sensitive young man. I am sure he will be gentle, but there will yet be moments when you may be surprised, even frightened. You must not be frightened—for no matter what happens between you, it is all natural, perfectly natural, and to be expected. Do you understand?"

She had agreed that she did, but she had not and did not. Understanding, she guessed, must soon arrive. She hardly realized that supper had ended until she looked down to find the dishes removed from the table. She was surprised when Gervais, bringing her hand to his lips, led her into the bedroom and disappeared through an adjoining door. She was also surprised when Phoebe came to help her change into a lacy nightdress. It was early to retire for the night. Outside, it was still twilight. She said as much to Phoebe and received only a giggle in response.

The bed was large and old. Its four posts were topped by a fringed canopy. Its curtains were damask. The sheets that covered it were blue-white and the pillows were in lace-edged cases. A satin comforter was pulled back, disclosing fleecy blankets. There was a faint smell of lavender, which, she knew, came from the sheets.

It was here that, according to the countess, she would await her husband. She had never slept with anyone before. She had mentioned that to the countess, who had frowned slightly.

"It is a great pity that your stepmother did not provide some necessary enlightenment, but . . ." She had looked at her oddly. "Perhaps, after all, that is just as well."

That snatch of conversation was in Rachel's mind as, assisted by a giggling Phoebe, she climbed into bed. The mattress was soft. It had been a wearying day, and were she alone, she would have fallen asleep immediately— but she was not alone. Rather, she realized with a slight shock, she *was* alone, for, unseen by her, Phoebe had left. The candles were burning low on the mantelshelf and a small fire in the hearth was dwindling. The ticking of the clock was accompanied by the crackle of the burning wood. Then she heard a different sound—a door creaked open and footsteps were coming across the floor.

Rachel looked in that direction and saw Gervais, attired in a long white nightshirt, approaching the bed. She smiled at him and wanted to welcome him, but nervousness clamped her words to her tongue.

"My darling," he murmured. "How very beautiful you are. Oh, my love, my dearest, dearest love, I am not sure that I am awake." He pulled back the covers and slipped in beside her, gently gathering her in his arms.

She was aware of panic and a wish to struggle. A small protest arose in her throat and was stifled by his long, invading kiss, and the thoughts that had been scurrying through her mind like so many frightened mice, were banished by a surge of excitement such as she had never experienced in her entire life. The excitement blotted out the fear, and Rachel, clinging to her husband and feeling his kisses on the throbbing hollow at the base of her throat, thought . . . But in another moment, all thought was banished.

6

In after years, when she would be called upon to describe her journey north, her wedding journey, Rachel was uncomfortably positive that she would not be able to furnish many specifics. They passed green fields, grazing sheep and cows, they passed horses and, occasionally on country roads, they halted to let sheep and cows pass them, meandering across the road while she, with Gervais's arms around her, watched and sometimes teased him out of his impatience.

Every so often, Rachel was aware of little Phoebe's eyes on her, looking at her wonderingly, looking at her, in fact, as if she hardly recognized her. There were times when she, glancing into a mirror in the bedchamber of one or another inn, hardly recognized herself. There were subtle changes in her face, changes wrought by happiness and a contentment she had never experienced before, not even in the years before Samantha came to live at the Court.

She had loved Gervais when they married, but she had known nothing about the state of being married. There had been none to instruct her regarding a passion so overwhelming, so all-encompassing that when she was together with Gervais, she lost all thought of self and the biblical words "cleave unto thy husband" took on an entirely different meaning. She was no longer lonely Rachel Villiers, she was Rachel Fenton—and she belonged with him and he belonged with her, for his happiness equaled her own. There were moments, in fact, when he confessed that he had never known what happiness meant until he had met her. There were times when he looked at her almost as if he were frightened, and said, "Nothing must ever come between us, my dearest. I could not bear it."

And she had answered wonderingly, "What could ever come between us?"

She was thinking of those words now, as she stared out of the window of the carriage. Gervais was dozing, but she was entranced by the character of the landscape. On this, the seventh and last day of their journey across England, there was a loneliness about the landscape. They passed vast stretches of greenery which Gervais called "moors." There were moors aplenty in Devonshire, but they were different. There were huge out-croppings of rock which she did not see in the North. There were rolling hills, but not many villages. Gervais had told her there would be Roman relics, including great stretches of the Roman wall.

They had seen the wall earlier this afternoon when they had stopped at a small inn for their midday meal. Hand in hand they had walked along an open field beside the winding wall with its carefully set stones that had remained in that same mortar for more than a thousand years. Gervais had told her a little about a boyhood spent in this distant part of England, and of his wonder once he had left his home to attend Eton and subsequently Cambridge.

"I returned to London for my holidays," he explained, "to the house where we will live come October."

"That is only three months away," she had said. "Will you want to leave your home so soon?"

"It is not soon, and you'll not appreciate this part of the country when autumn changes to winter. Now it is dressed in its best for my bride, but the face it will turn to her when the winds come howling down from Scotland will be less benign."

"But we will spend some part of the year here, will we not?" she had asked, vaguely distressed by she knew not what.

"That will depend on you, my dearest love. My mother, who came from Bath, hated it. She blamed two miscarriages on it and returned to Bath the moment my father died. She stayed with her sister-in-law, my Aunt Lily, and is buried there, having stated with what was practically her dying breath that she loathed our home while living and would haunt it were she to be interred in the family graveyard."

Rachel had shuddered and asked, "What do you think about it?"

He had hesitated, saying finally, "I will tell you . . . when you tell me what you think." Almost sternly he had added, "And I charge you, Rachel, you must be truthful."

As they turned onto the road that would eventually lead to the Hold, Rachel was excited and yet concerned. Did he love or did he hate his home? It seemed to her that he had spoken about it with some fondness when he had told her about Red Lizzie and the Border wars. Yet, judging from what he had said, he had spent little time there. And his mother had liked it so little that she had not even wanted to buried there.

Rachel wanted to like it, and she had liked, even loved, the country through which they had passed yesterday afternoon and this morning. Still, it was a lonely land, the villages scattered over a vast distance and the manor houses equally distant from each other. In earlier times, she guessed that those who lived in the great castles spent most of their life either in London or in Edinburgh when there was peace on the borders. She had a feeling that Gervais did love his home and that was why he had decided to spend his honeymoon there. Consequently, even if she did not like it, she would try to conceal those feelings for his sake. Indeed, she thought to herself with a loving glance at her dozing husband, were he to live in a castle of ice, she would praise it.

The coach was turning and they had arrived at a tall wrought-iron gate. Through its bars she saw the outline of a gatekeeper's cottage. It was sturdily built, and from the weathered look of its bricks, she guessed that a century or more had passed since it had been constructed. The coach had drawn to a stop and she heard the sound of the coachman's horn. A squat little man was hurrying out of the cottage and unlocking the gates.

"Malcolm, my man." Gervais had awakened, and as they drove through to pause at the cottage, the gatekeeper bowed and touched his forelock.

"Welcome home, my lord," he said obsequiously.

"This, Malcolm, is Lady Sayre," Gervais said with flourishes in his voice.

But she lies in Bath, Rachel thought strangely. Then, shaking herself, she smiled at the gatekeeper, who bowed again and grinned. Then the coachman was urging the horses forward once more, and Phoebe, roused out of a nap, was leaning out of her window, staring wide-eyed at a tree-bordered road—old trees: tall red beeches, maples, and chesnuts. The way to the house was long and winding. Gervais had already told her that, and Rachel, expecting it to be even longer, was not prepared for the immense red brick facade that suddenly came into view, nor for the adjacent mass of stone rising to one side of it, which, she knew, must be all that was left of the castle. Her eyes, traveling upward, sighted a high window and she guessed that it was from there that Red Lizzie, angered at her lover, had leapt, knowing in that swift descent a regret that did not end with death.

"Rachel."

She heard a touch of impatience in Gervais's tone and turned toward him, only to find the coach door open and him on the ground waiting to assist her down. She blushed. "I was thinking."

"Deeply." He smiled lovingly at her, adding unnecessarily, "We're here." He lifted her down. "What will you tell me about the Hold?"

In the recesses of her mind, a strange voice seemed to be whispering, "I'll be tellin' ye, my lord, that ye may have my person, but my soul's mine own." She shook herself and said lightly, "What may I tell you, my dearest, until I have seen it? From what I do see, I am impressed. It is even more beautiful than you led me to believe."

"Is it beautiful?" he said strangely. "My mother thought it overwhelming."

"Perhaps I, too, will be overwhelmed, once you have taken me through it," she said. "It is uncommonly long and large. I expect it must have been an act of defiance on the part of poor Christopher Fenton."

Gervais's arm, which was about her waist, tightened. He looked at her in smiling amazement. "How did you know that?"

She was not sure, but she produced an answer she hoped must satisfy him, more than her explanation that the air seemed to be laden with ghostly confidences. "I know how I would feel, were I to return to desolation and devastation"—her eyes strayed toward the ruined tower—"after all I had endured in exile. I am sure that your ancestor must have spent many a weary, frustrated hour thinking on the home he had left behind."

"And, of course, you'd not know that engraved on his tombstone are the words 'Here I lie, where I have longed to be,' " Gervais said wonderingly. He added, "I wanted you to feel the spell of this house. I did not think it would happen so quickly."

Rachel gave him a loving smile. She had had the response to her question regarding his feelings for his old home. He loved it and had brought her here because he had hoped against hope that she would not reject it out of hand, the way his mother had done. She said, "It is impossible not to feel its spell. I can hardly wait to have you take me through it."

"Tomorrow you will have a guided tour. Tonight . . ." His eyes lingered on her face. "Tonight I think we must retire early, do you not agree?"

"Entirely, my love," she murmured.

"And now, you must allow me to carry my bride across the threshold."

The front entrance of the house lay behind a pillared portico. The door, paneled and centered by a bronze knocker in the shape of a lion's head, was open. Standing in the aperture was a tall, portly old man whom Gervais greeted with obvious fondness. He said, "My love, this is Matthew, who has been at the Hold for close on forty years."

Rachel, meeting pale blue eyes under tufted gray brows, said softly, "I am pleased to meet you, Matthew."

The butler smiled. "And it's pleased I am to see the master's brought home so beautiful a bride."

Before she could answer him, Gervais had lifted her in his arms and carried her over the threshold into a hall, the size of which amazed her. It was even larger than that of the Court. It rose up three stories, and set in niches on either side of the massive door were huge Grecian statues, a cupbearing Hebe on one side and an Apollo on the other. Moving out of the entrance hall, they came to what Gervais called the Marble Hall. Facing Rachel was a winding stairway in marble, with a gently curving marble balustrade. The floor of black and white flagged marble stretched beyond the staircase and she saw an arched entrance to what she guessed must be a drawing room, and so it proved to be. The windows, also arched, stretched from floor nearly to ceiling and provided an excellent view of the drive with its framing trees. Before she had an opportunity to take in more of her surroundings, Gervais scooped her up in his arms, and ignoring her laughing protests, carried her up the long length of stairs, not stopping until he had arrived at a veritable bower of a bedroom.

Rachel, looking about her in amazement, saw that it was done in Chinese Chippendale similar to that in the room from which she had been so summarily ousted by Samantha. There were Chinese cabinets and delicately painted wallpaper. The bed had carved dragons over the canopy and there were more dragons crouching on top of a long mirror. Beside a chaise longue was a little lacquer table inlaid with mother-of-pearl.

"Oh, it's just like home," she breathed.

"Is it?" he asked eagerly. "I hoped it might be. When I went home, I carried but an imperfect picture of the room in which I had stayed."

"But it's so very similar, even to those dragons. I was always very fond of my dragons—of everything about that room!"

"Yes, I knew you loved it. That's what kept me an extra week—seeing that the artisans I had hired were well on the way to completing it before I left."

"Oh, my dearest . . ." She flung her arms around him.

He held her tightly. "I wanted you to like my home, my love. And I wanted you to feel at home in it. Do you? But of course, it is too soon to ask."

She said softly, "It is not too soon to ask. I loved it the minute I saw it, but I must tell you, that even were it not so grand, indeed, were it a hut in the forest and you beside me, there would be my home, Gervais."

To her surprise, she felt an actual tremor go through him. "May you never change, my angel."

She looked up at him adoringly. "I will change only when the stars fall from the skies, and the moon with them."

The following morning was given over to meeting the staff, assembled by Mrs. Holbeck, the housekeeper, who hailed from Yorkshire and still spoke its dialect. Fortunately, Rachel had a quick ear for nuances and was able to understand her tolerably well. She liked the housekeeper, a fair, round, rosy woman in her mid-forties, who breathed competence. She also liked her choice of staff. They seemed efficient and compatible. Their first meal, the previous evening, had convinced her that the kitchen was in good working order and the cook, a Mrs. Yardley, expert. More to the point,

Phoebe liked them and said as much, reassuring Rachel that she would not be lonely so far from her home.

Rachel was half-pleased, half-jolted by Phoebe's responses to question about her new surroundings. "Oh, I knew I'd like it fine, Miss Rachel . . . er, milady. Granny aid as 'ow I would. She told me exactly 'ow the 'ouse looked'n said I were to keep away from the tower'n so should you."

"The tower?" Rachel questioned. "How did she know about the tower?"

" 'Tisn't much Granny don't know, Miss Rachel. She 'as the gift. 'Er great-grandma were Scottish'n she 'ad the sight first . . . didn't do 'er no good, 'cause they found out'n 'ung 'er in chains. It's supposed to come every other time—my granny's ma, she didn't 'ave the sight'n then my granny 'as'n Ma didn't . . . but I don't either. Granny says it be all wore out, she thinks."

"I see," Rachel said. "And did your granny say why I was to keep away from the tower?"

"She said as it were sad . . . didn't say much else, never does, milady. She did say as 'ow yer stepmother'd rue the day she were ever mean to you."

A shudder ran through Rachel. It was ridiculous to credit such arrant superstition, and, she suddenly realized, it was equally ridiculous to imagine that ill-wishes could afflict those who uttered them. By that same token, no prognostications could keep her away from the tower. She had been drawn to it ever since Gervais had told her the disquieting tale of Red Lizzie. He had taken her to the supposedly haunted room and she had not experienced even the smallest psychic twinge. It was possible that the nurse had invented the tale to scare the child. Perhaps a great deal of Red Lizzie's story had been invented. Rachel could not imagine why a young woman who had borne a child out of wedlock would resent her successful capture, one that would have ended in marriage. If it were true, there had to be more to the tale than Gervais had told her, or, since she could not imagine him keeping back any of the story, more to it than he was aware of, especially if his ancestor had been anything like himself.

Strangely, she felt a reluctance to visit the tower in Gervais's company. It was something she wished to do alone, though she could not have explained the reasons—even to herself. Consequently, it was not until the third day following her arrival at the Hold that Gervais, being summoned to see one of his keepers regarding a prevalence of poachers, left her side. He had gone with obvious regret. "It would not do to bring you with me, my dear. There's no telling how long I shall need to be gone."

"You need not give me these excuses, my love," she had answered equably. "I cannot think that we can long continue to live in each other's pockets."

He had frowned. "Do I weary you, then?"

"No, of course you do not," she had answered in surprise. "I should think that that shoe would be firmly on the other foot."

He had not answered her immediately. Instead he had taken her in his arms and kissed her. Releasing her, he had said, "Does this answer all your questions?"

"All, my love," she had assured him.

With that exchange in mind, Rachel felt almost guilty at the excitement that claimed her when, at last, she stood at the archway leading into the tower. It was amazingly well-preserved. The interior of the keep was not. Once inside, Rachel was surprised to find it a mere shell, but of course, she reminded herself, she had expected nothing else.

Once it had risen several stories to a solid roof. Her husband had told her there had been a room on each floor and that the kitchens had lain on the ground floor. She guessed that the great square fireplace that still rose across from her had once been part of the kitchen. Looking upward, she found an arched window set several feet above the entrance and guessed it might have marked the third or fourth story. The roof was gone and weeds grew between broken masonry on all four sides. Despite the jagged opening once covered by the roof, Rachel felt chilled, as if the sun, currently bright enough to be blinding, was not there at all. Indeed, there were goose bumps on her arms. Furthermore, she felt almost compelled to look up at that window. Suddenly she was uncomfortably sure that it was the window from which Red Lizzie had leapt.

There had been stairs winding up to it, Rachel guessed. Lizzie had climbed them—not merely climbed them, had raced up them—while several men-at-arms, who had brought her there, and her lover, too, had watched, wondering at her wild cries, her denunciations, her hurt, which was not a physical pain but, for all that, was agonizing, since it spelled the end of love, the end of all that had held her close to the man whose child she had bravely borne out of wedlock, despite the fact that she was Scots and he English, ostensibly an enemy. He had not been an enemy when they had met, had not been an enemy during their secret, passionate trysts—but he had betrayed her. How?

Rachel shuddered, feeling an agony which amazed and frightened her. Coupled with it was grief, the wild grief that had sent Red Lizzie hurtling through the window to die at her lover's feet. Had she died in front of him? She had, Rachel knew, while her lover, that great strong man, had knelt by her side sobbing like a child, begging her forgiveness. Forgiveness for what? For having seized and carried her off. But that had always been part of their plan.

Rachel put her hand to her throbbing throat. Fear thrilled through her. What could she know of plans? Gervais had told her nothing of Red Lizzie beyond her leap. She would have to ask him, but she did not need to ask him. She knew how it had happened. Or did she? Suddenly she was trembling. She felt hot and cold, as if, indeed, she had a fever. Picking up her skirts, she ran out of the keep, standing there in the sunshine, grateful for its bright rays, wanting never to go into that chill ruin again.

Yet, a few minutes later, recalling the emotions, the suppositions that had seized her, she did not understand them. She had a sense of having been possessed or haunted by that ancient tragedy of which she actually knew nothing. Here, in the sunshine, the thoughts that had skittered through her brain were fleeing. She felt like herself again, and realized that while she had been in the tower, something had appropriated that self!

"No," she said aloud. "That is ridiculous. You have always had a strong imagination."

"*She's not telling lies, Mrs. James. She has always been a fanciful child and she's been much alone.*"

Those words, spoken by her father, had been addressed to one of her governesses. They were true. She did have a lively imagination, and in lieu of friends, there had been pretend-people, until Anne-Marie came into her life.

The feelings that had visited her in the tower were compounded of the tale Gervais had told her and of her own imagination. She had summoned up her pretend-people again, and the two of them had seemed as real as those she had invented when she was little. She had often frightened a younger Anne-Marie, she remembered, telling her the ghostly tales she had read in her father's books, retelling them as if they had been her own experiences. She had always embroidered them, and had done the same thing now, embroidering what Gervais had told her about Red Lizzie. He would tease her when he knew, but on second thought, she did not think she would tell him. She forbore to examine the reasons for that and excused it on the grounds that it was not necessary to confide every foolish thought that crossed her mind.

She smiled, realizing that of late she had been doing just that—telling him things that were not important, little things that occurred to her and would have been as quickly forgotten had he not looked at her quizzically, saying, "What are you thinking now, Rachel?"

"Why?" she would ask.

"You seemed lost in thought."

"I was not really thinking about anything save how happy I am to be here with you."

Her answers, invariably similar to that one, seemed to please and relieve him. Pondering on that, she wondered why he needed to ask and why her answers brought the release of what appeared to be a held breath. Was there something troubling him? she wondered. Something he, who wanted all her confidences, was not minded to confide in her? She shook her head and ran her hands through her heavy hair, a pair of gestures that was habitual and which her father had been wont to describe as "getting the cobwebs out of your mind, my dear."

Did Gervais have cobwebs in his mind too? She dismissed the idea as pure foolishness. They were merely getting to know each other. Despite the mutual passion that had come to them in a single night, the night they had met in the garden, they had been veritable strangers when they married. It still amazed her that everything had happened so quickly. Of course, her father had been partially responsible for that, wanting to get her out of the house for her own good and for the good of the woman he loved, who did not love her. Gervais's arrival had been marvelously fortunate. Her father must have been amazed that they had taken to each other so quickly. His arrival had definitely killed two birds with one stone! She was married and he could devote all his time to Samantha. Did he really love Samantha?

In the beginning he had; Rachel was positive of that. Now, naturally, he could not help being resentful of her attitude toward his daughter and her determined efforts to alienate her from all her friends and acquaintances. Rachel grimaced and determinedly pushed those memories away. She was far too happy to dwell on the unhappy past. Her main concern was Gervais, whom she loved and must get to know better, for, quickly or not, they were married, and unless she missed her guess, Gervais was as determined as herself to live "happily ever after."

"And here." She looked about her at the tall old trees

and the house she already loved. "I would like it to be here. I shall insist that we remain here throughout the winter. Indeed, I would like us never to return to London!"

She laughed, remembering that she had never been to London and that before they had come to the Hold, she had been just the tiniest bit resentful that Gervais had not wanted to drive through London—if not remain there, even though it was, as he insisted, the tag end of the Season. At this point in time, she did not care if she never saw it. There was a great deal to occupy her here in this magnificent house. Eventually there would be visitors, dinners to give, friends to invite for shooting and the holidays, and soon, she hoped, there would be a child, and another child, and another. She wanted four children, two boys and two girls, near enough to each other in age to be compatible. She had hoped that the symptoms of pregnancy, graphically described by Phoebe, would have already affected her, but they had not. However, there was Gervais, the house, and the coming winter, and perhaps by the spring, when the mares foaled and the young lambs made their appearance, she would be well on the way to bearing her first child.

Rapt in these thoughts, Rachel walked down the carriageway. As she reached the front of the house, she heard the sound of hooves and looked up quickly, expecting to see Gervais. Instead, there were two people riding in her direction. A young man was in the lead, and behind him there was a girl who, as Rachel watched, caught up with him and passed him with a wave of her hand. In another second he had passed her. Obviously they were racing, but who were they? How had they managed to pass through the gates without being stopped? As these questions arose in her mind, the two riders, nearing her and evidently seeing her, came to a stop so suddenly that the girl's horse snorted and reared. She controlled him admirably, and riding closer, stared at Rachel in a surprise that was also written large on the countenance of her companion, who, Rachel decided, now that they were nearer, must be her brother. Both were fair, blue-eyed, and, she guessed, close in age. The young man was handsome. His sister, whose nose and mouth were similarly shaped, was attractive if not precisely pretty. His hair was a rich gold, while hers was brown with gold lights. These impressions, flashing into her mind in seconds, were, she guessed, duplicated in her case. Both appeared extremely surprised to see her. She said, "Good morning."

"Er . . . good morning," the young man responded. His surprise was now less evident, Rachel thought. In fact, it appeared to have been replaced by disapproval. He said with a glance at his companion, "We had heard that his lordship was in residence."

"I think, Tony, that we'd best go," the young woman said uncomfortably, her eyes, cool and unfriendly, dwelling on Rachel's face and then shifting away.

"Um . . . yes," he muttered.

Rachel said quickly, "Are you friends of Lord Sayre's?"

"We are," the man said coldly, as if, having questioned her right to be there, he had come up with a displeasing answer.

Rachel understood their confusion. Gervais had not wanted to let anyone know they were in residence as yet. He had, he had told her, instructed the servants not to spread the word, which, she thought ruefully, was tantamount to trying to control the winds or hold back the gushing waters of a brook with one hand. These two were evidently near neighbors, or as near as anyone could be in this part of the country, and someone had told them he was here. Evidently they had not heard that he was married.

She said, "I imagine you must be friends of my husband's."

"Your . . . husband?" the girl said in a breath.

"I am Rachel Fenton, and you are . . . ?"

The pair exchanged a flashing look and then the man said, "I am Anthony Frazier and this is my sister, Charlotte. We are neighbors. In fact, we are your nearest neighbors."

Her guess corroborated, Rachel said, "I am delighted to meet you. Will you not let me have your horses taken around to the tables? Gervais is not here at this precise moment, but I expect he will be back presently. I am sure he will want to see you."

"Oh, no," the girl demurred. "We were not aware . . . But I must congratulate you, Lady Rachel."

"I thank you," Rachel said. It seemed to her that Charlotte Frazier had lost some of her bright coloring.

"Tony . . ." The girl glanced at her brother, who was frowning.

He started and his horse moved restively under him. He said, as he drew in the reins, "You have my sincere good wishes, Lady Rachel."

The look in his eyes, turned frosty, belied his words. His frown remained and there were questions in his eyes as well, questions which would remain unuttered in her presence. She imagined that Gervais would not escape so lightly, and in that moment heard the sound of hooves upon the road. She looked toward the gatehouse and was aware that her unbidden guests were doing the same. To her relief, Gervais had returned. He had been riding slowly, but then his horse snorted and suddenly picked up speed. He reached them in seconds.

"Charlotte, Tony!" he exclaimed in surprise. "You are back from London?"

"Do you doubt the evidence of your senses?" Anthony Frazier demanded coldly.

"We have been in residence for a fortnight. We heard that Eugenia was sick, so naturally we came home."

"Eugenia! Sick?" Gervais frowned. "Such a beautiful mare. I hope she's better."

"She died," Anthony said bluntly.

"Oh, dear, what a shame," Rachel breathed.

"Yes," Gervais agreed. "A great shame. She was a fine animal."

"Very fine," Charlotte said with a break in her tone. "There were times when she seemed more than a mere horse."

"Do you know what caused her death?" Gervais asked.

"A fever, contracted we know not how," Anthony said. "But enough of that. So you are wed, Gervais. When did this happy event take place?"

Gervais said, "I think you must have left London before you received my letter."

"I think we must have," Anthony agreed, his eyes on Rachel again. "That was the news contained in your letter?"

"Yes," Gervais said. He dismounted, and wrapping the reins around his hand, he moved to Rachel's side. "We were married in Barnstaple."

"In Barnstaple?" Anthony questioned. "I was not aware that you were acquainted with . . ." He paused and flushed. "Evidently I was wrong."

There was a flush on Gervais's face as he said, "Sir Harry Villiers, an old friend of my father's, lives outside Barnstaple. We met quite by accident, and nothing would do save that I come for a visit. And . . ." He broke off, adding, "Why am I telling you this, standing here in the middle of the road? Will you not both come in for—"

"No," Charlotte said quickly. "We are expected back at the house. However"—she smiled down at Rachel — "now that we know you are here and with so lovely a bride, we will arrange a time when you must visit us. My parents will want to meet you, Lady Rachel."

"I should love to meet them," she responded warmly. She liked Charlotte Frazier. Yet, at the same time, she felt very sorry for her—sorry especially for the letter that had not reached them in time. It was all too obvious that the news of their marriage had come as a most unpleasant shock to both brother and sister. Had there been some manner of understanding? she wondered uncomfortably.

"Please let me congratulate you, Gervais," Anthony Frazier said.

"I thank you, Tony." Gervais's smile was strained.

"And you have all my good wishes," Charlotte added warmly.

"You are very kind, Charlotte," he said in a low voice.

A few minutes later, as the brother and sister rode out of sight around a bend in the road, Gervais, meeting Rachel's questioning glance, said almost defensively, "They are our nearest neighbors. I have known them all my life. They live only six miles from here."

"That would account for their surprise," Rachel commented. "I thought that Miss Frazier—"

"Lady Charlotte," he corrected. "They are the children of the Earl of Dynevor. Their parents were friends of my mother and father. We grew up together."

"I see. It's a pity your letter did not reach them."

"A great pity," Gervais agreed. He frowned. "It might have kept them from a visit I consider most inopportune."

"Gervais!" she protested. "That is hardly the way to speak about your oldest and dearest friends."

The smile he gave her did not quite reach his eyes. "It is not a time when I wish to be burdened with my oldest and dearest friends. There'll be no help for it now. The visits will commence, and we must needs be host and hostess instead of honeymooners."

"Can we not be both?" Rachel asked lightly, the while she wondered unhappily if he were unwilling to present her to his friends, unwilling or fearful that some word of her mixed ancestry might have reached them. Yet, how would that be possible? Samantha, she knew, had no connections in the North.

"We can be both, of course, my dearest," he responded, "but I find I have grown very selfish, now that we have been together. I want you all to myself."

"If that is selfish, then I am even more selfish than you," Rachel said softly, happily. "Yet, unless we retire to a mountain peak or to a desert island, I think we will not have our wish."

He put an arm around her waist. "I will take Horace to the stables and then we'll go to the library and consult an atlas."

7

Desert islands and mountain peaks being out of the question, Gervais's fears were realized three days after Rachel's meeting with the Fraziers, with an invitation to Dynevor Hall. Finding it impossible to refuse, he accepted and Rachel found Lord and Lady Dynevor charming, if rather distant. Naturally, she responded with a return invitation, set, at Gervais's earnest request, a fortnight later.

Then, after what Lady Amelia Dynevor said was a delicious dinner, she said bluntly as they came out of the dining room, leaving the gentlemen to their wine, "I hear you have a voice."

"I sing a little," Rachel said a trifle reluctantly. She hoped her guest would not ask her to oblige with a song. It was not easy to sing after a full meal.

Quite as if she had read her mind, Lady Amelia said bluntly, "I understand that it is not easy to sing after dinner, but I am longing to hear you. We are starved for music in this part of the country. And Gervais says your voice is quite extraordinary."

"I do believe that he exaggerates," Rachel assured her.

"I beg that you'll let me be the judge of that," Lady Amelia said, her tone commanding rather than demanding. "Come, let us go to the music room. It's cooler than most of the other chambers on this floor. I

113

know the way blindfolded." Quite as if she were hostess rather than guest, she set off toward the room in question, with her hostess and Lady Charlotte trailing behind her, the latter visiting a half-regretful, half-laughing look upon Rachel.

The music room, pale green as to walls and with a ceiling depicting the nine muses gathered around Orpheus, was cooler than the rest of the house, and upon a servant lighting the candelabra on two tables and a candle near the music desk of the pianoforte, Lady Amelia seated herself at the instrument and said brusquely, "I am passionately fond of music but my daughter is tone deaf and gave her music master an attack of nervous prostration before he threw up his hands and threw down the music. Consequently, dinner or no, you must restore my faith in the human voice."

"Mama is speaking no more than the truth." Lady Charlotte sounded quite unperturbed by her mother's appraisal of her talents, or rather the lack of them. "Please do sing for us."

Rachel chose to sing, "The Last Rose of Summer" and Lady Amelia accompanied her quite creditably upon the pianoforte. When she finished, she found her ladyship in tears.

"Ah, my dear, you do have a voice. I could wish that poor Mr. Catley might have heard you. Do you not agree, Charlotte?"

"Entirely, Mama." Amazingly, Lady Charlotte also had tears in her eyes. "I have never heard a voice so beautiful."

"We will have to give a musicale," Lady Amelia stated. "And you will sing for us and for our friends who have been similarly deprived of good music. 'Tis seldom we are privileged to hear a voice of such extraordinary quality. I am quite amazed and entirely thrilled."

"Surely you are pleased to exaggerate," Rachel murmured.

She received a sharp look from her ladyship. "I beg

you will not dissemble. You must be quite aware that your voice is out of the ordinary.''

"Indeed it is," Lady Charlotte murmured. "It is not surprising . . ." she began, and flushing, paused, adding rather lamely, "that Gervais has praised your voice so highly. He has always been passionately devoted to music."

Rachel, thanking her, had a feeling that she had meant to say something entirely different. There had been, she noted, a pensive quality to the girl's tone, a note she had often heard whenever she mentioned Gervais or, indeed, spoke to him. Remembering the precipitate appearance of Charlotte and Anthony on that morning a month earlier and the surprise—or had it been shock?—with which Charlotte had greeted the news that she was Gervais's bride, she wondered if, at one time, Lady Charlotte and Gervais might not have been more than merely good friends. It was entirely possible that, having been raised together in this lonely community with its sudden storms that might have kept him in their house until the weather grew finer, as had happened to themselves on one occasion, that some manner of understanding might have been reached between a youthful Gervais and Charlotte. No, she assured herself hastily, that was impossible. Gervais was not a man who would have cried off and wed without telling her, had there been such an agreement. He was everything that was honorable. She would have staked her life on that.

Lady Amelia, having what her son teasingly described as "taken the bit between her teeth," wasted no time in arranging her musicale. She invited such families as could journey across a wide stretch of country, turned unexpectedly cold at the end of September, to be present at her home. Then, rather than accompanying Rachel herself, she had enlisted the services of Mr. Catley, who, as she had predicted, was enchanted. During a brief rehearsal, he had actually regarded Rachel with awe.

Much in the manner of Victor de Lascelles, he had said, "You are incredibly gifted, milady. It is a great pity that you can never be heard upon the professional stage."

"I confess to having thought the same thing myself once," Gervais, who had been watching the rehearsal, had affirmed. "But," he had added, "I am only grateful that our position in life precludes it. Else I would never see her."

On a morning some two months after the entertainment that had begun life as Lady Amelia's "musicale" and ended as "that time we were privileged to hear the extraordinary Lady Sayre sing," Gervais, looking up from a pile of invitations bidding them to routs, a house party, and several Christmas parties, smiled at his wife. "I am half-inclined to answer these"—he held up a handful of invitations—"by telling them that you have a sore throat. Otherwise, I am convinced that I will never have you to myself again."

His wife moved behind him and put her arms around his neck. "Shall I tell you a secret, my lord and master, whom I love beyond all reason?" she whispered.

"A secret, my angel?" he questioned, resting his head against her bosom. "What secret, my beautiful?"

"I will whisper it in your ear. That is the only way for secrets to be told." She put her lips against his ear.

"Rachel . . ." he breathed a second later. "Are you sure?"

"Phoebe is sure, and she has had the benefit of much advice from her grandmother. I should think that our secret will be due in . . . August. She tells me that he will be born under the sign of Leo, the Lion, or perhaps Virgo, the Virgin, but more likely—" She could not continue with her speculations, for her husband had risen and caught her in his arms, his lips stifling whatever else she was to say about lions or virgins.

"And so," she continued when at last he released her, "I would think that my singing services must needs be ending very soon."

"Immediately!" he exclaimed.

"No, I have promised Lady Amelia that I will sing for her friends at her Christmas party. She has been so kind, and Charlotte, also. I could not disappoint them."

His eyes were actually misty as he looked at her. "I do not deserve you, Rachel," he said softly. "You have breathed life into this house . . . and now you will bring it life."

She stroked his cheek. "You forget that I could have done neither without you. I sometimes think you saved my life."

He flushed. "And you saved mine."

Rachel, nestling against her husband in the post chaise, thought she had never seen anything so beautiful as the trees and ground coated with an unexpected fall of snow. The Hold had reminded her of an ice palace, and as they rounded the bend in the road leading to the Dynevor mansion, she found it almost as beautiful, even though she preferred the square outlines of the Hold to the Palladian house rising before them. She was looking forward to the evening.

In the past months, longing for Anne-Marie, she had found Charlotte a worthy second. She could not think of her in terms of a replacement, for, kind as she and her mother had been, they could not vie with Anne-Marie and the countess. There had been times when, despite her happiness with her husband, she had still missed them dreadfully. She sighed, remembering her dearest friend's disappointment that Rachel could not be present at her wedding to Douglas MacIvor, Lord Stirling.

Unfortunately, the event had taken place a scant month after her arrival at the Hold. The disappointment might not have been so hard to bear had not the bridegroom contributed yet another disappointment, which involved both herself and Anne-Marie. There had been talk of his settling in his ancestral castle, which lay in

Inverness and which would have made it relatively easy
for Rachel to visit Anne-Marie and for the latter to stay
at the Hold. Lord Stirling, who, despite his name, was
more French than English, did not like Scotland. His
ancesors had fled to France upon the beheading of
Charles I, and unlike Gervais's family, they had
remained in France until the Revolution. Shortly after
her marriage, Anne-Marie had written to explain that
Douglas would make his home at his château in
Provence, now restored to him by Louis XVIII. He had
also hired a house in London—but Scotland was out of
the question!

"Such a sigh," Gervais commented. "You look far
too unhappy for an arriving guest, my love." He
regarded her anxiously. "Are you feeling the thing? If
not, we will return immediately." He leaned forward as
if he meant to add a command to the suggestion.

"No." She hastily put her hand on his arm. "I was
thinking of something entirely different. 'Twill be
months before you need worry about anything." She
reached up a gentle hand to stroke his cheek. Seizing it,
he pressed a long kiss into her palm, and not being
satisfied with that, gathered her in his arms and pressed
an even longer kiss upon her lips.

"For shame," she reproved. "You make me wish we
were leaving, not arriving."

"I can tell the coachman . . ."

"No, I promised."

"We could say that you were suddenly stricken with a
virulent fever."

"No," she laughed. "I could not. This will be the last
time. After tonight, I will refuse all other invitations."

"On your honor?"

"Of course."

"I will hold you to it," he said happily. He added. "I
wish the evening were ending, not beginning."

"Come, love," she murmured. "They are your best
friends and mine. Besides, the time will pass swiftly
enough."

The house was decorated beautifully. The two columns that fronted the austere entrance were garlanded with pine branches, gilded cones, and red ribbons. As Gervais guided Rachel up the four steps and between the pillars, he bent to drop a light kiss on her cheek. The door was opened by a smiling butler and they came into a hall, again decorated with pine branches, ribbons, and holly.

Tall baskets of red hothouse roses stood in the drawing room, and Rachel could not help laughing to see that the two caryatids that held up a marble mantelpiece boasted red cheeks and dark eyebrows.

"Your paintbrush?" Rachel heard Gervais accuse Anthony. "I call that damned sacrilegious!"

"They're not goddesses. They are only nymphs. Your wife is the goddess," Anthony said, bending over Rachel's hand. Then Charlotte joined them with her mother, who took Rachel aside to ask about her selections as well as to admire her white gown, which, she said, made her look like a Christmas angel.

Anthony, watching Lady Amelia and Rachel moving away, said, "I agree with Mama. I do not think I have seen your lady looking so beautiful."

"I must agree also." Charlotte nodded. She smiled at Gervais. "And so talented. Mama is in ecstasies, as usual. She has always loved music, as you know, and mourns the dearth of it here in Norham. She said only tonight that it was as if Catalani herself had moved here."

Gervais nodded. "She does have a most beautiful voice," he agreed. "However, my dear Charlotte, tonight must needs mark her swan song—until, at least . . ." He counted on his fingers. "September, next."

Charlotte gazed up at him wide-eyed. "You'll not be telling me . . . that she is breeding?"

He nodded, adding proudly, "But remember, I have said nothing. She has insisted that I keep it a secret."

Anthony said, "Congratulations, Gerry." His eyes

were on his sister's face. "And do not go running to tell
Mama, either. She will be delighted, because she has
become very fond of Rachel, but she will be devastated
to learn that she is to face nine months of silence."

Charlotte said in rather a hurt voice, "I will not tell
anyone—but since we have become such friends, I think
that Rachel could have told me herself."

"It is rather new news," Gervais said. "I should not
have mentioned it, but it was rather hard to contain it."

Charlotte looked up into his happy face. "Nothing
can contain a cup that runneth over," she said softly.
Standing on her tiptoes, she brushed his cheek with her
lips. "I am very happy for you both. And now, I think I
must join Mama and Rachel in the music room."

"Remember, Charlie," her brother warned. "Silence
is golden."

"And diamonds and rubies, as well," she agreed.

In the music room, Charlotte found her mother
arguing with Rachel. "But they will not want only
carols to be sung in chorus."

"You must let dearest Rachel do as she pleases,"
Charlotte advised. "She is the artist." She slipped her
arm around Rachel's waist, somewhat to the surprise of
the latter, since she was not generally so demonstrative.
"You must not let Mama bully you," she added lightly.

"I am doing nothing of the kind," Lady Amelia said
warmly. "But I beg you will sing at least two by yourself. I have promised that you would."

"I will," Rachel said. "I have promised Gervais that
I will sing 'Greensleeves,' though it is not quite a carol,
and you have asked for 'O Holy Night.' "

Lady Amelia sighed, "Very well, I must needs honor
the whims of an artist, it seems."

"You must indeed, Mama," Charlotte said. "And
now, we have kept you imprisoned here long
enough . . . come and greet our other guests, Rachel."

Rachel smiled gratefully at her, thinking of Anne-
Marie. Charlotte, she realized, was almost of her same
coloring, if not quite as lovely. Yet she was pretty in her

own right, and tonight she, like Anne-Marie, seemed to radiate kindness. Indeed, everyone tonight had seemed the very personification of the season. And yet, she thought almost guiltily, she could not help looking forward to the end of the evening and the drive home with Gervais. She could almost hear the harness bells, hung there in honor of Christmas; they would be jingling and the horses' hooves would be adding their own accompaniment. Yet she could not think of that now—she was at the entrance to the drawing room and Gervais had detached himself from a group of other guests to draw her away from Charlotte and bring her to a chair—and everyone was smiling at her as if she really belonged, which, she thought was a slight shock, she did! In spite of her stepmother's cavils, she had been accepted and her loneliness was a thing of the past. She smiled up at her husband, who, in addition to being the man she loved and the father of the child she would bear, had acted as the architect of her future. Had he not come to the Court all those months ago . . . But she could not dwell on that. He *had* come and at present he stood by her chair smiling down at her with such pride and love in his eyes that it seemed to her that Christmas, which would not dawn until a week hence, had already arrived.

The grandfather clock in the corner of the hall was striking the hour of eleven when Rachel with Gervais and Charlotte beside her came toward the front door in the wake of the other departing guests. Everyone was talking at once, and the talk was laced with words of praise for the singer, who, in the opinion of one Lord Elphinstone, had embodied the very spirit of the season.

"And Mama says he is right," Charlotte murmured in Rachel's ear. "It was lovely. And it was kind of you to sing his favorite, 'Barbara Allen,' and all those other ballads."

"But was she kind to herself?" Gervais asked with a slight frown. He looked down at Rachel. "Remember, love, you have promised."

"I will remember," she looked up at him adoringly.

"You'd best watch your step," someone called as they emerged from the front door. "The steps have a coating of ice. It must have snowed again during the evening."

"You'd best let me carry you down the steps, Rachel," Gervais said worriedly. He put out his arms, and at the same time Charlotte stepped forward, and then, with a little cry of fright, suddenly slipped and fell heavily against Rachel, who, reaching out, grasped nothing and went headfirst down the four icy steps.

She was conscious of a great cry from Gervais, of agonizing pain, of horrified exclamations, of something warm coursing down her leg, and, more than that, she was aware of anguish as well as agony before she mercifully fainted.

II

8

"The Marquess and Marchioness of Sayre!" bawled the scarlet-clad majordomo.

Rachel, smiling at her husband, clutched his arm tightly as they climbed the marble stairs and emerged in the great ballroom of Carlton House. Before them stretched the shining polished floor on which couples who had arrived earlier than they were already dancing. She was thankful that they had finally traversed the marble floors and left the marble staircase behind them as well. Though these floors were certainly not icy and the chances of falling practically nonexistent, she was yet wary of them, and though she smiled brightly, the memories they still evoked on this, her second visit to the palace, could not be vanquished, try as she might.

She glanced at her husband. He, too, was smiling, but there was a little line between his brows that had not been there before on that night in December, four months earlier, the night when Charlotte, accidentally slipping on that icy porch, had fallen against her, sending her hurtling down the steps and inadvertently destroying what might have been a son or daughter.

The doctor, while shaking his head gravely, had told her that there was every chance that she, a healthy young woman, would conceive again. However, he had also muttered about shocks to her system and had suggested that she must be patient, for it would take time. She stifled a sigh. Gervais had heard far too many sighs from her. The disappointment had been great, actually crushing, and coupled with it had been the memory of Phoebe's sinister granny. Though common sense told her that it was ridiculous to believe in curses returning to plague those who had uttered them, she had felt accursed. It had been so grievous a blow, coming at a time when she had been so ecstatically happy.

There had been a short period after her fall that she had not wanted to look at Phoebe. Only common sense had kept her from dismissing the girl, the same common sense that had kept her from resenting, even hating, Charlotte. It had been very difficult, however, to receive her friend. Gervais had been similarly resentful, but both had agreed that it was wrong to blame her. Consequently, after Christmas, when they had met at the home of a mutual friend and Charlotte had fallen weeping into her arms, it had been she, Rachel, who had done the comforting and the friendship continued. She smiled a little wryly. Charlotte was in London, and Rachel needed her friendship, because Samantha was also in London, the mother of a fine baby boy whom she left mainly to the care of wet nurses while she busied herself with good works. Rachel wished Anne-Marie would return from Paris.

"My love," Gervais murmured, startling her out of her unhappy reminiscences. "May I have this waltz?"

Rachel made herself smile up at him. "Of course, my dearest, and all the others as well."

"I would gladly take them, but I would hate to deprive the numbers of gentlemen I see looking in your direction. They will think me a dog in the manger if I claim all your waltzes."

"Sir, I fear you jest," she teased.

"You have but to look about you," he said as he whirled her onto the floor.

Across the room, the Marquess of Dorne turned to the Princess Lieven, and raising a gold-handled quizzing glass, drawled, "Ah, young Lord Sayre is returned from the wilds of wherever he was, I see. And who might be the delectably lovely creature with him?"

The princess, who made it a point to know as much as possible about the members of the *ton*, on the off-chance that her husband, the Russian ambassador, might be able to utilize the information, looked in that direction. "Ah, I think it must be his wife."

"He is wed?" the marquess asked in some surprise.

It was the princess's turn to be surprised. "I thought you had in your head a register of births, marriages, and deaths, my dear marquess."

"Occasionally there is an oversight," he responded. "She is incredibly lovely. Is she a foreigner?"

The princess laughed. "One might say that she is foreign to these halls. Someone, I disremember who, knows her stepmother and received the confidence that Lady Sayre is partially of that ancestry that spawned Moses and Abraham. Her father, however, is Sir Harry Villiers, a charming man, wed to the most tiresome creature."

Though her confidence contained an invitation to probe further, the marquess did not take advantage of it. He said merely, "So it came about, then." He bowed over the princess's hand. "I thank you, your highness," he said, and much to her annoyance, excused himself and strolled away, his eyes on the crowded floor until at last he stopped and moved in the direction of Mr. Charles Osmond. The latter gentleman greeted him with considerable civility and a light in his eyes that suggested to the marquess that his crony was already in possession of the information he was about to divulge."

"A truly beautiful creature, the Marchioness of Sayre," he observed. "In common with felines, our friend has truly landed on his feet."

"Where did you obtain your information, my dear Osmond?"

"In Hatchard's bookstore," Mr. Osmond said. "I encountered the noble and noted Mrs. Hannah More in company with Lady Villiers. Since I never forget a name, I asked if she were any kin of Sir Harry Villiers and discovered that indeed she was. Having placed her, I made a point of inquiring after her stepdaughter and learned that the girl was wed to none other than young Lord Sayre, a fact that seemed to annoy her ladyship. Judging from all that Sir Harry told our friend on a certain spring night, her attitude was not surprising. The surprise, you will have to agree, came from other sources.''

Both gentlemen gazed across the floor, and having spotted the couple in question almost simultaneously, were silent, watching them. "She is quite ravishing," the marquess murmured.

"Agreed." Mr. Osmond nodded. "A most felicitous blending of bloods."

"And supremely graceful. A streak of luck, indeed! I am speaking of our friend Gervais. I almost begin to believe in prophecy."

"I understand from Lady Villiers that her stepdaughter has recently suffered a miscarriage. A fall on an icy step, or, as Lady Villiers is pleased to put it, 'God's judgment.' ''

"And the reason for this heavenly fire?'' the marquess inquired.

"She was lifting her voice in song at a Christmas party. Lady Villiers is of the opinion that entertainment of any description is profane.''

"Surely she does not include Christmas carols in that lexicon?'' the marquess asked with raised eyebrows.

"One of the ditties was 'Greensleeves' and another was 'Drink to Me Only with Thine Eyes.' ''

"Her ladyship appears to be exceptionally well-informed.''

"She has an all-abiding interest in her stepdaughter and has obviously found someone to gratify that interest.''

"And did you also manage to gratify it?'' the marquess asked.

Mr. Osmond's smile was unpleasant. "I did not resist

the temptation of dropping a few well-chosen phrases in her ears.''

The marquess regarded him coolly. "That was ill-done of you, Osmond.''

Mr. Osmond's smile did not waver. "Was it not?'' he agreed. "It did afford me the greatest pleasure, however. The Fleet is a most uncomfortable prison, and were it not for the extremely fortunate death of my uncle and the pittance I received in his will, I have no doubt that I should yet be cooling heels and the rest of my person behind its far-from-felicitous walls.'' He visited a pensive look on the marquess's face. "I should have greatly enjoyed seeing the Marquess of Sayre in my shoes. And on that night, it did appear to be a *fait accompli*.''

The marquess nodded. "I imagine I can understand your disappointment. I did not enjoy losing two thousand pounds to the fortunate Gervais myself.'' His eyes wandered to the dance floor. "She really is a most beautiful young woman. How very pleasant for all concerned that she is not encumbered with an infant.''

"She does have a husband, though.''

"Some encumbrances are more easily displaced than others—at least that has been my experience.''

"True,'' Mr. Osmond agreed. "And,'' he added musingly, "I have the utmost faith in Lady Villiers.''

"I, too,'' the marquess said softly. "Let us pray that our sanctimonious little 'saint' does not disappoint us, but now, you must excuse me, my dear Osmond.'' The music had come to an end and the marquess, moving more hastily than was his wont, was second among the several young men who had hastened to the side of the Marchioness of Sayre as her husband led her from the floor.

It was not to be expected that the hopes of the marquess and Mr. Osmond could be gratified as quickly as either hoped. These gentlemen met at an out-of-the-way gambling hell on an evening a week after the ball at

Carlton House. They spoke briefly about Lady Sayre's social success and her agreement, at the Regent's earnest request, to sing arias from *The Marriage of Figaro* and *Don Giovanni*. They agreed that her voice was indeed magnificent and then commented on the fact that some ill-natured soul had connected her with the deceased Miriam Medina Villiers and connected the defunct Lady Villiers with the house of Medina. The information had resulted in a falling-off of several young and older sprigs of the *ton*, whose association with the said house was not precisely felicitous.

"I have heard the *on-dit*, of course." The marquess nodded in answer to Mr. Osmond's query. "I wondered if it had been you who unleashed this tidbit."

"I wondered if it had been you," Mr. Osmond replied. Pointed stare meeting pointed stare, both gentlemen laughed.

"I presume we are guiltless," the marquess remarked.

"Entirely," Mr. Osmond agreed.

"Of course," the marquess murmured, "we are not the only ones to have been fleeced by Gervais."

"I am more inclined to beliveve it came from the female quarter."

"Lady Villiers?"

"I am not entirely sure." Mr. Osmond frowned. "She might have other enemies whom she counts as friends."

"Would you have any inkling which—?"

"Not at the moment. However, I shall make an effort to pursue the matter."

"And I," the marquess said, "will pursue the lady."

"Am I to understand that she has been encouraging?"

"I think she found me amusing and a trifle shocking. She is not used to being shocked, and I think it affords her some titillation. Furthermore, Gervais has encouraged our acquaintance."

"*You will never say so!*" Mr. Osmond said much more loudly than had been his intention, causing a gentleman who held a winning hand of cards to drop it and to utter a most terrible oath, meanwhile directing a slaying glance at Osmond.

The marquess and Mr. Osmond hastily withdrew to an anteroom. "You will never say so," Mr. Osmond repeated. "Furthermore, I cannot believe it."

"Believe that he has done his utmost to discourage the lady's friendship with the urbane and pleasant Marquess of Dorne, believe that he has not told her the reasons for his enmity, believe that the beautiful Rachel's curiosity is piqued. Believe that she believes me when I tell her that we had a most regrettable falling-out and that I am most anxious to make amends, for, after all, we were at Cambridge together. Believe that she is trying to act as a peacemaker."

"Excellent, oh, most entirely excellent," Mr. Osmond whispered. "But beware that he does not call you out."

"I have a feeling that she will be tentative and he discouraging, which, of course, will pique her interest even more. Poor Gervais has always lacked subtlety." The marquess stared pensively into space. "She is entirely lovely. I find myself almost inclined to write poetry. Unfortunately, I do not have the knack for it."

He received a piercing look from Osmond. "It appears to me that you are becoming uncommonly interested in the lady."

The marquess shrugged. "She is an uncommon lady, Osmond. My father would not have needed to bribe me into offering for her—were I the marrying kind, of course."

"Despite her . . . connections?"

"It might be rather profitable to be connected with the house of Medina, given its ruinous rates. I am inclined to believe that our young Gervais finds it so."

Mr. Osmond subdued his laughter. "I hope that for your sake Lady Villiers will not hold back her confidences much longer."

"I cannot believe she will. I presume you are acquainted with the process of spontaneous combustion?"

"I am." Mr. Osmond found his laughter rather more difficult to subdue. "I vow, you *are* a wit, Dorne."

The marquess and Osmond parted for the evening, each as pleased with the other as their natures would allow.

At that same hour, across several squares, Rachel, sitting at the piano in the music room of the commodious town house which had been in the Sayre family for generations, was singing. Seated in a chair beside the bench, Victor de Lascelles was listening raptly and, of course, critically.

As she concluded, he sighed, and receiving an anxious glance, was quick to assure her. "Your unfortunate illness has done nothing to harm your vocal chords, my dear. The voice is, if anything, richer than before. You have graduated from Elvira to Donna Anna." He could not restrain a sigh. "It would be a most notable *Don Giovanni*."

She laughed. "You are kind, Victor, but unfortunately—"

"I know," he interrupted. "Some dreams cannot be realized."

"And some can," she said softly.

He regarded her silently, caught between admiration and regret. "It was no more than you deserved, my dear Rachel." He paused and then added, "Will you remain in town long?"

Rachel ran her hands over the keys. "I expect we will stay here until the end of July. Gervais would prefer to leave earlier. He is not quite happy here."

"That seems to surprise you."

"It does. He rarely visited his home before, but now he seems anxious to return."

"And you are not?"

A cloud passed over her face. "I would prefer to be away a little longer, if only to greet Anne-Marie when she returns from Paris."

"Perhaps you and your husband ought to go to Paris."

"I have yet to know London," she protested. "It is a beautiful city."

"Paris is more beautiful," he told her. "I shall be going there soon."

"Will you, Victor?" Her eyes gleamed. "You have not been back for . . ."

"For nearly the whole of my life," he finished. "But as they say in certain plays, 'all is forgiven.' "

"Victor!" Rachel exclaimed. "You will receive your title again!"

"I have never been without it." He nodded. "But yes, I may now be known as the Comte de Lascelles and my château in Normandy will be mine if I choose to live in it."

"Which of course you will." Rachel clapped her hands.

He eyed her moodily. "I am not sure about that. Paris beckons me . . . the opera beckons me . . . ah, Rachel, if only you—"

"Shhh, Victor." She put her hand over his mouth. "We have agreed that—"

"Ah, *oui*, we have agreed!" he exclaimed. "But we have *not* agreed, only you have agreed. I myself will never cease to wish that you had been born in squalor."

Meeting eyes which had suddenly become blazing, Rachel tried to laugh. "That is not very kind."

"There is an even greater unkindness—that you, with all your talent and your incredibly beautiful voice, must be allowed to sing only for the privileged few. You were meant for the stage, Rachel. It was your destiny, your fate, and I will tell you that those who do not heed the call of their fate are in danger."

A shiver coursed through her. "Victor, calm down," she begged. "I cannot believe you know what you are saying."

"I know!" he cried, leaping to his feet and actually shaking his fist. Then he let it drop to his side. "I am sorry, Rachel. It is only that such a sound comes not often in a lifetime, and those who possess it should be more generous with such wealth. Yet, I know that your hands are, as you say, tied. At least you are not entirely gagged. I will take my leave now, and I hope you will receive me again, after my scolding.''

"I will always receive you, Victor," she said gently. "I do wish . . ." She paused. "But not really. Let me say that once I did wish that I might be heard upon a stage and act in roles rather than being merely a concert singer.''

"You were meant to be in opera, where you could harness your energies.'' He gave her a long look. "Here, you might get into trouble.''

"Trouble?''

"You are very trusting and there are too many jackals in this forest. If I were your husband, I would be inclined to keep you under lock and key.''

"You are pleased to jest.'' She frowned.

"Did you not go riding with the Marquess of Dorne this morning?''

She stared at him in surprise. "I did. How did you happen to hear about that?''

"A carrier pigeon dispatched from an adjacent rooftop, or . . . some other voice raised in song. You have no idea how swiftly news travels in London—at least to certain ears.''

"And it reached your ears. How?''

"You were kind enough to recommend me to Lady Charlotte. I understand that her brother saw you in the park.''

Rachel looked at him wide-eyed. "Anthony saw us and did not join us? I wonder why!''

"It is possible that he felt he might be *de trop*.''

"But that is ridiculous," Rachel said hotly. "I met the marquess quite by accident. I was riding alone.''

"Alone?'' Victor repeated. "Rachel! You are not at Villiers Court!''

"Gervais had planned to go with me, but he received a message from his aunt. I had ordered the horse and it was such a fine morning . . .'' She looked at him ruefully. "And so I have created a scandal.'' Before he could answer, she added with a short laugh, "But that has been done already, has it not? Some little bird has spread the news that I am closely related to the house of Medina. Charlotte was kind enough to tell me that. Perhaps that is why Anthony did not join us—guilt by association. At least the marquess did not feel himself defiled. And—" She stopped speaking, mainly because Victor had put his hand over her mouth.

"Defiled indeed!" He spat the words. "There . . . there are some of us who would be privileged to kiss the hem of your gown. I prayed that you'd not hear . . ." He broke off an stepped away, flushing.

"You have heard it too?" she stated.

"Gossip is the grist of London's mill," Victor said unhappily. "And you are far too beautiful to escape it. I beg you'll not let it trouble you overmuch. You will soon be replaced by some other nine-day wonder."

"Do you think I should not have allowed the marquess to join me?" Rachel faced him anxiously. "Gervais does not like him, I know, though I cannot see why. He is very pleasant company."

"How pleasant is pleasant?" Victor asked quizzically.

"He is amusing and keeps his distance. We talk of art and the theater. He knows Byron and has given me some amusing anecdotes about him. He has heard me sing and is extremely complimentary. He does not flirt with me. He is everything that is polite."

"There is always a calm before the storm."

Rachel said coldly, "There will be no storm. I do not think he has it in mind to create one, and I would not allow it."

"Rachel, my dearest, the waters in London are deep and there are many undercurrents to drag you down."

"You, too, are suggesting that I should not see him?"

"I am suggesting that you do not cultivate him. To see him, to exchange a word or two at a rout or a ball—"

"That is all I wish to do," Rachel interrupted. "I did

not *plan* to go riding with him. We met, as I told you, accidentally.''

"On your part," Victor said.

"Do you believe he was lurking behind a hedge waiting for me to appear?''

"Were I the marquess, that is what I would do—particularly if I were not welcome in milady's husband's house.''

"Oh, dear, complications upon complications. And he is charming. But I will take your word for it. I expect I should have discouraged him this morning." Rachel took a turn around the room. "It was just that I was missing Gervais.''

"And found him a worthy substitute?" Victor asked with raised eyebrows.

"Of course not!" she cried. "There is no one in the world that could replace Gervais. From the moment we first met—"

"I know," Victor said hastily. "And," he added meaningfully, "the marquess must also know."

"He does know," Rachel said. "I have told him so."

"When will Gervais return?"

"Late tomorrow.''

"And he is bringing back his aunt?"

Rachel smiled. "She has insisted that in order for our household to be proper, I must needs have a female companion. It is kind of her to put herself out. I understand she is quite an elderly lady. And I think she prefers to live in Bath.''

"Most elderly ladies do. They go to the Pump Room, gossip, and take those bitter waters. To me it is *incroyable*.''

"To me also," Rachel agreed.

He bowed over her hand. "At least she did not come this evening, else I must have been sent on my way. And will I be forced to conduct your lessons in the presence of this beldame?"

"This . . . beldame, as you are pleased to put it, is the dowager Countess of Beckford and was a great hostess in her day.''

"The Lord save us from past splendors. Your ears will be aching. I can only hope that for your sake, she will decide not to come."

"*Tu es très méchant,*" Rachel reproved.

"No, I am not wicked, I am only honest. *Bonne nuit, ma belle.*"

Rachel saw him as far as the hall. As the door closed on him, she sighed. She was not looking forward to the arrival of the Countess of Beckford. There was a painting of her in the drawing room. It had been done by Gainsborough and depicted her as a shepherdess—a shepherdess in silk and satin with fluttering ribbons caught in an imaginary wind, with a spurious sheep at her side. She had a lively, piquant little face that just missed true beauty. However, she had been very pretty. It was difficult to imagine what the shepherdess looked like at sixty-six. According to Gervais, she was rather formidable. And being the mother of the young man who would have succeeded to the title had anything happened to Gervais, she might very well resent his bride. Rachel was rather positive that the lady had not offered to come out of the kindness of her heart. Most likely, it was curiosity—and had she heard the gossip concerning Rachel's Medina connections? News did indeed travel fast, she was learning, particularly that sort of news.

She went slowly up the stairs to her chamber. The house was very empty without Gervais. It was, in fact, the first time they had been apart since their marriage, and she missed him quite dreadfully. She did not sleep in the big bed in his room. Again, for the first time since he had insisted on carrying her over the threshold of the London house too, she remained in her own chamber. Perhaps because the bed was unfamiliar to her, she did not sleep immediately, and when she did, her dreams were fragmented and vaguely disturbing. At one point she saw a girl with a great mane of red hair. She stood at a tower window screaming a violent denunciation. Her screams aroused Rachel, who sat up in bed with the sound still echoing in her ears. She found herself staring at curtains through which the sunlight was creeping.

She had a full recollection of her last dream. Red Lizzie had screamed as she jumped, but it had not been a scream of fear, and actually she had hurled herself from the tower window in anger or, rather, rage at the man she had once loved to distraction. Why? And why had the dream come to her at this time? She had no answers for that, and besides, it was only a dream.

Rachel tried to go back to sleep, but she was not successful. Eventually she summoned Phoebe, who brought her a breakfast of chocolate and a roll. As soon as the girl had helped her to dress, she went down to the music room to practice. Her art always helped her to soothe her troubled spirit—as did riding, but she did not want to run the risk of meeting the marquess again.

She began with exercises and had just started to study music that Victor had left her to peruse the previous day when there was a discreet tap at the door. "Yes?" she called.

The butler opened the door, looking surprised. "Milady, Lady Villiers is here and tells me that it is most urgent that she see you."

Rachel, glancing at the clock on the mantelshelf and finding that it was a scant five minutes past nine, looked at him in amazement. "At this hour? Is my father with her?"

"No, milady, she has brought her abigail only."

Considerably surprised and not a little alarmed, Rachel said, "Very well, I will see her in the library."

As Rachel hurried down the hall, her heart was pounding. What could have occasioned Samantha's second visit to the house . . . and at this hour in the morning . . . and with only her abigail? Had something happened to her father?

She came into the library and found her stepmother frowning up at the huge portrait of the late Marquess of Sayre, an equestrian painting that showed him on the back of a plunging white steed.

"Samantha," she said.

"My dear." Lady Villiers turned. Her eyes were wide and full of concern. "My dear Rachel, I have come because of a very serious situation. Believe me, I hesitated long before deciding to see you, but I feel it is my duty to make you acquainted with a piece of gossip that is going the rounds of the *ton*."

"A . . . piece of gossip?" Rachel's thoughts flew to her chance meeting in the park with the Marquess of Dorne.

"If you are going to tell me that I should not have gone riding with Lord Dorne, Samantha," she said coldly, "I have already been apprised of the fact and I will tell you that it was a chance meeting."

"Oh, no, I knew nothing of that, though unfortunately Lord Dorne is connected with what I must tell you. He is just as upset as I over it . . . and blames a man he knows for having spread the scandal. He assures me that word of it would never have left his lips. I vow, I have been awake all night trying to decide what to do. Your father, unfortunately, is away for the day, else I would have asked his advice. Yet, since he is so deeply concerned in the matter . . . Oh, dear . . . oh, dear, it is all a great shame and a storm you must needs weather. I know we have not always been in sympathy, but my heart goes out to you in this matter, it truly does. I cannot undertsand why Mr. Osmond chose to repeat this gossip, but since he has, my poor Rachel, you will need courage—and I pray you will not think unkindly of your husband. I—"

"My husband?" Rachel interrupted. "What of my husband?"

"Oh, I do hate to tell you, but you will hear it soon enough—a great many people have heard it already, and someone without your best interests at heart is sure to repeat it to you. Consequently, it is far better that you hear it from me. I beg you will sit down."

"Has . . . has something happened to Gervais?" Rachel cried.

"No, not that I know of . . . but, my dear, it is too shocking. Still, I pray that you will find it in your heart to forgive him. He does seem fond of you now."

"Fond?" Rachel repeated. "What are you suggesting?"

"Please, let me give you the whole of it," Lady Villiers cried. "And never think that I am doing this out of malice aforethought, for though it was a great sum to ignore, your father is well able to do so, and it was his suggestion, you must remember. I blame myself, too. I know I was being rather horrid to you at the time. I was expecting dear little Mark John James, such a darling, and so good, his nurse tells me. Dear Hannah thinks she is the most beautiful baby she has ever seen, a little angel in truth. But never mind that, do sit down, dear Rachel."

"What sum are you talking about?" Rachel demanded bluntly. "And what did my father have to ignore?"

Lady Villiers loosed a long sigh. "My dear, I know you will find this as hard to credit as I—but until a certain night at Brooks's last April, your father had never met Lord Sayre. They encountered each other at the club. Someone had told dearest Harry that Gervais was exceedingly lucky at cards. He had, in fact, what they called an inherited streak of luck. There was a story to the effect that it happened once in a generation. I am sure that must be a fable, but no matter, he was known to be a very canny player until he met your father, who seemed to have had a streak of luck himself, at least that night, and . . ."

As Lady Villiers, displaying all the sympathy and horror of which she was capable, continued with a description of that fatal night at Brooks's, Rachel listened in growing disbelief. When at length her step-mother came to the end of her account, she said coldly, "I am surprised that you would pay heed to such scurrilous gossip, Samantha."

"My dear, I only wish it were merely gossip." Lady

Villiers sighed. "But Lord Dorne corroborates this tale. And the debt was excused, my dear, else you would never have met Gervais. He would have been in the Fleet or the King's Bench for debt. He had lost everything, my love, even his stable. Had he chosen to continue the game, he would have lost his houses. As it was, he would have needed to sell or mortgage them. And it was then that your father suggested—"

"You have already told me what he suggested, Samantha. It is not necessary to repeat it," Rachel took a turn around the room. "You say that the Marquess of Dorne overheard my father's suggestion?"

"He did, and also one of the men employed at Brooks heard it. He was later paid to remain silent."

"But no one has paid the marquess, I see," Rachel said scathingly.

"It was not Dorne who spread the word, it was that ill-conditioned man Osmond. I dislike the creature immensely. He, it seems, has a grudge against Gervais, who won a great deal of money from him and did not think it his duty to return some of it to Osmond, thus saving him a stint in the Fleet. You can imagine how pleased he was to be possessed of this information."

"I can imagine that he made it up out of whole cloth!" Rachel cried.

"My dear, I thought so too, until Lord Dorne mentioned Lady Charlotte, who is a neighbor of yours, I believe, and a friend?"

"Yes, she is both," Rachel said. "What about Lady Charlotte? Have you been to her with this tale?"

"No, of course I have not," Lady Villiers cried. "I know we have not been in sympathy, but you *are* my stepdaughter and and my only concern in this dreadful business. We are united by family ties and those are not to be ignored. Please, Rachel, believe that I have only your best interests at heart."

"What does Lady Charlotte have to do with this situation?" Rachel demanded.

"My dear, they were on the verge of a betrothal. Lady Amelia was ready to insert the notice in the *Morning Post*, when Gervais cried off."

"I do not believe it. He is an honorable man. He would never have done such a thing and he would never have accepted such a proposition from Father. He . . . he loves me."

"I am sure he does," Lady Villiers said comfortingly. "And he is, by and large, an honorable man. If he made a commitment, I think he would abide by it."

"And I am that commitment. Is that what you are saying, Samantha?"

"I have reason to believe that he is quite fond of you, Rachel. Believe me, I would have said nothing were this story not making the rounds, thanks to Mr. Osmond. There will be talk, and it will undoubtedly be blown out of all natural proportion, the way gossip usually is. I thought you must be prepared. I hardly think Charlotte would have said anything, or even your father, who would feel that he had your best interests at heart. I think your best interest does not lie in ignorance but in the full knowledge of what occurred."

"I . . . do not believe it," Rachel said stonily.

"I expect that in your position I would feel much the same," Lady Villiers said sympathetically. "We are all inclined to wear blinders when it comes to those we love. I cannot approve dear Harry's actions. He must have known that the tale was bound to leak out—or perhaps not. He is not well-acquainted with London gossip. And as I have said, Osmond had a grievance. Obviously this tale was too good to keep to himself." She gave Rachel a commiserating look. "Naturally, I will say nothing to anyone. I do not believe in repeating 'scurrilous gossip,' as you have put it. I am a good Christian woman."

"I am much beholden to you, Samantha," Rachel said with a touch of sarcasm. "I know what it must have cost you to make me acquainted with this tale, the which, I do not mind telling you, I find entirely unbelievable. And have I your . . . er, Christianity to thank for spreading the word that I am connected with the house of Medina?''

Lady Villiers gave her a reproachful look. "I have never told anyone of that," she said in a hurt voice. "If your connection with the Medinas has been discovered, it was none of my doing. Perhaps you had best discuss the matter with your husband. It is very likely that despite your father's largess, his finances are in rather worse order than even Mr. Osmond knows."

Rachel moved swiftly to the bell-pull that summoned the butler and yanked it. "I will have Matthews show you to the door."

"You . . . you have the temerity to order me from your house?" Lady Villiers glared at Rachel.

"As you see."

"Your father will know of my treatment here," Lady Villiers said freezingly. "And being rude to your betters will not change your situation. I have always decried your father's first marriage, not because I am jealous of your late mother, but because I consider it an unfortunate aberration on his part. That has never been brought home to me more forcibly than at this time—when I, bound on an errand of Christian mercy, am summarily insulted."

There was a tap on the door.

"Come in, Matthews," Rachel called. As the butler appeared on the threshold, she added, "Lady Villiers is leaving. Will you be kind enough to show her out?"

Rachel could not remember a time when she had been so angry—not angry, she told herself, furious. That Gervais should be slandered and herself demeaned as no more than a debt discharged was terrible, and how to counteract the gossip? And had it really spread? There were those she could ask, and she meant to ask them. Moving out of the library, she ran up the stairs, and finding Phoebe at work on one of her gowns, said curtly, "Come, we have some visits to make."

The girl regarded her in surprise. "Yer ladyship, ye look all to pieces. 'Adn't you better 'ave a bit o'—"

"I want nothing, Phoebe. Kindly do as I ask. But first you had best comb my hair, and perhaps I should change my gown." She glanced at herself in the long mirror and saw that her eyes were unnaturally bright and her cheeks very red. Her hair was tousled where, upon Samantha's indignant departure, she must have pulled at it. She did not remember having done so, but it was her habit when disturbed. "No, never mind my gown, but my hair—please fix my hair."

A half-hour later, Rachel's post chaise stopped at the town residence of the Dynevors. Ten minutes after that, she confronted an astonished Charlotte in a sunny parlor at the back of the house. Her friend, she thought confusedly, did not seem as astonished at her unceremonious visit as she might have been. Did that suggest she had been anticipating it?

"Will you not sit down, Rachel?" Charlotte asked. "You do look disturbed. Pray tell me what's amiss."

"No, I would prefer not to sit down," Rachel responded. "I want only to hear from you if the gossip which my stepmother saw fit to repeat to me not an hour since is true. It concerns certain gambling debts incurred by my husband."

Charlotte said carefully, "I know that Samantha . . . er, your stepmother has said—"

"Enough. Then she has spoken to you. And is it true that you were formally betrothed to Gervais?"

Tears suddenly stood in Charlotte's eyes. She looked away quickly. "We . . . we were never formally betrothed," she murmured. "Mama was planning . . . but it came to naught."

"You did have some manner of understanding, then?" Rachel pursued with a sinking heart.

"It . . . We . . . we'd known each other from childhood, you see . . ." Charlotte spoke apologetically. "And, well . . . yes, we did have an understanding. But it had never been formalized. It happened when I was nineteen. You must not think badly of him, Rachel. He has come to be quite fond of you. He has told me so."

"He has told you he is fond of me," Rachel repeated

dully. She added in a low voice, "Did he also tell you that my father excused his gambling debts on the promise that he would meet me?"

"He . . . he told me nothing." More tears came into Charlotte's eyes. "I never knew the . . . the reason until Samantha . . ."

"I see." Rachel swallowed a huge lump in her throat. Charlotte's hesitancy, coupled with her anguish, was giving an unwanted credence to the tale. She had hoped, had expected, that her friend . . . But was she a friend? The terrible moment on that icy porch rose up to confront her. Had that been an accident, after all? Could Charlotte have been seeking revenge for Gervais's defection? No, it was unthinkable. She looked into Charlotte's agitated countenance. "I . . . had best go," she said.

"Rachel . . ." Charlotte put a hand on her arm. "You must not hold this against Gervais. He is, as I have said, very fond of you, and, I think, quite happy in his marriage. Whatever was between us is finished. And nor must you imagine that on the night I fell that 'twas done on purpose. I would never have taken so terrible a revenge—no matter how much I loved him. I cannot deny that I did have hopes that he . . . Well, until that night at Brooks's, we did have an understanding. We were to see each other the next day, and I expected . . ."

"You expected his proposal and your mother expected to insert an announcement in the *Morning Post*, an announcement of your betrothal," Rachel said flatly.

Charlotte nodded.

"And then, weeks later, you met me on the grounds of the Hold," Rachel said slowly, wondering why she should think of a girl with flaxen hair falling down her back and clad in a garment of rude sacking, weeping as she confronted a red-haired . . . With a feeling of horror she banished these telltale images. "You did not know of our marriage?"

"You must know that I did not," Charlotte admitted

in a low voice. "There was no letter—ever. I expect he feared to hurt me. Later, he told me that he had meant to explain in person."

"I am sorry. It must have been more of a shock than I realized," Rachel said bluntly. "I think . . . I must go. I thank you for . . . enlightening me further."

"Rachel . . ." Charlotte caught her arm. "Gervais does have a certain fondness for you. He has assured me of that."

"I see." Feeling as if her insides had suddenly vanished, leaving her hollow and empty, Rachel added, "I will bid you good-bye, Charlotte."

"I pray you will forgive me," Charlotte sighed.

"Why should you ask me for forgiveness?" Rachel asked. "It seems that I should be asking *your* pardon. But enough. I must go."

She hurried out of the house. As she came into her post chaise, she wanted nothing more than to sink into the ground. She had expected that Charlotte would provide her with reassurances. They were friends. Yet there had been that moment on the porch . . . But Charlotte could not have done that on *purpose*. And just now, she had obviously tried to be sympathetic, but at the same time, her words had been all too revealing. If she, Rachel, had been in her place, she would never have been so frank—or was that true? Charlotte had sustained a terrible disappointment, something she had been totally unprepared to hear from a strange young woman standing in the carriageway at the home of the man she loved. Yet Charlotte was not the person Rachel ought to have questioned. That person was her husband—and though she had been minded to actually pay a call on the Marquess of Dorne, she would wait and give Gervais at least the benefit of the doubt. With a sad little sigh she realized that until she had been to see Charlotte, she had not really entertained those doubts. Or had she? At this point in time, she was not sure. She was not sure of anything at all.

9

The rumors had reached as far as Bath. That was the intelligence awaiting Gervais when he arrived at his aunt's house in that city. Far from wanting to return to London with him, his Aunt Lily, small, angry and flanked by her four yapping spaniels, quizzed him as to his hasty marriage, talked about family honor and tradition, ending with a lengthy dissertation on moneylenders in general and on Shylock in particular.

The acrimonious visit concluded with the nephew telling his enraged relative that he was glad she had decided not to come to London because she did not deserve to meet his bride. She responded with a heartfelt wish that she might cut him out of the inheritance as he so richly deserved. She was hardly pleased to be reminded that since he was already the recipient of title and inheritance, she could do nothing. They parted with considerable ill-feeling. However, on the way back from that fruitless excursion which had wrested him from his wife's side for far longer than he wanted, Gervais congratulated himself on the fact that his Aunt Lily would not be returning to plague poor Rachel.

An unexpected and pelting rain kept him holed up in a miserable roadside inn for the better part of the day. Consequently, he did not arrive until early evening of the following day. Since he had guessed that Rachel had not been pleased by his aunt's offer to make a third in their household, Gervais, told that her ladyship was in the library, went there directly, without waiting to remove cloak or muddy boots. To his surprise, he found her seated there with not even a candle to combat the lengthening shadows of evening.

"My love, Rachel, why are you sitting here in all this darkness?" he demanded, coming to her chair.

"Is it dark?" she asked. "I had not noticed. I was thinking."

Her tone was dull and she had had no word of greeting for him. He said confusedly, "Is anything the matter?"

"I am not sure, Gervais," she responded, still in that dull tone so very unlike her usually vibrant speech. "Is your aunt with you?"

"My aunt . . . No, she decided that she preferred to remain in Bath, for which I am heartily grateful, as you must be, too."

"I see," Rachel said. "Then why did she summon you?"

"She had some bee in her bonnet. I'm damned if I know."

"I see," Rachel repeated.

"My dear . . ." Gervais moved forward and frowned. "What is amiss?"

"I am not sure," was her ambiguous response. "I am hoping that you will help me solve a particularly confusing conundrum."

"A conundrum, my love?" he replied confusedly.

"Yes," she said, still not rising from her chair. "My stepmother has been to visit me."

"Has she?" he demanded in a hard voice. "That must be the reason for your low spirits. I am sorry I was not here."

"I am sorry too, Gervais. I wish you might have heard what she had to tell me. There was further corroboration furnished by Charlotte—that is, if I wish to believe either of them." Rachel finally rose and faced him.

Even in that uncertain light, he could tell she was

pale. He said, "What did your stepmother have to say for herself?"

"She had a curious story to tell me—concerning a game of cards."

He tensed. "A game of cards?" he repeated. He essayed a laugh. "Has your stepmother become interested in card games, then? I thought it was against her religion."

"This has nothing to do with her religion. It seems that you and my father played cards at Brooks's one night, the night you met him for the first time . . . and he won, while you lost *heavily*."

Gervais took a step forward. "Where did your stepmother receive her information? I am sure that your father . . ." He broke off, realizing too late that that was not what he had intended to say.

Rachel was silent a moment. Then she said heavily, "Were you about to say that you were sure my father did not tell her about your card game?" Before he could respond, she rushed ahead. "There was a card game, then, at Brooks's? And he won?"

"There was a card game, yes," Gervais said. "And he won, yes, but—"

"I see," she interrupted coldly. "And afterwards . . . what happened afterward? Or should I tell you? Should I tell you how my father suggested that you come and meet his poor daughter, who was pining for a husband and there was none to offer for her because of her mixed blood, and since you had gone down so heavily and were in danger of being clapped into the Fleet, you agreed to meet this poor creature and see if you could possibly stomach a half-Jew?"

"Rachel!" he cried. "That was not the way of it."

"Was it not?" she demanded contemptuously.

"No, it was not. Your father seemed distraught, and I . . . I felt sorry for him. I—"

"Even though he had just won your entire fortune and your stable, you felt sorry for him. How entirely magnanimous, my lord!"

"I felt sorry for him," Gervais repeated angrily. "I

would never have gone had he not pleaded your case so—"

"My case. I see," she said shortly.

"You see nothing!" he cried. "You do not see how when I came back with him through the woods and met you it was as if . . . But why need I explain? You remember how it was with us that night!"

"When you were so kind, so sympathetic? Yes, I remember. I was very grateful to you. I did not know you had a very strong reason to be sympathetic . . . that there was your entire fortune in the balance, and a promised dowry on top of that!"

"I did not want to take your dowry!"

"But you did," she flashed.

"Your father insisted."

"What power is it that my father exercises over your will, Gervais?" Rachel spoke contemptuously. "I vow, 'tis most amazing. He had the power to remove your scruples and bring you to the Court to view his daughter and to see if you could stomach her, the alternative being the Fleet. How persuasive you were, Gervais, in making me believe you loved me, and how swift. Our courtship was a matter of *hours*! And this notwithstanding the fact that Lady Charlotte Frazier was expecting to marry you and her mother expecting to insert the announcement in the *Morning Post* when Charlotte and her brother, riding to the Hold, met a strange young woman, a young woman who turned out to be your bride—and they none the wiser. Have you no heart at all, Gervais?"

"That was not the way of it, dammit," he cried. "I had not offered for her. I had toyed with the idea, but I did not love her. We had been friends since childhood and there was no one else in the offing . . . but when I met you, all thoughts of Charlotte fled."

"And for a good reason, no doubt. You could not have afforded to marry her and no doubt her parents would not have welcomed a bridegroom from the Fleet—the days of Fleet marriages are long gone, are they not? And furthermore, my father had offered you a good bargain. Not only could you forget your debt, you had my dowry as further compensation!''

''Will you stop talking about my debt and that damned dowry. This is the way of it. I did accept your father's offer concerning the debt—''

''Ah,'' Rachel interrupted.

''But,'' he continued doggedly, ''I accepted it for one reason only. I accepted it because I had fallen in love with you.''

''Oh?'' she said contemptuously. ''You had fallen in love with me?''

''I had fallen in love with you,'' he repeated. ''And I would have done anything to possess you. Even the honor I had prized most highly until I met you, seemed a small exchange for what I felt. It seemed to me that I had been waiting for you all my life. I fell in love with you at first sight, Rachel. Surely you have heard of that . . . and did you not feel the same about me? Deny it if you can!''

''I cannot deny it,'' she said bitterly. ''You were also most persuasive, but of course, you had reason to be. All the reason in the world. How lucky you have been, Gervais, to lose and then to win, after all. But I think there must be an end of luck.'' Turning on her heel, Rachel walked swiftly out of the room and a few seconds later Gervais heard her ascending the stairs.

He sank down in a chair across from the one his wife had just vacated. After his long ride, his senseless quarrel with his aunt, and his delays on the road, he had been longing to see her—had loathed every minute spent away from the woman he loved with all his heart—and to come back to find her a contemptuous and angry stranger was a terrible shock, a stultifying shock that left him confused and helpless. How could he persuade her that the truth she had been told was not the real truth, but something twisted completely out of shape? And why?

Why had Lady Villiers thought it necesary to . . . ? But even as he began to question her motives, he had the answer. Jealousy, of course. She was jealous of her

beautiful stepdaughter, and there was her ugly prejudice
as well. Could not Rachel understand that? No, she
understood only that he, whom she had believed to be
honorable, had acted dishonorably. He *had* acted
dishonorably, but to win her, not to keep himself out of
debtors' prison. How might he prove that to her? Her
father . . . Her father knew the truth, had listened to his
arguments and replied to them with infinitely
reasonable arguments of his own—arguments that he
had won but would not have won were it not for Rachel.
He would have to see Sir Harry at once, and while there,
he would take Samantha's neck between his two hands
and twist it, as one might twist off a chicken's head. He
ground his teeth. He must needs calm down before he
saw anyone. He was not easily aroused, but when his
temper got the better of him . . . He loosed a long
hissing breath, striving for calm, but it was difficult to quell his anger against Samantha, against
Rachel, too, for not believing that he loved her, loved
her so much that he had done the unthinkable and
sacrificed his honor for that love. She had to believe
him. He would make her believe him!

He strode out of the library and took the stairs two at
a time, reaching her room. He turned the knob of the
door and found it unyielding. She had locked her door
against him! He went into his own room and through
the dressing room that stood between their chambers.
The second door was also locked. He tried to calm
himself, saying as coolly as he might under the
circumstances, "Rachel, I must speak to you. Please let
me in."

She did not answer.

"Rachel," he called furiously, "open your door, I
command it." He pounded on the door. Once more he
was possessed by rage, and coupled with it was hurt and
anguish. That he should need to come home to this,
when he was longing to see her, when he had
expected . . . He beat against the door with both hands,
beat and then in a near-frenzy kicked and pounded until

it finally yielded, crashing back against the wall with a force that caused some ornament to fall to the floor and shatter. He had half-expected to find Rachel standing there glaring at him, but she was not there. The door of her bedroom was closed. It had no key and he pushed it open, finding her huddled on the bed.

"Rachel!" he exclaimed. "Rachel, my love, listen to me."

She sat up, glaring at him. "Get out!" she said icily, staring at him as if he were a stranger, an importunate stranger whom she disliked. "Get out of my room!"

His temper rose at the tone. He glared back at her, his anger matching and even surpassing her own. "Nothing in this house belongs to you. This is my room, mine, do you hear? Your money did not purchase it. And I will not have your door closed against me. I am your husband."

"Bought with my father's money!" she said contemptuously.

"Damn and blast you for a bloody little fool. Can you not see that I love you?" he said gratingly.

"I can see that you were badly dipped, my lord, and willing to do anything to restore your fallen fortunes, even to taking to bed a stranger, and one of mixed blood, as it were. And—"

She got no further. Tearing off his garments, he flung himself on her, closing her mouth with a long invading kiss. Then, pushing her down on the bed, he subdued her furious struggles with hands and body, kissing her again and again, hard, hurtful kisses, his anger turned to fury, closing his mind to her cries and leaving him unmindful of her struggles or her sharp nails digging into his arms, his back, his chest. Then finally she stopped struggling, evidently aware that it was futile to try to contend against his fury, futile to try to prevent that inevitable, that ultimate possession.

"Rachel . . ." He finally lay beside her exhausted. "Rachel, can you not see that I love you?"

She did not answer. She began to cry weakly, and

turning away from him, buried her face in the pillow. He stared down at her, his anger and frustration leaving him. In their place was a combination of horror and remorse. This was not how he had intended to convince her of his love. He should have treated her gently, but instead, she had roused him to fury with her unfounded accusations, and he had ravished her.

"Rachel . . ." he said tentatively. "Rachel, please, I did not mean . . ." He placed his hand on her shoulder.

She trembled and shrank away from him. "Go . . . please go," she sobbed, her tones half-muffled by the pillow.

"Rachel," he said pleadingly, "I beg you will forgive me."

She did not respond, and eventually he left her and went to his own room, glad that she could not see the hot tears coursing down his cheeks as he fell on his bed and lay there contemplating what he feared was the wreck of his marriage and his life.

Rachel had not thought she could sleep, so filled was she with anger, hurt, and pain, but she did, awakening at a very early hour. The sky was still dark gray. She lay watching it, watching as a line of red began to stretch along the eastern horizon. Finally she rose. She found herself very stiff. Her body ached. He had hurt her. No, he had not hurt her, she told herself angrily, defiantly, nothing he could do would ever hurt her again. He was as nothing to her, this man whom she had believed she loved with all her heart. She had to respect the man she loved, and she could not respect one who had basely wed her to save himself from the Fleet and who had had the temerity to talk about love, even while he did not deny his action. Then, he had added to that, another action even more heinous. He had ravished her, and all was at an end between them. She would never, never forgive him, never as long as she lived! Last night, before she had fallen asleep, she had thought of leaving him, but she would not leave him. She would remain here and enjoy the benefits her money had provided for both of them.

She rang for Phoebe. She had to ring several times before the girl appeared, looking sullen and angry. Rachel made no apologies, no excuses. She said merely, "Please help me to dress. I am going riding in the park."

"At this hour, milady?" Phoebe questioned in surprise.

"At this hour," Rachel responded in frozen accents. She saw no reason to explain that she had one other destination in mind. She continued, "I want you to inform the coachman that I will be ready in a half-hour."

"But, milady," Phoebe protested, "you . . ."

"You will please do as I say." Rachel rapped out the words, ignoring the hurt look in the girl's eyes. "Go!"

It was not quite six by the time Rachel mounted on Aldebaran, the horse Gervais had bought for her when first they arrived in London. A white stallion, he was a beautiful creature. Mounting him, she remembered the moment when Gervais had take her out to the stables behind his house and shown her the horse. She had been so pleased, so surprised—she had not known, of course, that the animal had been purchased with her father's money. And last night, when he had brutally ravished her, he had dared to tell her that she was living in his house and, in effect, belonged to him as a chair or table might. But it was not his house! It would have been put up for auction if her father had not come forward with his generous offer and his lies—to tell her he had known Gervais's father, when, in fact, they had met at Brooks's on the night of that fatal card game.

Her anger increased. Her father, she guessed, would have done anything to rid himself of her presence so that he could enjoy peace and quiet with his bride, with the woman who had finally given him the heir he had wanted, the untainted heir, who was pure English. How pleased he must have been to have won the money and at the same time hit upon the plan that would remove

his unwanted daughter from his life and provide him
with the contentment he craved.

She had thought to see her father that morning, but
she would not. He was part of her past, just as Gervais
was part of her past. Tears filled her eyes. She blinked
them angrily away. She was not crying over Gervais.
She hated him, loathed him. She was crying because she
did not know what she would do with her future. No,
that was not true; she did know. She would enjoy herself. She would buy clothes, she would go to the opera,
and she would now accept invitations from the several
young men who had offered them. She grimaced,
remembering her shock at Gervais's explanation that it
was considered *de rigueur* for a married woman to have
escorts as long as they did not overstep the so-called
boundaries of polite behavior—and they would not!

However, the first thing on her agenda would be a
visit to a mantua-maker. She did not have nearly
enough gowns, and with the styles constantly changing,
some of the ensembles she had brought with her were
sadly out of fashion. She had intended to have a
seamstress make some of them over—because she had
liked the material and the color and because even
though Gervais had appeared to be wealthy, she had not
wanted him to believe her extravagant. However, now
that she knew the source of his wealth, she would not
stint on her purchases. There had been a love of a gown
on display . . . She paused in her thinking. She did not
care about gowns . . . she did not want to live in the
same house with Gervais. If only Anne-Marie were here,
she could have gone to her. Anne-Marie, her one true
friend, would have been glad to shelter her. But she *did*
have one other true friend—Victor!

He would be coming to give her a lesson tomorrow,
but she wanted to see him today. Now! He would listen
to her woes and she could depend on his advice. She
touched her horse lightly on the back with the ends of
her reins and headed toward the stables.

Victor de Lascelles had gone to bed late the previous

evening. As was his wont, he and some musically knowledgeable friends had repaired to the opera to hear Madame Fodor in *Orpheus and Euridice*, which naturally had necessitated an aftermath of musical discussion or, rather, dissection. Seated in a tavern not far from the opera house, Victor and his cronies, equally outraged, had first concentrated on the soprano. After disgustedly describing a robust physical appearance that contrasted most drastically with her role of a youthful beauty, they had proceeded to her vocal attainments, which had angered them excessively, especially given the glowing notices that had preceded her. However, they were willing to concede that if she sounded like a wounded screech owl, the tenor who had sung Orpheus had had more in common with a bat, being practically soundless in his upper register and painfully shrill when heard. They had mournfully discussed the great voices of the past, now silenced by age or death, agreeing that there was nothing to be heard in the present that could possibly match that golden era.

"There is one voice that could," Victor had stated. "A sound such as I have never heard before. If she were on stage, she would oust Catalani herself."

He had countered the round of guffaws with an earnest description of the voice, adding sadly that it must be forever denied a listening public because of the singer's position in life. He had been made extremely angry by one friend's contention that this was just as well, for he would not need to substantiate claims which were far too extravagant, at least in the opinion of the said friend.

Victor had been narrowly saved from calling out his onetime crony by the amount of brandy he had quaffed, the which had caught up with him and necessitated his companions bringing him home and throwing his semi-conscious form upon his unmade bed.

Consequently, after Rachel, confronting an astonished and suspicious lodging-house-keeper at a few minutes past seven in the morning, demanded Victor's attendance, he, embraced tightly in the arms of Morpheus, had been not only surprised but also indignant. However, being pressed to rise and speak to this elegant and evidently aristocratic young lady, who, despite the persuasions of the keeper, refused to leave, he did so with very bad grace, not troubling so much as to drag a comb through his tangled locks.

Rachel, sitting in the anteroom of the lodging house, was feeling extremely uncomfortable. The man who had admitted her had given her a most suspicious stare and he had seemed extremely disinclined to arouse his lodger. He had gone off grumbling, leaving her very uncertain as to the wisdom of calling upon Victor at this hour in the morning at his lodgings, even though he was her very good friend. Had Gervais known . . . But it would not matter if Gervais had known. Gervais did not matter. As of last night, he was nothing to her, nothing at all, nor ever would be again. Much to her anger and astonishment, the wall she was facing suddenly blurred.

"Rachel!" Victor cried in that same moment.

Rachel rose swiftly, blinking away her tears—which had not been real tears, but a condition left over from having the wind in her face as she had galloped through the park. She rose. "Victor, I must speak to you. I am sorry to . . . to come at this hour, but . . . but . . ." Much to her surprise and annoyance, more tears fell and she could not speak over the huskiness in her throat.

"Rachel, my dearest . . ." Victor put an arm around her waist and drew her down the hall to his rooms, which were, fortunately, just one flight up. He blushed as he led her into his disordered parlor, which was furnished with only a piano, a chair, and a rather rickety sofa. All the surfaces were at present covered with rolls of music and a few items of his attire. Several pairs of discarded shoes lay on the floor, and so did the coat he had worn the previous evening. "I must beg your indulgence, but I was not expecting—" he began.

"It does not matter, Victor," she interrupted. "And I should not have come at . . . at this hour in the

morning, but I had to . . . to s-see you. And . . .
and . . ." She swallowed convulsively. "I do not know
why I . . . I am crying. It is s-silly."

"My beautiful, my dearest . . ." He swept a pile of
scores from the sofa and pushed her down gently. "Tell
me, my sweetest girl, what is amiss?"

It was a moment before Rachel could stop sobbing,
another moment before she could speak. She began
slowly, hesitantly, but soon the words were rushing
forth, all her anguish, her shock, her indignation at the
cruel trick played upon her by father and husband.
Finally the torrent ceased and Rachel said bitterly,
"That is what happened. My husband was purchased
for me by my father."

"My dear," Victor said carefully, "it has been a great
shock, I know. However, among our circles, a dowry is
expected. In France, there is never a marriage
contracted without one, and—"

"I know," she interrupted. "I undertand about
dowries, but to . . . to pretend that he f-fell in love with
me at . . . at first sight, when all the time he was
p-promised that . . . that if he wed me he would not
need to forfeit all that he had lost . . . It was b-bribery,
and I . . . I thought it was love."

Victor swallowed a lump in his own throat. He was
indignant—more than indignant, furious—at Lady
Villiers for having divulged the tale. He was angry at
Gervais's action, but at the same time, he had seen them
together, and despite his own feelings for Rachel, he
was fair enough to admit to himself that Gervais had
appeared to be very much in love with his bride. It was
with that in mind that he said slowly, "Are you being
quite fair to your husband, my dearest?"

"Fair? Fair!" She stared at him incredulously. "Are
you suggesting that I should have p-played the understanding w-wife and . . . and for-forgiven him for
having made a m-mockery of our marriage? And I was
not the only one to be traduced. There was Charlotte,
who was affianced to him, and she was told nothing,

nothing at all. If she had pushed me down those stairs, I . . . I would have understood.''

"If she had pushed you down those stairs," Victor said coldly, "she should have been tried for attemped murder."

"She did not . . . How she managed to be my friend in those circumstances, I do not understand, but I am glad I did not bear his child. I want nothing of his, nothing, nothing, nothing!''

Victor sat down on the couch and gathered Rachel in his arms, patting her gently on the back and brushing his chin against her tangled locks. "My dear, you must calm down and look at this matter sensibly."

"Sensibly?" she questioned. "How—?"

"Shhhhh, listen to me, my darling. You have been grievously hurt, but I think you must yet give your husband a chance to tell his side of the matter."

"I know his side of the matter. He is not in the Fleet. He is living in affluence—thanks to my father, who was so anxious to rid his house of me that he s-sold me to Gervais.''

"That is nonsense!" Victor said sharply. "Your father was obviously unhappy because his wife did not like you. He thought the atmosphere in the house was hurting you, and it was. Do you remember when she thrust you out of the rooms you had occupied all of your life?''

"My father did not protest."

"Your father was between the devil and the deep blue sea.''

Rachel gave him a hurt and indignant stare. "You appear to . . . to sympathize with . . . with my f-father and Gervais.''

"I sympathize mainly with you, my dearest, but I think you have not thought this situation out. It is too new and—"

"If I were to tell you what Gervais did . . ." She put her hands over her face.

"You have told me, and I promise that it will be forgotten. My dear, you must go home."

"I do not want to go home," she cried passionately. "I . . . I want to go with you to . . . to France and become a singer. You have said often enough that a great t-talent was lost to the p-public . . . Well, I . . . I am ready to go!"

Victor was silent a moment, staring at her. Then he sighed. "No, my love, you are not ready to go. You are not thinking clearly. You must return home and go to bed."

"If you will not take me, I will go by myself!" she cried. "I will go to Anne-Marie!"

"Anne-Marie will be coming here by the week's end. I received the intelligence yesterday. She and her husband will be at Grillon's Hotel until their house is ready."

Rachel, momentarily diverted, stared at him in surprise. "She is coming to London at last? Oh, I must see her." She paused, giving him a stricken look. "But . . ."

"You must see her," he said insistently. "You must talk this matter over. You must do it calmly and at home. There is nothing I would like better than to have you share that golden voice with the public—with the composers, too. I think that Rossini would want to write an opera for you. I think that Von Winter would do so too. But I would not take you as far from this sofa as the pianoforte, not in your present mind. I will, however, see that you get home safely."

"My post chaise is below," Rachel said.

"Then I will see you to it, my love." He kissed her hand. "But I will not see you to France or Italy or Vienna, not until you have thoroughly thought out your situation—and I must tell you that I am of the opinion that Gervais, much as I hold no brief for his actions, loves you devotedly."

Rachel lifted her head and stared at Victor. "I do not love him," she said clearly. "I do not wish to be married to him. I am through with him forever and ever. You may not believe me, Victor, but I assure you that ˈ mean it, every word. He means nothing to me."

Staring at her, Victor felt a shiver run through him.

He had known Rachel a long time, and he had seen her in many moods. He had, however, never heard her speak so firmly, and nor had he ever caught that stony look on her face. He had no doubt that at this moment she was speaking the truth, and suddenly he felt very sorry for young Lord Sayre, the while he tried to subdue the hope that, after all, Rachel Villiers' glorious voice would not be lost to a public that deserved to hear it.

He did not, however, allow these feelings to manifest themselves. He said merely, "I will see you to your coach, my dear."

10

Sir Harry Villiers, roused from his bed at seven in the morning by his valet, who brought the disquieting news that a distraught Lord Sayre was below in the library, did not trouble to dress. Thinking only of Rachel, he flung on his dressing gown and hurried down the stairs. On entering the room, he thought his worst fears had been realized as he stared at the pale, unshaven young man whose clothes had evidently been thrown on without thought of anything save that they cover him.

"Rachel!" Sir Harry whispered. "What has happened to her?"

"Is she not with you?" Gervais demanded.

"At this hour in the morning?"

Gervais ran his hands through his already disordered hair. "She is not in our house, and nor is her abigail."

Sir Harry drew and expelled a long breath. "Why would that be?" he asked.

"She left at dawn." Tears appeared in Gervais's eyes. "I fear she has gone for good." He paused and then said angrily, accusingly, "That woman . . . What possessed you to tell her the circumstances attendant on our meeting? I did not want to accept your offer. I took it only because I could not have offered for her were I in debtors' prison. I knew it was dishonorable, but I . . . I loved her so much, from the very first moment that I saw her, and love her more now, but she will not believe me. There . . . there might have been a chance, were it not for my regrettable actions, but now . . ." More tears rolled down Gervais's cheeks. He put his hands over his eyes. "I am undone. Oh, God, why did you let that woman know?"

"What woman?" Sir Harry asked confusedly. "And what is amiss with Rachel? A quarrel? There are always quarrels, my lad. But here . . ." Sir Harry took a crystal decanter from a cabinet and poured brandy into a small glass, also taken from the cabinet. "Drink this and then try to calm yourself, so that I may know all that has happened."

A few moments later, listening to Gervais's broken recital, Sir Harry had turned pale himself. As Gervais came to the end of his account, omitting nothing and castigating himself for a brute and a fool, Sir Harry put a hand on his shoulder.

"Lad, I did not confide in her. I've no idea where she might have gotten her information, but I beg you to believe that I would never have provided her with such grist for her mill."

"Then how did she know?" Anger replaced the agony in Gervais's eyes. "And to . . . to tell Rachel . . . 'Twas done out of spite, not concern, and you'll never convince me differently."

"We will summon her and ask her," Sir Harry said grimly. Moving to a pulley, he paused, adding grimly, "I will fetch her myself, I think." He strode out of the room. In a few minutes he returned, looking grimmer than ever. "She pleads a sick headache. However, headaches cannot last forever, and I will exact the information and bring it to you at some time later today. Meanwhile, you had best go home. There is the chance that Rachel will have returned by now."

"Can you not speak to your wife?" Gervais asked insistently. "Can you not force the truth from her, headache or no?"

Sir Harry sighed. "She'll not answer. I know her very well, too well. I will come to you when I have more information, I promise you." He put his hand on Gervais's shoulder. "Cheer up, lad, I cannot think that Rachel will remain angry forever, given her love for you."

"She *loved* me," Gervais emphasized wretchedly. "I have told you what took place. I . . . I treated her like some doxy from the streets."

"You were not very wise, but when she is calmer and realizes that in her way she has been just as foolish, I think matters will be mended. Rachel has always had a hot temper, but her angers cool quickly enough."

Gervais stared at him doubtfully. "I wish I might be so sanguine." He shook his head, and turning, strode from the room.

Sir Harry's sigh was even longer than that of his son-in-law. He had not spoken to Samantha. His anger had been such that he had not trusted himself to confront her. In common with Gervais, he might have resorted to violence. Indeed, in his present mood, he would like to strangle her. He would need to wait until he had mastered his temper and then confront and ask her: Why?

He knew why.

In addition to her senseless prejudice, there was her jealousy of one whom she had hoped, he guessed, to keep under her thumb and make as wretched as possible. That his daughter had escaped, and had married a nobleman, must have infuriated her, and she had exacted a revenge as petty as it was cruel. He ground his teeth. All too often in the last months he had longed to be rid of her, had wished, indeed, that she had given him a pretext to put her aside. However, she went garbed in shining virtue and she was the mother of the son he had wanted, a bonny infant that he loved. Still, that would not restrain him from giving Samantha a piece of his mind. When he was done with her, he doubted strongly that she would be inclined to spread any more scurrilous gossip concerning his daughter's marriage. Meanwhile, his heart went out to Rachel and to Gervais. He hoped against hope that they would be able to settle this matter between them. Unfortunately, Rachel was stubborn, and though he had not said as much, she was very slow to forgive when she felt herself to be wronged. He had an uneasy feeling that he, too, must come under that same onus—else she would have come to him immediately with her woes.

Informed that her ladyship had returned, Gervais took the stairs three at a time and found Rachel seated at her piano in the music room. Her hands were on the keys, but they were idle. She was staring into space.

"Rachel"—he came toward her—"I have been beside myself with worry. Where were you?"

"I went riding," she said coldly and without looking at him.

"So early?"

"I was in the mood to ride."

"Rachel, about last night," he began.

He received a swift chill glance. "I prefer not to discuss last night, my lord."

"I was angry. I—"

"Your excuses do not interest me."

"Rachel, I beg you will believe that that slander—"

"Slander?" She stared at him then, her gaze fiery. "I have always been given to believe that slander suggests an untruth, but you have already admitted the truth—consequently, it cannot be slander."

"Rachel . . ." he said pleadingly.

She rose. "I will go to my room now, unless it is in your mind to ravish me again?"

He gave her an unhappy look and said in low, shamed tones, "I will not touch you again unless you wish it."

"Is that a promise, my lord?" she demanded icily.

"I swear it, on my honor."

"I would rather hear you swear it in God's name, Gervais. I have ceased to believe in your honor."

"I do not know you, Rachel," he said in a low, shocked tone of voice.

"I do not believe that I have ever known you, my

lord," she retorted coldly. "Will you swear as I have asked?"

"I swear it in God's name," he said evenly, and went out of the room, closing the door softly behind him.

She stared at that door and was pleased. Her shaft had found its mark. She was rather sure he would not trouble her again. A few minutes later she went to her chamber, and settling down at her desk, addressed a note to Victor, inviting him to the opera that night. Her mind remained unchanged, but she would stay in London, she told herself, until Anne-Marie returned. Meanwhile, she would have little to do with the man she had once loved. Suddenly Red Lizzie was in her mind. She shivered.

Had that kidnapped bride suffered a similar disappointment? Rachel was suddenly sure that she had, and so had stupidly leapt from the tower window. No wonder she had returned to haunt the place—or was it *her* that Red Lizzie was haunting, once she knew that Rachel was like unto herself? Rachel had found out about her foolishness too late, but Gervais was not worth such an act, and she doubted that his ancestor had been worth so much as a hair from his beloved's fiery mane.

She went into her bedroom, pulled open the doors of her wardrobe, and began to study her gowns, deciding which she would discard. But she knew without looking. Those that Gervais had admired the most must go. She would order several new ensembles—she had decided that earlier, she remembered. She must think about . . . The Marquess of Dorne suddenly came to mind. She must speak to him. He had been present on that fatal night and doubtless there was much he could add to her stepmother's account. She thought of dispatching a note to him, had determinedly stepped back into the sitting room, but she paused as she reached her desk. Undoubtedly she and the marquess would meet somewhere—in the park or at an assembly—or perhaps he would seek her out.

Gervais had warned her against cultivating Lord

Dorne. He had said that no young woman was safe with him, married or single. A bitter little smile played about her mouth. At the time of his warning, she had flung her arms around him and told him that no one, no one in the world, could ever pry her from his side. Resolutely she banished that unwanted memory and concentrated on the marquess. Had Gervais been telling the truth? Probably not. He and truth were strangers, it would seem. Lies came very easily to him, and he was particularly adept . . . Or *had* it been particularly adept, making a lonely, love-starved young girl believe that he had fallen in love with her at first sight?

"I was a fool," she muttered. "He did not love me. He came to the Court with Father because he wanted to preserve his fortune and his stables."

She could imagine that he had been almost as unhappy about the possible loss of his horses as he had been about his fortune. He owned some truly beautiful cattle—purebred, too, which was more than he could say for his wife. A tiny curlicue of a thought told her that she was being unjust and unkind. Angrily she banished that thought. Gervais did not deserve so much as a shred of magnanimity from one whom he had wronged so cruelly! Indeed, she had half a mind to dispatch a note to Lord Dorne, inviting him to the house. No, undoubtedly they would meet, and soon.

They did meet at the end of a fortnight, during which time Rachel had managed to keep remarkably busy. With Phoebe in tow, she had visited a number of shops, coming home with all manner of amusing and sometimes expensive trifles. Among them was a love of an Indian silk scarf, a white silk spencer from France, a delight of a bonnet made from white French gauze, and a pair of gold combs that were, said the mentors at that popular publication *La Belle Assemblée*, exquisite for evening wear. She also bought a sprig of snowdrops for her hair, the snowdrops being fashioned from pearls and the leaves from emeralds. It was the most dear of all her purchases and she half-expected that Gervais, seeing the bill on his desk, must make some comment. However, somewhat to her disappointment, he did not, thus keeping her from delivering a withering set-down concerning her right to spend *her* money.

In addition to her newly acquired habit of shopping, something that grew rather tedious upon repetition, she also visited mantua-makers and spent hours revolving on platforms while sewing women either fitted or finished her new gowns. Early each morning she rode in the park with a groom in attendance. She had hoped that she might meet Lord Dorne on one morning or another in the first week after her stepmother's confidence had destroyed her marriage. However, she did not meet him that week or the next, and nor did she meet him at a Carlton House dinner she attended with her husband.

Oddly enough, despite the *on-dit* Samantha had described so vividly, the invitations continued to pour in. Some of these were from old friends of Gervais's family, and at his tentative question, she agreed to go. Her desire to leave him remained unabated, but until the opportunity presented itself, she would act the happy wife in public and no one save Gervais would know that her door remained closed and locked against him—just as her attitude remained cold and contemptuous to the point that he took to absenting himself from the house and not returning until late at night. She had no idea where he went, and nor did she care. The memory of his perfidy was with her night and day, and if she ever relaxed and did not think about it, it was brought home to her by someone's curious stare or an overwise look from one female acquaintance or another. Since she was determined not to see Charlotte, she had no close female friends, would not have any until Anne-Marie returned to London.

Two weeks to the day after Samantha had seen fit to unburden herself concerning Gervais's betrayal, Rachel encountered the Marquess of Dorne at the opera, as she had hoped might happen, and at a time when Victor, having met some friends during the interval, had gone off to argue the merits of Madame Fodor, who had redeemed herself that evening. Victor had asked her—actually he had begged her—to join them, but Rachel, weary of their endless and acrimonious debates, had preferred to remain in her box.

She was looking particularly well that evening. She had been assured on that point by Phoebe as she dressed her in a yellow silk gown cut low across the bosom. Rachel had chosen to wear her mother's cameos with it, and Phoebe had dressed her hair beautifully. Victor had gazed at her with his heart in his eyes, and his friends had been obviously envious at his good fortune in escorting one whom they did not hesitate to describe as the most beautiful woman in the house. Rachel, having had additional confirmation from her mirror, had been pleased about that—since she had not been at her best that morning. The dinner to which she and Gervais had gone the night before had been heavy and not particularly palatable. She had half-feared the effects of it might last throughout the day, but they had worn off by noon and she was quite herself again.

The Marquess of Dorne obviously agreed with the dicta of Victor and his friends. His silver-gray eyes widened and he said in tones of amazement, "You must tell me why the most beautiful woman in London is alone in her box."

Rachel would have preferred that he eschew these obligatory compliments, but to say so would have been churlish on her part, so she must needs join in the comedy. With an interior sigh she made play with her little ivory fan and said, "I am not acquainted with that woman. You must point her out to me."

"I beg you will not dissemble, milady. You must be entirely aware that there is no one in this house who can equal you in either wit or beauty."

She laughed lightly. "Compliments come very easily to your lips, Lord Dorne."

"Alas, that is only too true. However, what does not come easily to my lips is truth, and you have inspired that, Lady Sayre."

"Then I am complimented," she said, hoping that her concession would put an end to this small talk.

"I am pleased that you have admitted it. Might I take this chair until your churl of an escort has returned?"

"He is not a churl," she defended laughingly. "He begged me to accompany him, but I preferred to remain here."

"Were I your escort, nothing would dislodge me."

Rachel concealed another sigh. Unless his stream of gallantries was stopped, he would continue to mouth them until Victor returned. She said bluntly, "I understand from my stepmother that you were party to a . . . situation at Brooks's a year ago last spring."

He raised his eyebrows. "Surely," he said with an amused glint in his eyes, "you do not expect me to remember whatever might have taken place at Brooks's last year? My dear Lady Sayre, my memory is not so elephantine."

She had seen understanding flash in his eyes and she guessed that he was either reluctant to tell her what she wished to know or, what was more likely, he was being deliberately provocative. Neither attitude appealed to her. She said even more bluntly, "You heard my father urge the man who is now my husband to accompany him to the country to meet his daughter."

"On the contrary, my dear Lady Sayre, I heard nothing. It was my friend Charles Osmond and one Luke, a servant employed there, who listened. I do not believe that Luke is employed there at this time."

She dismissed Luke. "My stepmother tells me that Gervais lost heavily."

"Very heavily," the marquess confirmed. "It was an entirely new experience for the poor lad. Until that evening, he had had the greatest success in the often uncertain game of piquet. His expertise with cards was said to run in the family. Indeed, your Gervais was hard put to find anyone willing to play with him. Your father, being a stranger to London, was not aware of his . . . er, luck.''

"You . . . you are suggesting that he cheated at cards?'' Rachel breathed.

The marquess was silent a moment, seemingly turned thoughtful. "I am suggesting that he was uncommonly lucky," he said at last, "but no more than that, and, unfortunately, his luck ran out that night, or so it appeared at the time.''

He had told her no more than she had expected to hear, but, surprisingly, a feeling much akin to pain ran through Rachel. One hand crept to her throat, but she took it away quickly, lest he believe her shocked. "I see," she said, and in her mind was an image, an image of a great door which had been slightly ajar, irrevocably closing on a hope she had not known she had entertained.

The marquess studied her face in silence for a moment before saying softly, "I have missed our rides in the park, my dear Lady Sayre.''

Rachel managed a smile. "I have ridden," she responded. "I have not seen you there.''

"I have been out of town, family matters," he explained. "I hope you are suggesting that you have missed me?'' Before she could comment, he continued, "But, as you see, I am back. Might I hope for another early-morning canter?''

"I ride in the park every morning, Lord Dorne. Generally, I am early," Rachel responded.

"Ah, I see your friends are returning." He rose and kissed her hand. "Now that I am returned to the city, I hope that I will be able to see more of you, Lady Sayre.''

"I am often at the opera," she murmured.

"Did I ever tell you that I am passionately fond of music?" he inquired. "Particularly when it comes garbed in yellow.''

"My lord . . .'' She frowned and would have given h'm a set-down had not Victor and his friends come to stand at the back of the box. There was an exchange of greetings, cool on Victor's part and amused on the marquess's, and then he was gone.

Victor, taking his seat beside Rachel, said in a low voice, "If I had known that Dorne was going to join you, I should not have left you alone."

"Come," Rachel protested. "He is entirely charming."

"So was the serpent of Eden," Victor growled.

"You are being ridiculous," she chided.

"Better ridiculous than foolish," he said meaningfully.

"I pray you will not lecture me, Victor." Rachel had a mulish look in her eyes. "I find the marquess very good company."

"I doubt that your husband would agree."

"Are you taking his part now?" She stared at him indignantly.

"I would take the part of the devil against Lord Dorne."

"You do not know him."

"Nor do you."

Unfortunately, Victor's strictures did not have the effect for which he had been striving. They succeeded only in intriguing Rachel. In the next few weeks she met Lord Dorne in the park for rides and for races, which he only occasionally won, annoying Rachel, who accused him of giving her an edge when she reached a given mark first. It was an accusation he hotly denied, surprising her the more by saying, "You would be the last female to whom I would give an edge or an inch."

"And why would that be, sir?"

"Because of your . . . natural ascendancy."

"And what," a puzzled Rachel had asked, "would you be meaning by that?"

"I hope the explanation will present itself to you without my aid."

This and other equally enigmatic comments fascinated Rachel, and naturally she could not help being flattered by his constant attention. Were she to attend a rout, he would gravitate to her side the moment he saw her there and stay with her far longer than with any other female in the room. Since she was still constrained to arrive at Carlton House functions in the company of her husband, the marquess, nearly always arriving alone, would find an opportunity to engage her in conversation and leave without so much as taking notice of the other females who vied for his attention. At one Carlton House ball, Rachel allowed him no less than three waltzes, a country dance, and a cotillion.

On bringing his wife home, Gervais had not, as was his wont, left her side immediately they entered the house. Instead, he confronted her in the upper hall, saying coldly, "Your name, as I am sure you know, is being coupled with that of Dorne. I must needs remind you that in our circles, smoke is generally accompanied by fire. Since you are yet my wife and bear my name . . ."

Rachel had given him a long cold stare. "I find the marquess extremely amusing, no more. If, however, I were interested in him, you would have, I think, no cause for complaint. You have been well-reimbursed for the use of your name."

He had turned white. His hand had risen and then fallen to his side. Turning, he had stridden away from her into his own room.

Rachel, reaching her chamber, had been half-exhilarated, half-frightened by the impact of her remark. Before going to bed, she had had a drowsy Phoebe place a chair under the doorknob on the chance that, Gervais's rage increasing, he might try to knock down her door again. However, there was no such attempt, and in the morning she discovered that his lordship had had his clothing and other personal items removed to a chamber at the far end of the corridor. That move was not the only distance he put between them. Indeed, considering that they still occupied the same house, it was remarkable how very little she saw of the man she had once loved so deeply.

He contrived to be away by the time she breakfasted, and if she did not dine alone, the meals they shared were silent. Fortunately, his defection had little impact on her social life. She continued to see the Marquess of Dorne, and on nights when she did not see him, there was always Victor and the opera. Indeed, as she told a concerned Anne-Marie upon her much-awaited return to London, "I am having a really splendid time."

Anne-Marie had given her a long, worried stare. "You are looking rather peaked, my love. Are you sure that all these late nights agree with you?"

"Oh"—Rachel had shrugged—"I will allow that I have been eating too many rich foods of late. I fear they have wrought havoc on my constitution. I have heard the same sort of complaint from various of my friends. We have agreed that the French, having lost the war, are getting their revenge through the chefs employed in our kitchens." Belatedly remembering that Anne-Marie was French, she had blushed and added, "No offense intended."

"And none taken." Anne-Marie had regarded her anxiously. "Victor is worried too. He says—"

"I know what he says. He does not like Lord Dorne. However, Victor does not know him as I do. He is truly charming."

That exchange was not the first, nor was it the last that she had with Anne-Marie. Indeed, much as she loved her friend, Rachel began to avoid her company, mainly because Anne-Marie insisted on taking up the cudgels for Gervais.

"I had occasion to see him at the house of a friend," Anne-Marie had told her. "He looks so very unhappy. I wanted to speak to him, but he left before I had the opportunity. I do not think you have treated him quite fairly, my dear."

"I have treated him as fairly as he has treated me," had been Rachel's icy response.

"My dear, he loves you. I am sure of it."

"If he loves me, it is the same love that a dog has for the master that feeds him," Rachel had retorted coldly.

Her response had infuriated Anne-Marie. "You are a fool, Rachel, and one day you will know how very foolish you are and have been. I hope that this lesson is not learned too late."

Two days after that unfortunate meeting, Rachel, rising early, felt far from well—the which she blamed on another heavy dinner at the house of Lady Griselda Hobart, a new friend whom she had met while riding with the marquess. Lady Griselda's husband, a friend of Lord Dorne's, was Sir James Hobart, an official in the East India Company, which, complained his wife, forced him to visit the country. He was currently in Madras and would not be home for another half-year.

"And that, my dear, is a dead bore," Lady Hobart had complained. "It leaves me practically a widow."

She had seemed extremely taken with Rachel, and though Rachel considered her rather flighty, she could not help liking her. However, she had not liked the dishes served by her cook, an Indian from Calcutta, who prepared very exotic meals, replete with curry, ginger, and other spices. Still, aside from the dinner, the rest of the evening had been very interesting. Lady Hobart's house contained many fascinating artifacts and furniture from India. Upon Rachel's commenting on them, her hostess had made a little face.

"I am sure India is an interesting country . . . it should be, with its three hundred million gods and its plethora of sacred objects, including those huge cows or bulls or some such that wander unmolested in the streets. Poor James loathes the place, but, my dear, I hear from the marquess that you have a beautiful voice. Will you not sing for me? I can play the pianoforte tolerably well."

Rachel, though feeling rather ill from having consumed so much odd food, had obliged, with the result that her hostess had gone into raptures. "Oh, I quite understand that the dear marquess means—you ought to be singing in opera. Such a shame that your position in life precludes it. My dear, might I beg that you come tomorrow night? I am having a few people to dinner. They all share my passion for music. Indeed, I cannot form friendships, deep lasting friendships, with those who do not share my interests. I am sure that you are well acquainted with what our noted Shakespeare had to say about those who do not love music?''

"I am." Rachel had smiled and quoted softly, " 'The man who hath no music in himself nor is not mov'd with concord of sweet sound is fit for treason, strategy, and spoil—the motions of his spirit are dull as night. And his affections dark as Erebus. Let no such man be trusted.' ''

"Ah, you have conned it better than I, who was inclined to leave out various words and rush to the end," Lady Hobart said ruefully.

"The play from which it is taken is a favorite of mine," Rachel had explained, and felt a warmth on her cheeks, wondering if Lady Hobart knew of her mother. She thought it unlikely that she did not, and was sure of it when her hostess said, "I am of the opinion that *The Merchant of Venice* is one of Shakespeare's greatest works and Shylock by far his most tragic creation."

Rachel had felt very much like embracing her for those kind sentiments, but she had said merely, "Yes, he is truly a tragic character."

"And Anthony a dreadful prig, besides being deucedly full of himself," Lady Hobart had added. "However, we are getting far from the subject of your voice. I hope that you will sing some operatic arias for us. I am quite devoted to the works of Peter von Winter, so prolific a composer, do you not agree?

"I do agree," Rachel had returned carefully, not wishing to offend her hostess by mentioning that Von Winter, though popular, was to her mind the inferior of Mozart or Rossini. "I have not, unfortunately, learned any of his arias. My teacher favors the Italian school, though he is, of course, very found of Mozart."

"Ah, Mozart," her hostess had said soulfully. "Exquisite music. If you will choose selections from

Mozart and Rossini, I know my guests will be transported.''

"Very well," Rachel had assented. "I will sing '*Dove Sono*.' " Even as that title left her lips, she had felt a strange little pain in the vicinity of her heart as she remembered she had sung it for Gervais on an evening long ago—too long ago to be even recalled, she had told herself angrily. "I will also sing some French songs."

"Excellent," Lady Hobart had said. "I am expecting my company at nine o'clock." She had clasped her hands. "Oh, I am excited. I can hardly wait for them to hear you."

But now Rachel, thinking of another dinner such as had been served to her the previous night, actually cringed. She longed to cry off, but she did not want to disappoint her new friend. She did not, however, believe she would ride this morning. The marquess would be waiting for her, but she must disappoint him if she were not to disappoint Lady Hobart's guests, and it would not hurt him to wonder where she was. Consequently, she surprised Phoebe by teling her that she would have her breakfast in bed that morning, and aside from a few social exercises, she decided she would rest for the better part of the day. She did feel amazingly lethargic, and when the hot chocolate and biscuits she had ordered arrived, she found herself unwilling to partake of them and sent the tray away.

Midmorning, Rachel was aroused by a light tap on her door. "Yes," she called edgily, and opened her eyes wide as she found Gervais standing in the doorway.

"Phoebe tells me that you are not well," he said coolly.

She sat up quickly. "I am only tired," she responded in tones even colder than those he had employed.

"It is possible that you have been doing too much. You are looking pale. I suggest that you cancel whatever engagements you have for the rest of the week."

"I thank you for your . . . concern, my lord, but I am the best judge of my strengths and weaknesses."

He took a step into the room. "I wonder if that is entirely true."

"I assure you that it is. And I will be the better if I am allowed to rest."

"Rachel," he said pleadingly, "can we not find some way of mending matters between us?"

She sighed. "There are some fine silks, my lord, which are destroyed even by the prick of a needle. And . . ." She paused, suddenly finding herself looking at a door that had closed, leaving her alone in her chamber. She swallowed an obstruction in her throat, and yet it remained, requiring several more swallows before it was gone. She had also to blink several times before the wetness in her eyes left them.

"One day you will regret your implacable attitude," Anne-Marie had told her.

Rachel, her symptoms having disappeared, glared at the door through which Gervais had gone. She muttered, "Not yet, Anne-Marie, not yet."

By evening she felt much better. She had felt almost recovered at noon, but she had still eaten lightly from a tray sent to her room. As she sat at her mirror, she agreed with Phoebe that the rest had done her a great deal of good. Her color was brighter and her eyes had lost the tinge of redness that had been apparent earlier. She had elected to wear one of her new gowns. It was the very latest thing and daringly exposed her ankles. For the rest, it was a blue that her abigail insisted was an exact match for her eyes. It was also a bit fuller than the silhouettes of the previous year and her mantua-maker had told her that by January 1817 she would see the skirts considerably wider, though of course they would never approach the fullness of the early 1790's, just as it was equally unlikely that they would see a return to the wispy muslins of that period when the English ladies were following what they called "Ancient Greek" and which the mantua-maker had dubbed "plain indecent."

The fact that she was garbed in the very latest style also helped to cheer what Rachel stubbornly refused to

identify as her "flagging spirits." She was wearing a
new turban with peacock feathers sewn in front and
seemingly held there by a band of brilliants. Her little
blue satin reticule was also new. She was particularly
pleased that Gervais was nowhere to be seen as she
descended the stairs. Their brief confrontation that
morning had, for some unknown reason, lingered in her
mind, this despite the fact that nearly two months ago
she had decided that his past and present actions had
rendered him a negligible factor in her life.

At present, however, she had ceased to harbor even
the slightest regret over the attitude that Anne-Marie,
deeply in love with her own husband, must have
deplored. However, Anne-Marie's husband had not
been constrained to marry her because of his debts
to her father, and nor, she was sure, had he cruelly
ravished her at a time when he should have exercised the
understanding that he, Gervais, unfortunately, did not
possess! A quavering sigh escaped her as she thought of
that terrible moment when all her illusions had been
stripped away like the branches from a tree that was
soon to be chopped down. Did they strip the branches
from such trees or did they chop them down intact? She
was not sure. The analogy was apt, she thought as she
went out.

There were not as many carriages before Lady
Hobart's door as Rachel had anticipated. Yet, perhaps
she had been too prompt. She had arrived precisely at
the hour of nine and she had previously learned that
many of the *ton* were not so prompt. Indeed, it was
considered fashionable to arrive late. Gervais, she
recalled, had never been in agreement with that
particular fashion. And why was she still letting
Gervais's opinions crowd her mind? Rachel, directing
her coachman to return at midnight, went up the stairs
and was shown into her ladyship's exotic drawing room.
It was, as she had noted the previous evening, furnished
beautifully, though some of the pieces were much at
variance with the formal look in her own house and in
most of the houses she visited.

There were deep sofas covered with velvet, and wide wing chairs. Everything seemed designed for comfort. Indeed, she was reminded of rooms she had read about in history books. In the seventeenth century, hostesses had often received their friends while lounging in beds hung with gold silk or fine tapestries. These sofas might bear, Rachel thought, some resemblance to the beds. It would not be difficult to sleep in them. There were paintings of strange animals on the walls, and there were exotic statues from India—a goddess with a multiplicity of arms and another of a man with an elephant's head. There were figurines, too, in bronze and ivory. One chair was fashioned from elephant tusks, and the carpets, too, were very thick. Furthermore, the smell of incense she had noticed the previous evening was even heavier tonight, as if, indeed, it were burning in more than one holder. The light coming from two tall standing lamps was soft and diffuse.

As these impressions seeped into her mind, Lady Hobart, clad in a flowing gown of some Indian silk, hurried in. She looked both nervous and apologetic. "Oh, my dear, how delightfully prompt *you* are. I have had the most fearful upsets today, but please, did not Mohammed remove your cloak?"

Rachel, who did not remember seeing the servant, shook her head. "I—"

"Oh, dear," Lady Hobart interrupted. "This house is in a shambles, and I expected . . . But fancy, at the very last moment two of my guests have sent notes . . . so absolutely rude, shocking really. You must let me take your cloak and turban, so pretty, really, and the very latest from France, I am sure. I feel quite, quite dowdy beside you." Before Rachel was quite aware of what was happening, Lady Hobart had deftly removed the cloak and turban. "Now, my love, I will leave you momentarily. I must see what has happened to Mohammed. Indian servants, you know, totally undependable. Ah, I think I hear a pounding on the outer door. I shall be back in a moment, my dear. I do hope that these are the Vernons, I do want them to hear you.

I know they did not believe me when I told them you were far superior to Catalani . . . but they must agree with me before the evening is at an end." So saying, her ladyship hurried out of the room.

Rachel, finding herself alone, was surprised and not entirely pleased by an informalty of a kind she had never before experienced. It seemed to her that a hostess who felt constrained to stand at the door like a butler and greet each guest was not quite the thing. Furthermore, Lady Hobart had appeared strangely lacking in poise. Rachel did not want to be overcritical of her newfound friend, but actually, she reasoned, she knew very little about her. She had a definite feeling that Gervais, meeting her, would not have approved. Nor would he have found the overfurnished room to his taste, she realized. It *was* overfurnished, and she did not care for the cloying scent of the incense. She moved toward the balcony, but at that moment she heard Lady Hobart's voice in the hall, raised in greeting. Another guest had arrived. She released a breath of relief and took a minute to examine that feeling. The fact that no one had been present save herself had been strangely unsettling, though why she had felt that way, she was not quite sure, but there was little time to rack her brains for an explanation, for the door was being pushed open and the Marquess of Dorne entered. He was looking very handsome and entirely correct in his evening suit of black and white, attire dictated by Beau Brummell, now absent from London's scene since May and not likely to return from his safe-harbor in Calais, according to Gervais, since he too was in danger of debtors' prison. As the marquess bowed over her hand, she was glad to dismiss the subjects of the Beau and Gervais.

"My dear, what a delightful surprise," he exclaimed. His brilliant eyes held just the lightest hint of reproach. "I had expected to see you in the park this morning."

Rachel met his gaze steadily. "I was not feeling quite the thing."

"Oh, I am sorry to hear it, but I am pleased you have recovered. You must be recovered, for surely I have never seen you looking more lovely. That blue almost rivals your eyes, but not quite. I challenge any mortal to duplicate their magnificent hue."

"My lord . . ." Rachel was caught between laughter and a trace of indignation. "I fear you grow fulsome."

He looked down at himself immediately. "No, never, I swear I have not put on a pound in either figure or speech. And I am known to speak the truth at all times."

"Ah, you have found her." Lady Hobart had returned. "Can you believe that I have just had another message from the Vernons. They have been delayed, but will be here inside of an hour."

"They have been delayed, and I am dismayed. I was looking forward to a 'concert' after dinner, and now it must be postponed." The marquess looked crestfallen. "Would it not be possible to give me a brief recital at this moment?"

"I am sure that Lady Sayre would prefer to dine," Lady Hobart began.

"No," Rachel exclaimed, and flushed. Though she was no longer feeling queasy, she had no great desire to taste of the exotic viands which had had so unsettling an effect on her digestion the previous evening. Consequently, the straw offered by the marquess was one she was only too pleased to grasp. "I would quite like to sing now."

"But my other guests will feel entirely deprived if they do not hear you," Lady Hobart protested.

The marquess laughed. "I am sure that she has more than one song to her bow."

"Indeed, I do," Rachel hastened to assure him.

"I fear we are imposing on the poor child, but if she is inclined to be gracious, I, too, confess that I would love to hear that magnificent voice again. Oh, dear, why are people so unmannerly? It was not so in my mother's day. Then it was not considered fashionable to arrive

late, it was considered ill-mannered." So saying, Lady
Hobart moved across the floor. "Come," she invited
gaily, "we will repair to the music room—and you may
entertain his, er . . . majesty"—she winked at the
marquess—"until our guests deign to honor us with
their presence."

"Another glass of wine, my dear?" The marquess
lifted his hands from the ivory keys of the pianoforte
and smiled up at Rachel. "You must be thirsty again."

Rachel stared down at him vaguely. She had, she
realized, lost track of time, something which often
happened when she sang. Furthermore, she had had
more than one glass of wine, and that, coupled with the
fact that she had eaten very little that day, was making
her dizzy. The room, in fact, had a disquieting way of
blurring every few seconds, but rooms, she thought, did
not blur—it was her eyes. Her tongue felt thick and
furry.

"Another glass of wine, my dear," the marquess
urged. "Come, my beautiful one, you have more than
earned it." He rose, and lifting the bottle which stood
on a nearby table, filled a goblet with ruby-red liquid
and held it toward Rachel. "Let us toast the finest artist
to have appeared in many an age."

"The guests . . ." Rachel murmured, remembering
that there were to be guests, other guests besides herself
and the marquess. Her head felt most unpleasantly
heavy. She shook it and realized that it was aching, an
ache that shifted from side to side like wine in a tilting
glass. "Where are the guests?" she murmured.

"We are the guests." The marquess smiled at her.
Putting his arm around her waist, he led her to one of
Lady Hobart's large soft sofas. "Will you sit down, my
dear?"

She was glad enough to obey him. She was not quite
so pleased when he sat down beside her. He was too
near her. It would have been more courteous had he
drawn up a chair, but he had put a pillow behind her
head and that did feel very comfortable. And not far

away from her was an open window. A breeze had risen and was fanning her cheeks. The coolness pleased her. It seemed to be driving the cobwebs from her brain. She smiled at a vagrant memory, but could not quite place it.

"You are so beautiful when you smile, my Rachel," the marquess murmured, moving closer still and again slipping his arm around her waist.

The breeze ruffled her hair—or was it his hand? Rachel tensed. He was very, very close to her, and his hand had slipped from her hair to her shoulder. In his other hand he held a glass of wine.

"Drink, drink, my sweetest girl," he murmured.

A shiver went through her. "No more," she managed to say.

"Perhaps not now, my sweetness, but later," he murmured, and setting down the glass, kissed her full on the mouth, an invading kiss that filled her with repugnance and anger. She brought up both hands and tried to struggle, but he was too strong, too determined, and he had pinioned her on the sofa with his hands, with his mouth, and with the full length of his body pressing her down. Fear rose in her, and with it, comprehension.

Her friend, her new friend, whom she had met through the marquess, was in fact *his* friend, and as his friend had decoyed her to the house, to this room, and she must needs get away soon, as soon as the hateful caresses came to an end. Yet, how quickly and how much wine had she drunk? Not enough to entirely cloud her mind, no, but enough to swoon or be affected by the drink. It would depend on her capacity for wine, which, she now realized, was stronger than he knew—for her mind was becoming clear. She was, indeed, possessed of a terrible clarity and knew that unless she was very, very clever, she must suffer the consequences.

Finally the hateful pressure on her lips ceased. Finally he lifted his head.

With a little moan, Rachel said, "Oh, my lord, I do feel so . . . so terribly ill." She coughed and gagged very realistically.

He rose swiftly. "My dear, the hair of the dog . . . just wait." He moved to the pianoforte and picked up the bottle. In that same moment, Rachel, rising with equal swiftness, glanced hastily to her left and saw what she half-remembered glimpsing, a slim bronze figurine on the table near the sofa. She grabbed it, and as the marquess turned toward the sofa, staring at the place where she had lain, she slipped behind him and brought the figurine down on the back of his head. He fell without a sound.

Not stopping to examine him, she fled toward the door, but stopped. Were she to go into the hall, Lady Hobart might see her, or she might encounter one of the soft-footed native servants. She glanced desperately about her again and saw French doors opening onto a balcony. She hurried out, but on looking down, moaned softly as she measured the distance from there to the ground. However, her eyes brightened, for there was a tree nearby. She had done a great deal of tree-climbing in her lonely youth, and this particular tree was an oak with projecting branches. She did not stop to think. She crawled up on top of the marble railing of the balcony and lowered herself to the branch. In another few moments she had made her way to the ground. She stifled another little moan as she saw that the gates to the carriageway were closed, but on reaching them, she discovered that they were not locked. A minute later she had gained the street.

Hardly knowing where she was going, she picked up her skirts and ran away from the Hobart mansion. She had turned down another street and then another before she was forced to stop by a lamppost and catch her breath and, at the same time, try to ascertain her where-abouts. Her breath was coming in great sobbing gasps, but the exigencies of her situation had completely cleared her mind and she knew what she must do. She must go, as she had done once before, to Victor de Lascelles! For that she needed a conveyance—a hackney. She looked about her. She did not see any vehicle on this quiet street, but she must find one. She started to walk, then came to a stop, remembering with a pang of fear that she had no money. Her reticule was with her cloak and her cloak was wherever the perfidious Lady Hobart had hung it. However, she did have the sapphire ring she had chosen to wear that evening, and around her neck was a small string of pearls. The driver of the hackney, were she fortunate enough to find one, could have either or both. She must get to Victor. Again, he was her only hope.

Victor de Lascelles stared at Rachel incredulously. Her tale of deception and attempted seduction sounded like something concocted by one of the indifferent writers employed by publishers whose standards were several degrees lower than the Minerva Press. Yet there was no doubting her—not when one looked at her torn gown and the leaf stains on her satin sandals. He had no doubt that everything had happened exactly as she had recounted it. Rachel and Anne-Marie, too, had not been above climbing trees in their youth, which, he reminded himself, was no more than five or six years back. The one difference was, of course, that Rachel, who had seldom wept in those days, was drowned in tears and barely coherent as she recounted her night's adventure. To his logical suggestion that she go home and put the matter before Gervais, she had shaken her head and said, "I could not. He would call out the marquess."

"And so he should—so he must," Victor had snapped. "*I* would. Indeed, I *will*—"

"You will not. He has the reputation of being a master swordsman and he is equally proficient with pistols. I will not have one hair of your head harmed for my folly, or . . . or Gervais's either. He and I are finished. Victor, I want to go to Paris. I want to sing."

"But, my love, you are yet a marchioness."

She stamped her foot. "Have you not listened to me? Even if I wished to return to Gervais, which I do not, he would not have me back after tonight. I want to go to Paris. I have no money, nothing but these clothes and this ring . . ."

"That need not concern you." Victor seized her hands. "Are you serious, Rachel? Are you willing to face the consequences of your decision? The doors that were open to you will be shut, and the friends you knew . . ."

Her tears and anguish seemed to melt away, "I am . . . oh, I am, Victor. I have only two friends—you and Anne-Marie. You will not desert me. Tonight I sang and sang, and I was happy while I sang. The world was not with me then. It was only later, when he attempted to . . . to ravish me." She sighed. "I thought him a friend."

"You were warned," Victor reminded her, his expression grim.

"Yes, but he was so charming. They are all charming on the surface: that woman Lady Hobart, who also wanted to be my friend, and Charlotte . . . even my father. But underneath, they . . . Oh, I have had enough of the *ton*, enough of my so-called high position! I am only half a person when I do not sing—and it is not the better half. Victor, I must practice my art. Surely you, above all others, can understand that! You must believe me."

He seized her hands, and kissing one and then the other, he said, "My dearest Rachel, I do believe you now, and as soon as it is possible, I will take you to Paris."

"I want to leave immediately!" she cried.

"My dearest, arrangements must be made. You will not want to go without Phoebe. And you must have some of your garments."

"Yes, she could bring them to me. I know she would say nothing to the rest of the staff. But I do not need an abigail."

"You will need a *dresser*," he emphasized. "And Phoebe loves you."

"But how . . . ?" She faltered.

"Leave all that to me, my Rachel, and never fear, we will be in Paris before the week's end!"

III

11

"Fabri! Fabri! Fabri!" chanted the audience. "Fabbbbriii!" They screamed the soprano's name from all parts of the Théâtre Italien.

"Madame . . ." The harried manager had inserted his plump, panting form into the doorway of the soprano's dressing room. "Madame Fabri, *per favore.*"

She turned a weary face in his direction and pointed to her dressing robe and to her maid, who had just put her costume on a hanger. "*Non è possibile,*" she said clearly. She added, "*C'est impossible. Je suis très fatiguée.*"

"*Oui, oui, oui, Madame est très fatiguée, comprenez-vous, s'il vous plaît?*"

"*Mais, Monsieur le Comte,*" the manager protested. "*Madame partira demain—écoutez!*"

The clapping, the cheers, and the screams to which he was referring were as loud as they had been when the curtain had dropped fifteen minutes earlier, signaling the end of the fifth and final act.

"We hear," Madame Fabri said, lapsing into her native English. "But it is impossible." She stared into the manager's uncomprehending face and sighed, wondering, as she often had during the last two years and four months, why the manager of a major European opera house rarely troubled to learn more than his native tongue. Her command of French and

191

Italian was definitely improving, but when she was tired, when she had just sung the long, taxing leading role in *Fastrade*, a work written especially for her by Lorenzo della Gracia, everything seemed to fly from her mind. She stifled a sigh as she thought of the coming ordeal of the green room. It would be over an hour before she could escape her devoted following, some of whom had trailed her all the way from her last engagement at the San Carlo Opera House in Naples. Tonight her fans would be particularly demanding, for it was well known that Francesca Fabri would be leaving for London on the following day to appear at the King's Theater in the English premiere of *Fastrade*. She threw a glance at Victor and received a roll of his eyes and a shrug of his shoulders.

He had, she realized, left the burden of refusing to appear before the curtain one more time entirely on her shoulders. Two years ago, when she had been a trembling neophyte, she would have acceded to the manager's request. However, as Victor was constantly reminding her, she was Francesca Fabri, who had been winning plaudits almost from the very hour she had first stepped upon the operatic stage.

In her trunk were effusions from newspapers in Italian, French, and German. True, some of those who had penned the earlier articles had chafed at acting that did not quite match her miraculous tones, but in the last eight months her acting had also been praised. She used this latter talent to good effect as she suddenly rose and said in the deep tones of the thespian who had performed the title role of *Phèdre* at the Comédie Française two nights previously, "*Pardonnez moi, s'il vous plaît, monsieur, mais c'est impossible.*" Though she had uttered practically the same words a very short time ago, her delivery and her Phèdre-esque glare obviously made an impression upon the manager.

"*Très bien*, Madame Fabri," he said nervously and obsequiously. "*J'expliquerai.*" He bowed and moved slowly from the dressing room, his bearing not unlike that of a convicted criminal going to his death. Madame

Fabri, watching him, smiled, and upon the door closing behind him, observed, "I vow, Victor, he should be a member of the Comédie Française himself."

As usual, Victor did not pretend to misunderstand her. "Is there an opera called *Phèdre*? If so, you should be singing the title role."

Madame Fabri laughed, albeit wearily. "Do not wish another new work on me, Victor. It was difficult enough learning this one . . . and such a silly plot. I am hard put not to giggle each time the tenor stabs me."

There was a real giggle from Phoebe. "He does look fierce, 'e does. I watched 'im from the wings tonight. 'E looked particularly fierce after ye got all that applause for yer fourth-act aria. I were 'alf feared 'e were ready to do it in earnest."

Madame Fabri rolled her eyes. "Tenors," she said succinctly.

The ordeal of the green room was even more prolonged than the artist had feared. It was close on one in the morning when her numerous admirers finally dispersed and she could return to her small apartment in a street conveniently close to the opera house. As usual, Victor came with her and waited in her tiny sitting room while she hurried into her bedroom, where Madame Dubois, the elderly nurse in charge of her child, watched over him. The old woman had been dozing, but as Madame Fabri opened the door, she became alert immediately.

"*Ah, madame,*" the nurse said in a half-whisper, "*voici, le petit ange.*"

Madame Fabri directed a loving glance at the sleeping boy and winked at the nurse, "*Un petit ange . . . quand'il dort.*"

"*Mais non, Madame Fabri,*" the nurse said in a reproving whisper. "*Il est bon, toujours.*"

Madame Fabri bent to kiss the boy's tousled black curls and then moved out of the room. She loosed a quavering sigh and looked at Victor. "I wish . . . But it is impossible."

Victor said, "It would not be impossible if you would allow it."

She shook her head, saying firmly, "I could not, my dear, though you are kind to suggest it and I know that Paul would enjoy the country. Still, he would miss me and I would miss him. We have always been together, but of course it is not necessary to give you such explanations."

"There is the chance that his father . . ."

"Anne-Marie has written that his father is in the country."

"Now," Victor said warningly. "In the past three years he has not remained in any part of England long." His gaze was semireproachful. "It is my opinion that he is searching for you."

"I have a strong feeling that after three years, he has given up his search." Madame Fabri frowned. "And it is well that he has. I am no longer Rachel Fenton, Lady Sayre. I renounce her. I am Francesca Fabri, and when I am in England I shall remain in seclusion, save when I visit Anne-Marie and her family. I am sure they will not betray my secret."

"You cannot wear a mask."

"I can wear Fastrade's flaxen hair until I leave the opera house. And I have had a blond wig made."

"And a mask?" Victor demanded caustically.

"I will not need a mask. They are looking for Rachel Villiers Fenton, who had blue eyes and dark hair—poor Rachel, who slipped away three years ago and has not been seen since. A mystery that remains unsolved. Those who come to the opera house will not be looking for a silly child of twenty and they will not find her. I pride myself that I have changed a great deal in the past three years. And when I have obtained the divorce I seek, the process of change will be completed."

"He will never know that you have borne his child?" Victor demanded.

Madame Fabri looked at him with pardonable annoyance. "You know my feelings on that count,

Victor. You even know the circumstances attendant upon that birth." She suddenly looked quite fierce. "He deserves to know nothing—and nothing is what he is going to know." She added edgily, "Why do you quiz me on this so often, Victor? Have you changed your mind?"

He moved forward and took her hand. "You know that I will never change," he said earnestly. "You know what you mean to me. You know that I have waited for this return to London for three years. But I wish to be sure."

"Is it not enough for you that everyone else is sure that we are lovers, *mon ami*?"

"No," he said angrily, "it is not enough to have the name without the gain."

"When I am free, you will have both," Rachel said softly. "And we will settle down—"

"Stop it!" Victor cried furiously.

She regarded him in surprise. "What is the matter, my dear?"

"Sometimes I think you have no understanding, none at all," he growled. "Or else there is in you a wish to tantalize and torment those of my sex."

"Victor!" She opened her eyes wide. "I was only anticipating our happy future."

"The future, the future!" he exploded. "We, you and I, live in the present, the empty present." Meeting her blank stare, he groaned. "But it is no good to rail at you. You have no understanding beyond your music—otherwise you might have been able to forgive much. But I should not be surprised. It is always thus with singers. They have room in their heads only for the sound and the music."

"My saving grace," Rachel retorted. Her own anger was uppermost. "Am I supposed to be full of Christian charity toward him, who might not have even regarded me as a Christian, who saw me, in fact, as a way to keep out of debtors' prison?"

"That is an old, a meatless bone, that you have gnawed far too long."

She glared at Victor. "I begin to think that you sympathize with him."

"I have begun to sympathize with anyone who has had the ill-fortune to love you."

She gave him a glance full of the understanding he had just accused her of not possessing. "I think you are afraid that when we return to England there will be a reconciliation with Gervais. And I say that you are being ridiculous. It has been three years. I am a wife who has deserted her husband. If he has not divorced me *in absentia*, it is only because he is not sure whether I am alive or dead. That is why he has searched for me. It is all pretense with him, pretense and pride."

"Pride?" Victor questioned.

"Yes, pride!" she flashed. "He would like to convince himself and others that he cared for me. I am sure that shoddy bargain with my father must yet irk him. He is a Fenton and a Sayre, proud old family of which he is the last member. I am sure he does not like to dwell on that."

Victor gave her a long look. "I begin to believe that your bitterness has crippled and blinded you, Rachel."

"Nothing of the kind!" she exclaimed. "It has strengthened me and given me the power to see with utmost clarity—or it would, were I not so weary at this moment."

He smiled a little wryly. "I accept the hint. I will see you in the morning." He bowed over her hand. "*Bonne nuit*, Madame Fabri."

"*Bonne nuit, Monsieur le Comte*." She gave him a grateful smile. "Thank you, Victor, for bearing with me. I admit to being . . . nervous about this English debut. Indeed, I fear I was very rash in accepting the engagement, but the remuneration was difficult to refuse . . . or, rather, impossible."

"It will be a triumph," he said softly.

After he had gone, Rachel emitted a long sigh. There were times when she did not wish to be alone, and this was one of them. In the silence of her sitting room, her thoughts developed wings and darted at her like a swarm of angry bees. Try as she had to vanquish her feelings, a return to England did not spell an opportunity to triumph upon her home ground; it meant only Gervais, who had wronged her, who had trampled on her feelings and made it impossible for her to trust or love anyone, even Victor, and whom she could not exorcise from her mind, not when she was faced with the son born out of that night of anger and unleashed passions. Would they meet or would Gervais remain in the country? Certainly he must surface when she began proceedings for a divorce, a most unusual act for a female, she knew, and one that would distress her father. She swallowed a lump in her throat.

She had not been in communication with Sir Harry, mainly because she had feared he must confide in the husband he had provided for her. She could find it in her heart to forgive him. She no longer believed he had made his proposition out of a desire to be rid of her. He had been impressed by Gervais, even as she had been impressed. He had seemed so honest, so trustworthy . . . which, of course, spoke very little for her insight. She had trusted her friend Lady Hobart, too—Lady Hobart, who had been nothing more than a procuress. Rachel dismissed her quickly from her thoughts. She must needs concentrate on Gervais and the divorce. She wished that he had instituted those proceedings. Certainly she had given him reason enough, and she was positive that it was his pride that had prevented him from doing so. And if she must needs be the one to set those wheels in motion, would he insist on a meeting? And what about the child, who had something of the look of him in his gray-green eyes—would Gervais dare to demand his son?

"No," she whispered. "He is mine, mine alone." She blinked then, and was furious because the tears that had sprung to her eyes were silent proof that despite her herculean efforts, she had not quite exorcised every vestige of the feeling she had once had for Gervais. As she went to her bedroom, she prayed that her dreams would not torment her as they had been doing ever since she had made the decision to accept the munificent offer from the manager of the King's Theater, bringing her images so vivid that she would wake in fear that she must yet find him at her side.

In another part of Paris, a gentleman who had been a member of the audience that had cheered the great Francesca Fabri that night at the opera sat in his cold little room, five narrow flights up from the street, and by the light of a single guttering candle wrote a letter to an old friend. It read in part:

And so, my dear Dorne, I am happy to inform you that Madame Fabri, as she is pleased to call herself now, will be in London no later than the tenth of the month. She is engaged to perform in that rather indifferent work *Fastrade*, which concerns the sufferings of one of the nine wives of Charlemagne, a libretto even sillier than that of *La Scala di Seta*, which I had the misfortune to hear upon its premiere in 1813. (Was that really six years ago?) Rossini's work, however, has improved mightily. *Il Barbiere di Siviglia* is enchanting. I do not know but that I prefer it to *Le Nozze di Figaro*. However, if the gods and various helpful factions are kind, della Gracia will be hissed off the stage along with Madame. But I run on too long. I meant only to tell you that *she* will be back, and since I, unfortunately, prefer not to set foot on English soil, I will let you make what you choose out of this information. I am sure that Lady Villiers would appreciate it. I remain,

Yours,
Charles Osmond

P.S. I can think of another female who might also be very pleased at this intelligence. Is it true that Lady Charlotte remains on the vine? However, I am sure that you will have also held a similar thought. I hope the headaches have finally ceased. Or should I not have let you know that our mutual acquaintance, the obliging Lady Hobart, confided that information to me? I swear she was moved less by malice than concern. She described your sufferings to me in the most sympathetic terms.

C.O.

The commodious traveling coach bearing Madame Fabri and her young son, as well as her abigail and her manager, rounded a corner, and Madame Fabri, leaning forward, said excitedly, "There is Grinling Gibbons' statue of Charles II, my darling." She touched her son's shoulder and pointed. "That is the hospital founded by his majesty."

Victor regarded her with amused affection. "Do you think he can share your excitement at these landmarks?"

Rachel flushed. "I expect not," she admitted. "But oh, it is good to see them again. I am glad we are going to stay in Chelsea Village, too. It is really such a charming spot."

"Yes, it is far enough away and near enough at the same time."

"*Maman*," the little boy cried. "*Voici le cheval. C'est grand, n'est-ce pas?*"

"Yes, my love, he is a very large horse." Rachel glanced at the steed in question. "But since we are in England, we must needs speak English now."

"*A me non piace parlare inglese.*" Paul gave her a roguish look.

"How he picks up all that foreign lingo!" Phoebe marveled.

"But he must speak English." His mother directed a mock-reproving glance at her son. "I mean it, Paul. English at all times."

He moved restlessly on her lap. "I want to go out."

"We will be arriving soon." She ran her hand through his hair.

"When?" he demanded.

"Soon, *mon enfant*," Victor assured him.

"*Voyez! Mon Oncle Victor parle français*," the child cried.

"Your Uncle Victor must also remember that he, too, is upon English soil," Rachel said reprovingly.

"His Uncle Victor is entirely aware of that," Victor said testily. "And . . ." He paused as the coach drew to a stop.

"But have we arrived, then?" Rachel demanded.

"If this is Cheyne Walk," Victor said, "we have."

"The river!" Rachel exclaimed, looking out of the coach window. "We will be facing the river!"

"And here is Anne-Marie," Victor added softly.

Rachel turned back and stared out the other window. Tears filled her eyes, for there was Anne-Marie, her skirts caught up in her fingers as she ran down a flagstone walk toward the coach. In no more than a minute, the coachman had opened the doors, and Rachel, not even waiting for the steps to be let down, leaped to the pavement and flung her arms around her dearest friend. A moment later she was also embracing the Countess de Lascelles and marveling because neither looked a day older.

"Oh, I did not expect . . ." she began, and then could not speak at all for the sobs that were escaping her.

"Oh, it is entirely lovely," Rachel said some thirty minutes later, her calm restored. She was standing in the small back parlor of the house and looking through the window into a garden bright with rhododendrons, azealeas, and tulips, all of which would soon be coming to the end of their blooming.

The countess indicated the peonies and the rambler roses. "These will presently be at their best, but enough. Now that our dear Victor has departed, we must remember tht we are not here to discuss horticulture.

Let us hear about you, my love, and your adorable son whom I wish you'd not left with his nurse.''

"It is past time for his nap," Rachel explained. "And he does become fractious."

"He seemed very good-tempered to me, especially for one arriving in a place he has never seen before."

"He is used to arriving, used to leaving," Rachel explained. "Ours is rather a hectic life. I am glad we will be staying here for at least a month."

She received a concerned glance from the countess. "And no longer, my dear?"

"I anticipate that we will be returning to France as soon as my engagement is at an end."

Anne-Marie said bluntly, "And you do not intend to let his father know of his existence. I have told you how very miserable Gervais is, and how he has looked everywhere for you . . . from the Highlands of Scotland to Land's End."

Rachel said coldly, "A belated attack of conscience, perhaps. But," she continued before Anne-Marie could respond, "I ought not to credit him with a conscience."

"And I tell you," Anne-Marie retorted hotly, "that you mistake him. He loves you, has always loved you. Your pride, your overweening pride, has shut your eyes and sealed your ears, Rachel."

"That is true, my love," the countess agreed. "If you were to see him, Rachel . . ."

Rachel said stubbornly, "I am delighted to see you both again, but I beg you will not mention those with whom I have broken completely."

"But," Anne-Marie began, "if—"

"My love," the countess interposed gently, "do not say anything more. Rachel has made up her mind. And now"—she smiled at Rachel—"do let us talk about the great Francesca Fabri, for whom composers write operas and about whom we have read much and heard much, but not from her own lips. Only you can tell us, my love, how it feels to be a famous opera singer."

The light from the window facing the garden had grown considerably dimmer when at last Anne-Marie

and her mother bade farewell to Rachel and were seen
by her into their waiting post chaise. They waved at her
until the vehicle turned a corner, and then Anne-Marie
put her hands over her face and began to weep. The
countess, too, had tears in her eyes, but she wiped them
away angrily, saying with the ferocity she usually
reserved for discussions of Robespierre and Napoleon,
"It is a shame. That woman—I saw her the other day,
quite by accident, on the street. Her expression was so
self-satisfied that I wished to go up and hit her."

"I," Anne-Marie said, "would like to wring her
neck. She has wantonly destroyed two lives and perhaps
a third. That child needs his father. If only I might tell
Gervais!"

"You have sworn on your honor that you will not. I
have sworn also," the countess reminded her.

"If only she would listen to us," Anne-Marie said in
the accents of deep frustration. "And if she had not
made us swear that we would say nothing to Gervais
concerning her arrival in the country, I would go at once
to him."

The countess nodded. "But we have sworn we will
not." She cocked an eye at her daughter. "However,
my dearest, we did not promise that we would not ask
him to join us at the opera when Madame Fabri makes
her debut."

"Ah, of course we may do that!" Anne-Marie
clapped her hands. Then she frowned. "Is the Marquess
of Dorne in the city?"

"Wretched creature, I think not. I heard that he was
in the country. He, I might mention, is the reason that
there may yet be hope."

"For Rachel and Gervais?" Anne-Marie looked at
her mother in surprise. "I do not follow that reasoning,
Maman."

"It is what she told Victor on the night she came to
him," the countess said meditatively. "She feared that
Victor might call the marquess out. Also, she feared
that Gervais might do the same. I happen to believe that
her fears were mainly for her husband. My poor

Victor . . ." She shook her head. "Yet, I am not sure he does not know he loves in vain."

"She will never admit it," Anne-Marie said positively. "She is so uncommonly stubborn."

"She has been so hurt," the countess reminded her gently. "Until she was eight, Rachel knew neither mother nor father. Sir Harry attempted to right that wrong, but he was late and her nurse was harsh and possibly prejudiced. You remember what Rachel was like when we met her—very suspicious of us. It took us a long time to win her over."

"Did it? I hardly remember—we have been friends for so very long," Anne-Marie said musingly. "Ah, yes, she was wild and violent . . . always she had to protect herself even against me." Anne-Marie frowned. "And then, just about the time that Sir Harry won her trust, he met Samantha."

"It was later than that," the countess said thoughtfully. "Rachel was turned sixteen, but was yet a tender age to be faced with that sanctimonious wretch."

"Was she not satisfied with thrusting poor Rachel out of her home?" Anne-Marie demanded rhetorically. "Why was she so determined to carry her enmity so far?"

"She had an ax to grind, as the wise Benjamin Franklin has said. There were too many axes, I think." The countess frowned. "Gervais has explained Osmond's ax."

"But Osmond is out of the country, and I understand that he must needs remain where he is, else he will be arrested for debt. Consequently, his claws are clipped," Anne-Marie said thankfully.

"And Dorne, being away, has no knowledge of Madame Fabri's presence, which is all to the good. He is, as you know, very fond of the opera. I hope his accommodating mistress is with him." The countess looked quite fierce. "If I had my way, Lady Hobart, as she is pleased to call herself, would be whipped at cart's tail like any common drab."

Anne-Marie's mobile features reflected her mother's

ire. "I do wish that Rachel had struck his lordship harder."

"Do not repine," the countess said consolingly. "The blow to his pride would have been enough."

Anne-Marie turned a worried face toward her mother. "Then we must pray that he remains in the country." She paused and then said thoughtfully, "And what of Sir Harry—will she see him?"

"*Sacrebleu*!" the countess exclaimed. "Can you imagine . . . my head was so full of poor Gervais's woes that I never mentioned him."

"Nor I, but I have a feeling that she is no more receptive to her father than she is to her husband."

"Which, of course, is the way Samantha wanted it. Damn the creature, she ought not to be allowed to exercise her wicked wiles without interference from anyone."

"Hannah More would not call her 'wicked,' Maman."

"And is Sir Harry so bamboozled by her angelic countenance—" the countess began furiously.

"I think," Anne-Marie interrupted, "that he is not so bamboozled as trapped." She flung her arms around her mother. "I do thank you for refusing all those who demanded your hand in marriage here."

A shadow passed over the countess's face. She said softly and with a tinge of an old grief, "I was wed once . . . and forever."

"And I . . . which is as it should be."

The two ladies smiled mistily at each other and went on to speak of other things.

Much as she loved them and had longed to see Anne-Marie and her mother throughout most of the time she had been away, Rachel found herself wishing that they had not come. They had brought with them an unwanted and all-too-pervasive presence: Gervais.

He had hovered over them during the two hours of their visit. He had been there in their questioning glances and in their unspoken comments. It was only natural that they would wonder about him, but they might have been deterred from that underground of partisanship if they had not seen little Paul.

Rachel grimaced. Though Paul did not actually resemble Gervais, he did have his large green eyes and cleft chin. Her legacy to him was the greater. He had inherited her black hair, her nose, and her high cheekbones. Mentally Rachel examined the term "legacy." By her decision not to tell Gervais of the child born out of his furious assault on her the night she had confronted him with the truth, she was keeping her son from inheriting the title that would be rightfully his. Would Charlotte's children eventually stand in his place?

Anne and her mother had not mentioned Charlotte. Did that mean that she and Gervais were not planning to be married as soon as he was free? But, she reminded herself caustically, they had not mentioned Gervais because she had forbidden any reference to her past misery. The conversation had been of her devising. They had listened while she discussed her operatic debut, her experiences while easing into the profession, her encounters with temperamental impresarios, composers, tenors, and baritones, not to mention the declining race of castrati, poor maimed creatures more feminine than masculine. She had aroused her friends' pity for them and had made them laugh, too—but Gervais had lurked behind their laughter, Gervais and the son he did not know—*would* not know, she thought decisively now, title or no title. And certainly he must have reached an understanding with Charlotte. Yet how cruel he had been to the girl, callously bringing her together with the wife who had apparently usurped her place in his life.

Rachel ran her hands through her hair. She must not dwell on the painful past now. She must remember why she was here. She smiled wryly. On the face of it, she had come because of the money she could no longer

afford to ignore. She had known from the outset that
her return to England would be difficult, but until the
visit from Anne-Marie and her mother, she had not
known just *how* difficult. Three years away from
England had, in a sense, dulled her perceptions of what
she might expect once she returned.

In Italy and France, faced with the exigencies
attendant upon her life in opera, she had been able to
forget her previous existence for days at a time, but here
it was rolling over her like a juggernaut. Everywhere she
went, she would be weighed down by the memories she
had so determinedly tried to put aside . . . and must she
see Gervais again? She guessed that Anne-Marie and her
mother believed she must. As she had already decided,
they were snugly in his corner. He could always make
women like him. None knew that better than herself.
Yet Anne-Marie was fully acquainted with the reasons
he had married her. As her best friend, she ought not to
have wanted to plead his cause, but she had been
burning to do so, and so had the countess, this despite
the fact that they knew Victor wanted to marry her after
her divorce.

Victor.

Rachel groaned. "No," she muttered, and was
aghast, but in that moment she knew what she must
have known ever since Victor had proposed to her and
she had tacitly accepted him. She could not marry him,
had never loved him the way she had once loved
Gervais. She stared out at the darkening landscape. Had
her return to England crystallized these thoughts, or had
they always lurked at the back of her mind? She had a
feeling that the latter was true. She had always known
she could not marry Victor. She had made that half-
commitment at a time when she had felt particularly
bereft and alone—because Paul had been a mere infant,
held in the arms of his wet nurse.

Then what of Paul, who was fond of Victor and
needed a father? Rachel grimaced. Years ago, she had
needed both father and mother and had had, in their

place, a grim, cold nurse of Methodist persuasion, who had disapproved of her late mother and had read her homilies on Christian conduct as well as cautionary tales about bad children who died young, and good children who also died young but in an odor of sanctity that kept them from burning in hell. Rachel grinned. She had always preferred the bad children. Paul, however, would never become acquainted with either.

"He will survive," she muttered philosophically. "I did."

Gervais was following the crowds to the King's Theater. He was feeling weary and scarcely in the mood for an opera. He had arrived back in London only that afternoon, after having ridden most of the way from the Hold and letting his valet have the post chaise to himself. By the time his servants welcomed him at his London house, he was weary, puzzled, and dispirited. However, he had no time to cosset himself. He had been held up in an unanticipated summer storm on the road and had reached his home only in time to dress for the opera.

Three hundred miles was a long way to come for an opera, yet he could not have ignored the strange communiqué he had received from Anne-Marie. She had invited him to join her husband, her mother, and herself at the King's Theater to hear a new opera called *Fastrade*, by a composer unknown to him and with a prima donna who, Anne-Marie had explained, was making her debut after considerable success on the Continent. She had told him that they had taken the liberty of purchasing a ticket for him and had added the surprising information that her mother was particularly hopeful that he would join them.

That they had wanted him to travel so far to view an opera had at first caused him to wonder if they had taken leave of their senses. His second thoughts had, however, brought a flicker of hope, a hope that they might have had news of Rachel. He still held this hope, but as the miles between him and the Hold had lengthened, it had diminished. If they had heard anything about Rachel, would they not have told him so? They knew of the long fruitless search that had occupied the greater part of his time in the last three years. The Countess de Lascelles had, he remembered, tried gently to discourage him from that endeavor. Indeed, though she had vehemently denied it, he had the feeling she knew Rachel's whereabouts. That feeling had estranged him, rather than bringing him closer to them. If they knew anything, he had reasoned resentfully, they should have passed that information to him.

The fact that after some two years of silence they had invited him to the opera seemed to indicate a change of attitude. He was of two minds about that possibility. On the one hand, he was resentful, and on the other, he was hopeful. If they knew anything at all, they ought to have told him—but perhaps they had been unable to do so. Perhaps, out of loyalty to his wife, they had sworn they would not. Rachel was quite capable of having exacted such a promise. He had had more than a taste of that side of her nature. Her attitude once her stepmother had made her acquainted with the "reasons" behind their hasty marriage had been one of implacable anger.

Of course, he had invited that anger through his own desperate reactions. When he had seized her and forced himself upon her, his purpose had been to show her how much he loved her—but her resistance had incited him to fury and he had ravished her! That had been the beginning of the end—the end that had resulted in her inexplicable disappearance and the disappearance of Phoebe, the abigail that had been with her since she had been a very young girl.

That latter disappearance was the one factor that had given him hope. If Rachel had taken Phoebe with her, she had had a destination in mind—but where, where, *where* had she gone? He had hired Bow Street Runners and they had searched everywhere, to no avail. Rachel had seemingly dropped off the face of England. He had toyed with the idea of going to the Continent, but in the end, he had not. He would have met with even greater difficulties there, for he had only a smattering of French. He had moved restlessly between his two houses, trying to improve matters on his northern estates. He had built a road and built better cottages for his tenants. He had made some changes in his London house, but he had steadfastly refused the invitations that had piled up on the silver tray in the hall, and he had had a furious quarrel with his Aunt Lily.

He was still thinking about that quarrel as he walked toward the King's Theater. A year after Rachel's disappearance, she had summoned him to Bath and dared to suggest that he divorce Rachel and marry Lady Charlotte, for whom she had always had a soft spot. It was time, she had told him, that he settle down and think about an heir. She had started to cite Charlotte's impeccable background and bloodlines, speaking as if she were a prize mare rather than a woman. She had also mentioned a visit that Charlotte had paid to her during which the girl had admitted her love for him, suggesting that it had been of long duration. In deference to her age, he had stifled the retorts that had sprung to his lips until she had dared to suggest that it was well Rachel, with her mixed blood, had left him. His anger, or rather his fury, had been such that he could not even remember what he had said to her before he had slammed out of her presence. It was quite possible, he thought, that his anger had been partially predicated on the fact that he had been visiting her when Rachel's stepmother had come with her poisoned load of gossip. He had not seen his Aunt Lily since—he hoped never to see her again.

"Gervais, my boy!"

Gervais came to a stop and found himself facing Sir Harry Villiers. A second wary glance showed him that his father-in-law was not accompanied by Lady Villiers. It was because of her that Gervais, after several anguished visits to Sir Harry's London house in the futile hope that her father might have heard something about Rachel, had ceased all communication with him. During two of those visits he had seen Lady Villiers, and the look of smug satisfaction on her face had made him long to take her by the shoulders and shake her, or worse.

". . . the opera?"

Gervais reddened. He realized that Sir Harry was looking at him interrogatively and must have asked him a question. Caught in his flood of memories, he had not been attending. "I am sorry, Sir Harry," he said. "I fear I did not hear you."

"The noise is distracting," Sir Harry said understandably. "I asked if you were going to the opera."

"Yes, and you, sir?"

"Yes. I had an invitation from the Countess de Lascelles. We have not spoken in quite a while, but she thought I might enjoy this particular work."

Gervais digested this information in silence. Questions by the score leapt to his mind, and with them was hope. He was now reasonably sure that Sir Harry, in common with himself, had been invited to the opera for a purpose that had nothing to do with music. He said cautiously, "Lady Villiers is not with you, sir?"

"No." Sir Harry smiled. "The countess did not send her a ticket. She knows and understands my wife's disapproval of theatrical entertainments."

Gervais's hopes rose even higher. He said, "I would not think that onus would extend to the opera."

"My wife," Sir Harry said, "feels that the human voice should be used only in sacred song." Rather unnecessarily he added, "I myself do not agree." His face clouded. "Rachel has been much in my mind tonight. I remember her great love of music, and her voice—so beautiful."

"The music of the spheres," Gervais said softly, and blinked, hoping that Sir Harry had not seen the sudden wetness in his eyes.

He had seen, however, for he put an arm around Gervais's shoulders. "Lad, I am sorry," he said in a low

voice. "As I have told you repeatedly, I cannot understand how we came to be overheard that night. Unfortunately, I can understand my wife's eagerness to
impart that information to Rachel." His voice quivered
with suppressed fury. "And to twist it so cruelly. There
are times when I . . ." He suddenly clenched his hands
into fists and then thrust them down at his sides. "Shall
we join our hosts?"

"I think we must hurry. The crowds are thinning out,
and I am sure the opera must soon commence."

Sir Harry and Gervais reached the box where Anne-
Marie and her family were already ensconced. There
was time for no more than a brief exchange of greetings
before the music began.

The audience was restive during the overture. Gervais
could understand why. The music was all too rem-
iniscent of other composers and he could not like the
preponderance of violins. The first act began with a
great deal of incomprehensible dialogue between the
bass, who sang the role of Charlemagne, and the tenor,
who appeared to be the lover of Fastrade. Then
Fastrade was heard before she was seen, and he came to
attention. The sound was beautiful! Then she entered, a
tall blond woman in medieval robes, and Gervais knew
why he had been invited!

He exchanged a glance with Sir Harry and read an
amazement in the latter's eyes that he knew must be
reflected in his own. He also became aware that Anne-
Marie had turned in her chair. She was sitting directly in
front of him. Meeting her eyes, he nodded almost
imperceptibly, wondering at the same time how he could
sit there so quietly when with every fiber of his being he
wanted to rush down to the stage and, notwithstanding
the audience, take Rachel—for it *was* Rachel—in his
arms.

From the moment she made her entrance, the
audience leaned forward to drink in that beautiful
soaring voice. Gervais glanced at the program and noted
with an interior groan that there were no fewer than five
acts—five acts before he could go the green room. He

cast a harried glance around him and longed for the days when seats had been placed on the stage itself, and young sprigs of fashion wandered up and down at will, ogling and even addressing actors and actors while they were in the midst of a scene. A split second later he realized that not for the world could he have interrupted her. The voice that had shown such promise three years ago had matured and, if possible, was even more beautiful than when he had first heard it. He continued to listen entranced until the curtain fell, until he looked at Anne-Marie and her mother, and until all the thoughts which her singing had held in abeyance flooded back into his mind.

He turned a frowning gaze on Anne-Marie's face. "Why did you not tell me?"

Regretfully she said, "We were under oath not to tell you. It was never suggested, however, that we might not show you what we, my mother and I, were of the opinion you must needs see and hear."

Lord Stirling, a fair young man, was red about the ears. He cast an uncomfortable and reproachful look at his wife and mother-in-law. " 'Twas their idea, my dear Lord Sayre."

"Yes, my dearest Douglas"—the countess turned a determined gaze in his direction—"I was of the opinion that Rachel's father and her husband had been punished far more than either deserved. Rachel, unfortunately, did not understand how very much she was adored by both. The account she was given was full of distortions and out-and-out lies. Though I am not entirely sure of all the particulars of the situation, I am of the opinion that Lady Villiers and also Lady Charlotte were misinformed by those who originally spread the tale."

"You need not try to spare my wife." Sir Harry spoke for the first time. "I am of the opinion that she herself furnished many of the distortions. She prides herself on telling the truth at all times—however, her truths have often a most elastic shape."

Gervais turned toward the countess. "We . . . I am sure I speak for Sir Harry when I say that we are much in your debt, Countess. And in yours too, Lady Stirling."

"If that is so," Anne-Marie said earnestly, "I beg that neither of you will mention the . . . er, happenstance that resulted in your being present at the opera this evening. Our box, if you will note, is on the side, and I doubt that dearest Rachel has been able to see all its members."

She received a hasty acquiescence from both her guests and quite noticeably relaxed as she leaned back in her seat.

In the crowded pit of the house, a gentleman who had arrived even later than Sir Harry and Gervais surveyed the audience with a quizzing glass. His attention was necessarily riveted on the boxes where most of his friends or those who called themselves his friends were located. His stare, much magnified by the glass, as he noted Sir Harry and his son-in-law, was such that a young girl some distance away shivered and made a sign that caused her escort to regard her in some perplexity.

"Why'd you do that?" he whispered.

" 'Twas for 'im," she muttered. " 'E 'as the evil eye."

"Eh? 'Oo?"

She darted another look in the direction of the gentleman and said with some relief, "H'I don't see 'im no more."

Her companion remarked in some embarrassment. "We better get up there, ye've seen down 'ere like you wanted."

"Right away," the girl said. She shivered. "H'I don't want to be nowhere in 'is vicinity."

Unfortunately, as the girl and her companion edged toward the outer door and the stairs that must bring them to the top of the house, she saw the slim figure of the man with the quizzing glass and came to a dead stop, causing her escort to glare down at her. "Now wot?" he whispered angrily.

" 'E's gone," she muttered. "H'I don't think 'e

means to stay for the rest o' it. Oh, H'I am glad. 'E 'as the evil eye.''

The man with the quizzing glass strolled out into the street. He glanced up at a three-quarter moon and ascertained that by the time the woman calling herself Francesca Fabri sang again, that white orb would be full. Quite unconsciously, he put one slim hand to the back of his head, almost as if he could still feel the welt caused by the bronze figurine that had come in violent contact with it. His smile was unpleasant. Upon receipt of the letter from his erstwhile friend he had visited the home of his mistress, riding whip in hand. He had left her with shoulders so badly lacerated that she would be scarred for what remained of her life. He had further informed her that her ill-advised confidences to one Mr. Charles Osmond had lost her an affluent protector.

Upon his departure, he had said to the wretched, moaning woman, "I am not in agreement with dear Charles that your motives in describing the outcome of my meeting with young Lady Sayre were sympathetic."

He had not heeded her groans or her protests of undying love. He had merely strolled out of the house. On the following day he had dismissed the servants and put the establishment up for sale, informing a bailiff to wait upon the woman who called herself Lady Hobart but who had no legitimate claim to a title other than plain "Mrs. Hobart." The officer was instructed to tell her that she was allowed to take with her only those garments and such few personal effects as she had brought with her. He had thoughtfully made a list of these. Her jewels, for the most part, were to be confiscated. He had not neglected to alert several mantua-makers that he was no longer responsible for "her ladyship's" debts and that any outstanding bills were to be settled by herself. He rather thought that she would be quickly removed to the Fleet or some other sponging house.

He was thinking of that explusion with some pleasure as he went toward the home of a lady he intended to visit that night. She would not be nearly so accommodating as Lady Hobart—but the visit promised him even greater pleasure.

The final curtain had fallen and the response of the audience was such that Victor de Lascelles, conferring with a delighted manager, was assured that Madame Fabri was worth every cent of the exorbitant salary he had exacted in her behalf.

"A voice for the ages, my dear sir, my very dear sir," the manager cried. "We are delighted. The curtain calls . . . ah, Madame . . ." He broke off as the artist, looking weary but happy, came toward them. The sound of the applause was still continuing, but only sporadically now. Those out front were reminded that there would be difficulties in getting away from the house—a mass of vehicles, neighing horses, and swearing coachmen awaited them. A need to join in the fray and escape without injury to life or limb was suddenly paramount.

The manager approached the singer. "Ah, Madame, my felicitations. I kiss your hands." He proceeded to carry out his threat.

"I thank you, sir." She smiled at him. A second later she cast an appealing glance at Victor. "Please, may I go to my dressing room? And where is little Paul? I saw him with Phoebe in the wings. I cannot imagine what prompted her to allow him to remain there for such a long time! I must speak to her."

"I beg you will not," Victor said earnestly. "She had little choice. Paul has a voice too, and it was raised in sound each time we attempted to take him back to your dressing room."

"Oh, dear, I will not bring him to the theater again," she said apologetically.

"I expect that would be best," he agreed.

The ordeal of the green room was not something to which Rachel looked forward with anticipation, at least not on this night. The plaudits, music to her ears from time to time, were not enough to combat her extreme weariness.

This night, though one of many similar opening nights, had been full of the tension of being on her "native ground" before a "jury of her peers." Though her name cloaked her identity, and with her dark coloring she could easily pass for Italian, she was English, after all, and though she had enjoyed a triumph akin to those she had had on the Continent, it had left her exhausted.

On most occasions she would have gone to some little café and celebrated with Victor until the excitement was dissipated and she was ready to sleep, but tonight she knew she would sleep immediately she returned home, and that must be soon. The sound of the river would be in her ears and she would pretend that she was being borne on its bosom down to the sea, a childish fancy, but incredibly soothing after the anticipation, the realization, and the resulting excitement. That there were other factors contributing to that excitement, she would not acknowledge, even to herself.

She said to Victor, "You insist that I leave within minutes after I arrive in the green room. You may explain that there is Paul to consider. Indeed, I give you leave to bring him in there. On Wednesday, I promise, I will behave like a prima donna, but tonight . . ."

"You need give me no explanations," he said sympathetically. "Can you imagine that I do not understand what tonight has meant to you?"

She smiled up at him. "You must forgive me, Victor, my dearest. My brains, if ever I possessed any, are entirely scrambled."

The green room was filled with those privileged members of the audience who had once been allowed free access to the stage. Barred from that pleasure, they, for the most part gentlemen, regarded the door with anticipation, many of them ogling the young women, especially the dancers, as they drifted in from their dressing rooms. There was applause for the tenor and baritone, but of course it was the prima donna whom they awaited.

Gervais, arriving ahead of Lord Stirling and his party, a mark of grace on the part of Anne-Marie, the countess, and Sir Harry, stared nervously about him. His heart was beating close to his throat, or so it seemed. His thoughts were in a whirl. He could not deny the fact that despite the kindness of Anne-Marie and her mother, he resented them. They should not have allowed him to suffer for three long years. Promises or no, they should have revealed Rachel's whereabouts. Yet his common sense told him that they had acted in loyalty to his wife. Still, should a mere promise stand between man and wife? He could not dwell on these feelings, not when he was about to see her, speak to her, whom he had loved at first sight—but how explain to her that that was the truth? Given her pride and her anger . . . He could not dwell on that either. Something brushed against his legs. He looked down and found a child staring up at him out of huge gray-green eyes.

"Why, who are you?" Gervais smiled at the little boy. "Surely you are not one of the singers?"

"Paul, you naughty boy, where are you?" demanded an irate voice. Various people turned around, and a few laughed.

Gervais bent down and picked up the child, raising him to his shoulder. "Are you looking for this young man? He . . ." He paused, staring amazingly at a young woman he had not seen in three years, not since she had mysteriously disappeared from his household one night, the night after his wife had not troubled to come home. "Phoebe!" he exclaimed.

"Did you find him, Phoebe?" asked another woman, her tones full of anxiety. "I told you . . ." Her words were drowned by the applause that resounded through the room.

Gervais, still holding the child, turned to face his wife—his wife, who was holding out her arms for the child, her dark blue eyes stormy in her white face. The boy, he noticed, had her black hair and other features in common with her. "This is your boy?" he asked in frozen tones.

Unmindful of the applause, unmindful of the people beginning to crowd around her, Rachel, looking into her husband's eyes, nodded and said steadily, "He is my child, my lord." She added coolly. "We must discuss a divorce."

He said dully, "I will have my solicitor wait upon you." He thrust the child into her arms and made his way quickly through the crowds and out of the green room, out of the opera house, out into the heated air of the summer night. The questions that had troubled him for three years, that had troubled and tortured him, were answered at last.

12

On that same night that her husband had astonished her by declaring that he was going to the opera, a form of entertainment she held in abhorrence, Lady Villiers was bidding farewell to an unexpected but, as it had turned out, a most welcome visitor.

She was very beautiful, the visitor decided dispassionately. Filled with the information he had just vouchsafed, she looked not unlike an angry angel or, he thought amusedly, an avenging angel, and he had no doubt that she would live up to her image. He did feel it incumbent upon himself to say, "I beg that you will say nothing."

Her vivid blue eyes widened. "You have had my word, Lord Dorne. I quite agree with you that discretion is the better part of valor, especially in this regrettable situation."

He had one more question. "You will have only a day and a half—will it be time enough?"

"I assure you that it will." Her expression was one of righteous indignation as she added, "There are many who share your opinion, Lord Dorne. London is a wicked city, as we know, but the 'fear of the Lord is the beginning of wisdom.' Fools, however, despise wisdom and instruction. There are many fools in London, but there are those who are passing wise."

"And will respond to instruction, I hope."

"They will know that they must avoid the strange woman, 'for her house inclineth unto death, and her paths unto the dead,' " Lady Villiers quoted glibly.

"Ah, yes," he murmured. He bowed over her hand. "I will hear from you on Wednesday?"

"In the afternoon," she promised, her beautiful eyes alight with anticipation. "I do thank you for having come to me with this information. How true it is that the Lord moves in mysterious ways."

"Quite," his lordship acknowledged, and thankfully bade her ladyship a second farewell.

Gervais did not return to his house immediately. Prompted by he knew not what impulse, he went to Brooks's, a place he had not visited since that night four years earlier when he had played cards with a stranger named Sir Harry Villiers.

Despite his lengthy absence, the proprietors appeared delighted to welcome him. He himself was not sure why he had come—but as he entered the gambling salon, he knew. It was here that his life had changed four years back, and now he had arrived full circle, a man alone or, rather, soon to be alone. He wondered caustically if there were another middle-aged man with a nubile daughter waiting for him. His Aunt Lily would no doubt recover from her anger and be at him to marry again once he had divorced Rachel. He wondered bitterly who had fathered her child.

"Ah, my dear Gervais," someone drawled. He turned and stiffened as he met the Marquess of Dorne's amused gaze. Before he could respond, the marquess continued, "Is there none will challenge you to a game of piquet? Or whom you might challenge?"

In spite of the hot words crowding to his lips, in spite of his interior rage, Gervais managed to say with remarkable calm, "I have only just arrived. Should you care to play with me, Dorne?"

"Despite your fabled luck?" his lordship inquired, his eyes bright with malice.

"Surely you must know by now that the tale is entirely apochryphal," Gervais responded.

"To my certain knowledge, you have lost but once—at least here in Brooks's."

The implication of his remark gave rise to a fury that held Gervais silent for a brief moment. Then he said softly, "I will yet challenge you to a game, Dorne. Of course, you do have the option to refuse me."

"I will not, however, refuse you," the marquess responded. He signaled to one of the servants and ordered the cards. Piquet, he reasoned, was a game that required not only skill but also the utmost concentration. Judging from Gervais's expression, he had a great deal besides cards on his mind. Although he himself had much to occupy his own mind, he could easily put it aside. It was only too obvious that his opponent had suffered a cruel disappointment this night—one that must be eating into his very soul. Undoubtedly his concentration would be sadly impaired.

Toward morning, Lord Dorne put down his cards. He said calmly, "I should have known better than to challenge the famous Sayre Luck. Truly, my dear Gervais, you are favored of fortune."

Gervais regarded him with an ironic smile. "I had some surprisingly good hands."

"One cannot dispute that." The marquess rose. "I will need to consult with my man of business. You will have your twenty thousand pounds by Thursday if that is agreeable."

"It is quite agreeable, my lord." Gervais nodded.

Despite the danger of braving London's streets so late at night or, rather, so early in the morning, Gervais chose to challenge the fates and walk home. He arrived at his house without mishap. Once admitted by a sleepy porter, who was within an hour of rising and who looked at his master with considerable concern, Gervais went on up the stairs. He paused at the room adjoining his own and went inside.

Nothing had been changed. The bed, turned down by Phoebe three years ago, was still turned down. Those clothes that had not been removed from the closet yet hung there. Rachel's silver toilet articles were on the dressing table and her jewel box yet contained the pearls, the sapphires, and the diamonds that he had given her at one time or another. The entire suite was, indeed, mute evidence that she was away only briefly. However, this night he had another explanation for the condition of the room. It had remained unchanged because the wife he had adored was dead. Tears rolled unchecked down his cheeks. Later, in the morning, he would order his housekeeper to dismantle the room.

Anne-Marie was quarreling with her husband. She faced him defiantly, while Lord Stirling, who rarely disagreed with her, said in the French that came more easily to him when he was disturbed, "You have interfered enough. You will not tell him the truth. This I wil not permit."

"And so the child will grow up without a father?" she demanded angrily.

"It is what your friend wishes."

"She still loves him. I know she does," Anne-Marie contended. "And you could see that he loves her."

"He loved the woman he married," Lord Stirling said. "She cannot be his wife again, even if she so desired. He is a peer of the realm and she is an opera singer. Were she to return to him, she would never be received in polite society, and very likely her son would also be ostracized."

"How can you be so hidebound, Douglas?" Anne-Marie cried.

"I do not speak for myself, I speak for others. She and her son are beyond the pale. It is better that she weds your cousin, who loves her and the boy."

"Victor also has a title!" Anne-Marie reminded him hotly.

"Yes, but he has seen to it that he has a foot in two worlds. The Fentons of Sayre are a different matter, and besides, your friend does not want to return to her husband. She, I think, is wiser than you."

Anne-Marie tossed her head. "You do not know her as I do. Rachel is stubborn, but she loves him still. I am sure of it."

Her husband said firmly, "You must promise that you will not interfere. If this marriage is meant to resume, it must be decided by no one but the participants."

"Very well," she capitulated. "I will move no more mountains. But I will hope for the best."

At that same moment, a few miles away, Sir Harry was being pricked by the horns of a dilemma very similar to that of Anne-Marie as he faced his daughter in her small parlor. "Paul's resemblance to Gervais is obvious to me," he was saying. "And it would have been to Gervais had you not so swiftly got rid of him."

"I have told you what was said. He did not give me a chance to explain. He merely said he would send his solicitor," Rachel said coldly.

"You implied that the child was illegitimate," Sir Harry said insistently.

She stared at him coldly. "I do not think of him as Gervais's child," she responded.

"Rachel," he sighed. "We have never discussed that night at Brooks's—"

"And we will not discuss it now," she said stubbornly. "That was my stipulation when I agreed to see you, Father. I have heard all I wish to hear about that night."

"You have heard lies!"

"Then you did not win at cards? You did not suggest that he come to see me? You did not tell him that I was ill-used by my stepmother? You did not hint that the debt might be excused and his stable restored to him? All that has been told me is completely untrue?"

"It is not precisely untrue, but—"

"I do not wish to hear any more, Father," Rachel said firmly.

"Even though there were mitigating circumstances?"

"I cannot believe that there were any mitigating circumstances," she responded icily.

Sir Harry regarded her helplessly, and then he was suddenly stirred by a vagrant memory that carried with it a vivid imagine, that of a tall, handsome, middle-aged man with cold dark eyes under knit brows. That man had faced a much younger Sir Harry from the doorway of his luxurious office. He had said, "My daughter, Sir Harry? I have no daughter. She is dead to me."

"Esdras Medina," he muttered.

"What did you say, Father?" Esdras Medina's granddaughter inquired in the same icy tones.

"Nothing, child," he sighed. But he could not leave it at that. Pleadingly he added, "If you would but listen to me . . "

"Would you care to hear about my experiences as a singer?" she asked, quite as if she had not heard that plea. Her tone was hostile, her gaze chill. Sir Harry sighed. He wished he had the courage to continue the argument, but the image of Esdras Medina hung in the air between him and his daughter. Resolutely he put his sympathy for Gervais aside and said, "Yes, I am anxious to hear about it, of course, my love. Tell me."

Rachel's eyes mirrored the relieved smile that curled her lips. "It began in Paris, Papa . . ."

It was Lady Villiers' morning hour with her little son. She had come to the nursery with Sir Harry, who usually joined her on this after-breakfast visit. The boy, whose looks were a felicitous combination of both parents, had just celebrated his fourth birthday. As Emma, his nurse, a motherly woman in her early forties, looked on with the proprietary and slightly jealous stare she could not quell even in his mother's presence, Samantha ruffled his golden-brown hair. "Ooo is Mama's pwecious 'ittle one, isn't oo?" she cooed. She looked up at her husband. "I do believe he is getting taller, do you not agree, Harry?"

Sir Harry nodded and smiled briefly at his son. He was still mulling over the astonishing request that

Samantha had made at breakfast, a scant quarter of an hour since. It was one he was far from eager to honor. It would interfere with his plans for the evening. Yesterday he had agreed to meet his daughter backstage and take her, his grandson, and Victor de Lascelles to a late supper. He said deprecatingly, "I cannot imagine why you would wish to attend the opera, Samantha. I thought you believed all such entertainment to be anathema."

She said, "I have heard that the composer has also contributed hymns and an oratorio to the literature. Hannah More has told me that she holds him in especial esteem and she has praised this particular opera highly. She told me that I ought to conquer my prejudice against opera. She insists that it is not in the least like theater."

He had an odd feeling that she was not telling him the truth. He gave her a searching glance and asked, "When did she give you this confidence?"

"Yesterday, when I attended her lecture on *Christian Giving*," Samantha explained. "She offered me a seat in her box, but I thought that since you are always urging me to attend musical events, you might want to accompany me."

Sir Harry allowed some very angry, not to say vindictive, thoughts to drift in the direction of the saintly Miss More. He said as graciously as he might, "Very well, my love, I will see if I can procure tickets."

"If you cannot procure them, would you mind if I go with Miss More?" Samantha asked.

"Of course not, but I believe I will be able to purchase them," he said uncomfortably, thinking it far better for his wife to make what was bound to be a most unpleasant discovery while in his company rather than that of her good friend Miss More. There was no telling what her reaction might be. There were times, and this was one of them, when he wished . . . But it did no good to dwell on those wishes. He had made his bed, and though since the birth of his son he rarely shared it with his wife, he was still bound to her. He moved toward the door. "I had best go to the theater now—the young woman who is singing the title role made quite a success on Monday evening, you know."

"Harry," Samantha said resentfully, "you have not even bade farewell to little Mark."

"Have I not?" He turned back and ruffled his son's curls. "Good-bye, lad," he murmured, and strode from the room.

A second later, Samantha, with a grim look on her face that surprised Emma, also left and, much to the nurse's amazement, did not visit so much as a backward look upon her son.

"Never you mind, lovey." She smiled at the lad. "You 'ave Emma."

The child, apparently undisturbed by the defection of both parents, said merely, "I want to go to the stables and see my pony. May we, Emma? See, I have finished my breakfast."

"That we will, lovey," she said. The nurse and her charge arrived at the stables just as Lady Villiers' post chaise was rattling out of the gates. Emma stared after it in some surprise. "Where be she goin' at this hour in the morning?" she muttered. She made a face. " 'Nother of 'er errands of mercy, no doubt."

"What did you say, Emma?" inquired Mark.

"Nothin', lovey, let's go see your pony," she urged, wondering, as they went toward the stall, how Lady Villiers had managed to dress so hastily. "She's got somethin' on 'er mind this mornin', I'll be bound," she remarked. She had little respect for Lady Villiers, for all she was known as a Lady Bountiful to London's poor. In her lexicon, charity began at home, and Lady Villiers was at home only on those increasingly rare occasions when her husband chose to remain there. However, it was unlike her to shorten her morning hour with her child. "I wonder—" she whispered, but was not allowed to speculate further. Mark was calling her.

In one of those dim alleyways that lie cheek-by-jowl

with the fine houses fronting the wide streets of Mayfair, a tall, slim gentleman, clad in garments that had cost him enough to feed the ragged denizens of this area for weeks, strolled along. He fastidiously avoided piles of manure and human excrement as well. The bold rats scurried through other refuse, and gaunt scavenger cats slipped past them like shadows. The gentleman held a fine lawn handkerchief to his aristocratic nose. In his other hand he clutched a small pistol. Reaching a battered door, he tapped three times, and in a few moments he was confronted by a pair of ragged young men whose thin feral faces pronounced them inhabitants of this area. He spoke briefly with them, but long enough to provide a description, a location, and a promise that they would be well paid for their services. In parting, he added, "I suggest that you wait until the excitement is at its height."

"Aye, we knows wot to do," muttered the older of the pair, a thin, pale, starved-looking lad of seventeen.

"Aye, us knows," agreed his companion, who might have been fifteen.

"You know where he is sitting?" the gentleman felt it incumbent upon himself to repeat.

"Us knows," said the younger lad.

"Us'll be meetin' you afterward," said the older boy.

"Very good," the gentleman commented. He moved away, and a few minutes later was thankfully walking down a broader thoroughfare toward his home.

Near the hour when the doors of the King's Theater were due to open, Gervais walked quickly in the direction of that building. In spite of the shock he had received when he had seen the child, he was fighting a desire to rush backstage and see Rachel. The thought of waiting the three hours and more until the opera ended was almost more than he could bear. Yet, in deference to her art, he must needs control his eagerness. Had she relented? She must have relented, else she never would have sent him that hastily scrawled note and the ticket to a seat in the pit, only three rows from the stage and on an aisle. He had searched his heart and found that he did not care what she had done. He loved her. He wondered what could have caused her change of heart. The note gave him no clue. It had stated only, "My dearest, I wish to see you again, after the performance. Here is a ticket. I will look for you." It was signed "R."

He had almost reached the doors of the theater. They were open now. If he might go backstage . . . But he had better not. He went inside, one of the first to arrive, but up in the gallery a pair of lads ensconced in the front row stared down at him. "There 'e be," muttered one.

"Aye," said the other, fingering a thin-bladed knife. "Us mustn't lose sight o' 'im," he added warningly.

"Won't," said his friend. He looked about him. "Place's beginnin' to fill up." He wrinkled his nose. "Phew, some o' that stuff stinks like 'ell." He cast an eye over the bags that some members of the audience were carrying.

His companion looked back at several rough-looking individuals who had sat down in the row behind them. "I seen 'im afore," he whispered.

"Which?" The older boy looked over his shoulder.

"Big burly 'un wi' the broken nose'n the ears. 'E usta be a Pet o' the Fancy till 'e were knocked out. 'Append in the nineteenth round. Ain't ever been right in 'is noggin since."

"They are turning them away," Victor said excitedly to Rachel as she sat at her dressing table while Phoebe adjusted her long blond wig. "Every seat in the house is taken, the manager informs me."

She nodded. "I know. Can you imagine, even my stepmother is present." She grimaced. "We will not be meeting my father after all."

"She has come to hear you?" Victor demanded incredulously.

Rachel held up a sheet of white paper. "I think not. According to this note that Papa left at the stage door, she was inspired to come here by her mentor Hannah More, who has praised the composer."

Victor raised an interrogative eyebrow. "Odd," he commented. "I did not know that Signor della Gracia was much celebrated beyond the borders of Italy and, more specifically, his native Milan."

"You must tell him about it when next you write to him, or I will. It is sure to please him," Rachel said. She added, "Papa has explained that Samantha does not know that I am singing."

"Oh." Victor grinned. "And what will happen when she finds out?"

"He is in hopes that my blond wig will be disguise enough. If she does recognize me, I think he can count on a hasty departure."

"That woman . . . to have caused so much havoc!" Victor exclaimed.

Rachel's face darkened. "She considers it her Christian duty."

"Had she lived in the times of the good Christ, she might have been among those to cast the first stones." Victor grimaced. "But I will leave you . . . you should not be expending your energies on this useless talk. I will see you after the first act, my dearest."

"We will be sitting downstairs?" Samantha asked as she and her husband came into the theater.

"Yes, my dear, 'twas all I was able to procure. They told me at the ticket office that there was an untoward demand for tickets this night. We were fortunate to get these."

"The house does seem full," she murmured. She stared up at the boxes and her eyes widened. "That young woman," she gasped. "Her gown and . . . and her jewels, a veritable collar of diamonds, and that bracelet. She . . . she must be . . ."

"Very likely," Sir Harry agreed uncomfortably.

"Oh, she is shameless!" Samantha gasped. "And ogling the gentlemen in that horrid bold manner."

"Who are, in turn, ogling her," Sir Harry observed with a smile.

"I do not find it amusing, Harry," Samantha told him stiffly. "It is a shame that the opera and all other places of amusement are frequented by these wanton creatures. They ought to be closed one and all. They are no more than dens of iniquity and vice."

"And yet your mentor, Miss More, does not frown on all of them. She was a friend of David Garrick, and was the author of several plays for the wicked stage herself, unless I am misinformed."

"That was when she was younger and had not seen the Light," Samantha responded stiffly.

He regarded her with no little surprise. "And still she has a box at the opera this night?"

"I have explained that the composer is her friend," Samantha said quickly. She scanned the boxes. "She has not arrived yet, I see, but many have." A slight smile played about her mouth but was quickly erased.

Sir Harry gave her a questioning look. His wife was in an odd mood this night. Several times on the way to the theater he had addressed a remark to her and received no answer. She had seemed to be deep in thought. Once, he had put his hand on her arm and she had started as if frightened. He had suspected that she was fighting off her qualms at attending an entertainment she had always believed to be shocking and immoral. Yet at present she seemed to be fighting a sort of suppressed excitement. Perhaps Miss More had succeeded in changing Samantha's mind to some degree. Some years back, he would have had reason to be grateful to the lady for softening that implacable attitude. In those days he had blamed that on her strict upbringing. He had also thought that her beautiful face had been the reflection of an equally beautiful soul. His awakening had come swiftly—but, he thought bitterly, not swiftly enough. He had not been happy at the time he had met Gervais, but he had not been actively miserable. Now, only the fact that she was the mother of his son kept him at her side. Had it not been for little Mark, he would have left her at the time she had seen fit to ruin his daughter's happiness with those cruel revelations culled from Gervais's enemies.

He sighed. If only he might have spoken for his son-in-law. He was fond of the young man and desperately sorry for him. Gervais had aged far more than his years since Rachel had deserted him. There were strands of gray in his ruddy locks and a look of settled disappointment in his eyes. Now there would be a divorce and Rachel would live with her new husband on the Continent. If only he had had the courage to tell Gervais that the boy, whose gray-green eyes were replicas of his own, could be none other than his son . . . But Rachel had forbidden it. He shot a resentful glance at his wife and was startled. She was smiling and her eyes were agleam with excitement. Meeting his questioning stare, she flushed and said, "I . . . think it is about to begin. The musicians have just come in."

He looked toward the proscenium. "Yes, I think they are about to begin," he agreed.

In the gallery, the two youths stared down at their quarry.

"Matt, us'd better be gettin' down soon," said the younger one.

"Not yet . . . 'tisn't time. They might chuck us out. When she comes in . . . then nobody won't notice us," Matt cautioned.

"We'll 'ave a time gettin' down to where 'e is."

"We'll find 'im," Matt said grimly. "An' nobody the wiser."

The music began, and some gentlemen who had been walking up and down, quizzing glasses trained on the boxes, hastily slipped into their seats. That there were some who did not follow their example was not surprising to anyone. That sparkling sisterhood which boasted among its membership such heartbreakers as Hariette Wilson were as much an attraction as the opera dancers and the singers onstage. However, a hush did come over the audience when, toward the end of the first act, the beautiful Francesca Fabri entered singing her first aria. The hush did not last long.

Just as Matt poked his friend and muttered, "C'mon," a howl arose in the gallery and the two boys did not escape a rain of ill-aimed rotten tomatoes as they hurried out. The howl increased, and in the pit a wild-eyed long-haired man arose and made his way through the musicians to leap onstage.

"Beware the scarlet woman!" he screamed. "Beware the whore of Babylon." He confronted Rachel. "Jewess!" he thundered. "You are shameless, immoral, flaunting yourself before us, you and your lover." He reached out gnarled hands to grab her at the same time the tenor tried to come to her aid and was hit by a well-aimed rotten tomato. A hail of stinking fruits and vegetables was hurled from the gallery toward the stage. Many of these missiles landed in the boxes, where there was pandemonium as screaming women tottered toward the doors.

Matt and his friend had threaded their way to the pit, their eyes fixed on their quarry, but as they started down the aisle, they were met by panic-stricken men and women rushing at them.

Gervais, meanwhile, had pushed his way forward, toward the stage, where a group of rough men had suddenly appeared as Rachel and her terrified colleagues tried to make their way past the interlopers who still milled about the stage screaming their epithets. He never quite knew how he had managed it, but suddenly he was there as one of the men catching Rachel's costume tore at the flimsy material. In one leap Gervais reached her side and put his arm around her. In that same moment he felt a sharp pain in his other arm. He took no notice of it, but in the audience a burly man had seized another man and was holding him in a viselike grip. The pistol he had just fired had dropped from his hand and lay on the floor.

"Let me go, damn and blast you," cried the man as he struggled with his captor. In another moment a blow to his jaw had silenced him, and the burly man, lifting his unconscious victim, pushed his way through the crowd and out an adjacent door.

Samantha was screaming loudly as Sir Harry tried to forge a path up an aisle crowded with terrified patrons running in all directions. In the melee, he was summarily separated from his wife, who, still screaming, fell beneath the feet of those who had blindly rushed toward the door.

"Rachel!" Gervais had managed to get her offstage, and meanwhile the heavy canvas curtains had been dropped against further invasion. The harried manager was nowhere to be seen, but Gervais, his arm around his wife, used his other arm and hand to good effect, elbowing and shoving his way to one of the dressing rooms. Behind him was Victor, who closed the door and stood against it. Fortunately, though there was still yelling and screaming in the halls, no one had followed them.

"Rachel," Gervais cried, "are you hurt, my love?"

She looked up at him, her eyes wide in her pale face. She seemed hardly aware that her costume was hanging in shreds about her. "I . . . do not understand how you . . . Oh, my God, Gervais, my dearest, you . . . are bleeding!"

"Bleeding?" he repeated blankly.

"*Sacre nom de Dieu*!" Victor gasped, staring at Gervais's arm. "We must remove your coat. There's a hole in it."

Gervais was suddenly aware of pain, a throbbing pain. "I . . . I . . ." He looked blankly at Rachel, and then an encroaching darkness suddenly washed over him and he knew no more.

He awakened to pain and voices rising and falling about him like the waves in an ocean. He was also aware of movement. Something was moving under him, jarring him, and his shoulder hurt badly. The pain grew worse and he felt faint. He treid to fight against the feeling—because his memory was furnishing images he wanted to consider—but the blackness came again.

When he opened his eyes once more, he saw the ceiling of his bedchamber and was conscious of deep disappointment. He had dreamed . . . What had he dreamed? Rachel. Yes, he had dreamed of Rachel, and she had spoken gently to him as she had in the days before they had quarreled and she had fled. He had been reminded of that time years ago, when they had been at the Hold and were so happy.

"We were happy," he muttered. "And I love her so much. How could she think I did not love her? But if I had not accepted the . . . the terms, I could not have met her," he explained to someone he could not see—mainly because he could no longer keep his eyes open. His eyelids felt weighted. "I sacrificed my honor, I accepted her father's terms—because I would have done anything. I loved her, love her . . . but she does not understand."

"She understands now," someone whispered.

"No, for she has gone away. I have searched everywhere . . . but I cannot find her."

"She is here. You have found her," said the whisperer.

"No . . . she looks at me as one looks at a stranger," he insisted, and felt weak. The blackness returned.

"He has fainted again." Rachel turned to the doctor at her side. "It is a swoon, is it not?" she added fearfully.

"Yes, that is all," the doctor assured her. "He has a slight fever from the wound. It is deep, but fortunately it missed the bone. He is strong and young. He should mend rapidly, Lady Sayre."

She flushed slightly as she heard the unfamiliar title. She said, still anxiously, "You are sure of that?"

"I am positive," he said. "One does not succumb to a flesh wound unless infection sets in, and I have cauterized the wound. I wonder who it was shot at him. A great shame, this riot. These Evangelicals—fanaticism rampant." He gave Rachel a concerned look. "You must rest, you know. You have another performance, I understand."

"No, there will not be another performance," she said. "As I am sure you know, the theater has been closed for a week, while the chandeliers are replaced and the flooring mended. There was considerable damage, as you know."

"That is not unusual, Lady Sayre," the doctor said. "I can remember a time when Madame Catalani refused to appear. The theater was also closed for a week and the chandeliers replaced."

"I think that as soon as my husband is better, we might go to the country," Rachel said firmly. "I should like our little boy to see the estate."

The doctor's gaze was questioning, but being far too much in awe of the only marchioness he had ever met, he did not dare question her as to the meaning behind that rather odd statement. A few minutes later he took his leave and Rachel resumed her seat beside Gervais's bed. She put a gentle hand on his forehead and was pleased it did not seem so hot. She wished that he would wake. She had so much to tell him.

"Hurry and be better, my darling," she whispered, and shivered slightly as she thought of the shot that had gone awry. If that burly Bow Street Runner had not made his move before the Marquess of Dorne could take better aim, Gervais would have been dead. As it was, the Runner, who had been summoned to help quell the riot, had saved Gervais's life. He had also arrested the marquess, who was in prison awaiting trial on a charge of attempted murder.

Why had he tried to kill Gervais? she wondered. And why had he urged Samantha to instigate the riot? She herself had two answers to that latter question.

One, he had never forgiven her for the blow on his head that had frustrated his fell intentions, and two, he had intended to use the riot as a blind while he shot Gervais. Two boys, who had also been arrested, had laid information against the marquess, saying that he had hired them to kill her husband. She shuddered and leaned over the bed of the man she had treated so badly and who, she realized, had never stopped loving her.

"And I have never stopped loving you," she confessed. "Will you ever forgive me for my blind pride, my dearest love?"

But of course he had forgiven her; his every broken word was proof of that. She bent over his bed and brushed back a lock of hair that had strayed toward his eyes. "Wake, my love, wake soon, that I may tell you how much I love you."

Toward evening, Gervais opened his eyes. He moved restlessly, remembering now that he had been hurt, remembering bits and pieces of a conversation that had seemed to seep into his mind—from where, he did not know, but he had recognized a voice, a woman's voice.

"Rachel," he murmured.

"Gervais," came the quick response. "Oh, at last you are awake."

He started to sit up, and then groaned at a pain in his shoulder. A gentle but determined hand pushed him down against his pillows. "You must lie still," insisted the voice that was Rachel's.

He turned his head toward the sound and saw her, a dim shape in the twilight. "You *are* here," he said wonderingly. He sighed and shook his head. "I must be dreaming."

"No, you have been dreaming for the greater part of the day, but you are awake now," she assured him softly.

"But you are here," he whispered. "You would not be here. You went away."

"I have returned, my love," she said, "and here will stay, if you wish."

"If *I* wish. If I had my wish, you would stay with me forever, but you are an artist."

"No," she said. "I am your wife. And I beg you will forgive me for the past. I did not understand anything."

"It was my fault, my love," he said. "All mine . . . and I want you to know that whatever has happened in the years you have been away from me does not matter to me. The little lad. I will give him my name. I—"

He was silenced by her hand over his mouth. "Your son will appreciate your name, my dearest, for surely he comes by it honestly enough."

He stared up at her. "You are telling me . . ."

"I am telling you that his mother's been with no man save her husband," she said firmly. "You will believe me when you look into his eyes."

"Oh, Rachel," he said brokenly, "I believe you now." With his good arm he reached up to bring her face down against his.

L'envoi

"My first question was going to be, have you ever regretted leaving the opera?" Anne-Marie said as she walked with Rachel in the gardens of the Hold. She, her husband, and their two children had just returned from an extended stay in New Orleans, whence they had gone to visit Victor and the beautiful young singer he had recently married. "But"—she gazed at the gardens that Rachel had just announced were her pride and joy—"I am inclined to believe that you do not miss it."

"Not for one moment of those that have gone to make up the last four years," Rachel said softly. "I still sing for our friends, of course." She smiled at Anne-Marie. "Despite Gervais's Aunt Lily's croakings that I would never be accepted by the *ton* again, there are few who can resist my husband's charm."

"You are too modest," Anne-Marie chided, "and you have never looked more beautiful, my darling."

"You can say that at this time?" Rachel demanded incredulously.

"These fuller styles hide your figure—but nothing hides your face. Motherhood becomes you. What do you wish for this time? A daughter or a son?"

"Paul insists that he does not want another girl, and of course Marianne, at three, does not want a brother, since Paul teases her so. Mark agrees with Paul, and Gervais says he will leave it up to God."

Anne-Marie laughed. "That is very wise." She added, "I see that Mark is still with you. Will he remain here?"

"I wish my letters had not gone astray," Rachel

complained. "I can see you know very little about anything."

"I did hear that the Marquess of Dorne shot himself," Anne-Marie said. "I read it in the American newspapers."

Rachel said soberly, "Yes, just after he was released from prison. They could not keep him very long, but still he was disgraced. He could not face it."

"Once a coward, always a coward," Anne-Marie said contemptuously. "But you've not explained about Mark."

"He will be with us only until Papa returns from the Grand Tour, which will be soon. In his last letter, which came to us from Vienna, he writes that he cannot bear Austria and adds that no country pleases him as much as England."

"I expect Samantha is still living with her parents?"

"Yes, Papa refuses to have her back."

"She should have been imprisoned, instigating that riot!" Anne-Marie said roundly. "Is her leg any better?"

"The breaks have healed, but she cannot walk without a cane. She walks very little. She's a confirmed invalid—that is why she does not want Mark with her—not that Papa would allow it, even if she did."

"I expect one must feel sorry for her." Anne-Marie grimaced.

"I am extremely grateful to her, and to the late marquess as well." Rachel smiled.

"And why would that be, my love?" Gervais inquired, stepping around a large oak.

Rachel gave him a startled look. "Were you behind that tree all this while?" she demanded indignantly.

"I cannot deny it."

"You know the fate of eavesdroppers."

"I've not suffered it." He put his arm around Rachel's waist. "I repeat, why are you grateful to Samantha and Dorne?"

"You know very well why. Will you make me repeat it?"

"Yes." He winked at Anne-Marie. "And I am sure that our guest would like to hear those reasons too."

"But I know them," Anne-Marie said gaily. " 'Tis the silver lining to the proverbial gray cloud."

"I would still like to hear you repeat it," Gervais insisted.

"Because, my one and only love, had it not been for the riot which nearly put period to your existence, we would not be back together again. Are you satisfied?"

"Entirely and forever," he said fervently. He might have said much more, had not little Marianne come rushing up to her mother, weeping loudly. "Mama . . . Mama!"

Rachel knelt and put her arms around the child, smoothing back her tangled red locks. "What is the matter, my love?"

"M-Mark and P-Paul say there's a ghost in the t-tower 'n I went 'n disturbed her and now she'll come 'n chase me!"

"What ghost is that, my love?" Anne-Marie inquired.

"The g-ghost of Red L-Lizzie," Marianne sobbed. She directed a beseeching look at her mother. "She will not come after me, will she, Mama?"

"You do not need to be afraid." Rachel stroked the child's hair. "That ghost is long laid, and besides, she would never have hurt you. She only hurt herself."

"Why was that, Mama?" the child demanded.

"Because . . ." Rachel ceased to look at Marianne. She stared into space, saying slowly, "I think that Red Lizzie might have been confused and misinformed and led astray by those who were jealous of her. Yes, I am rather sure of that."

"As am I," Gervais said.

"Poor ghost," the little girl said. "To fall such a very long way!"

"You need not pity her, my dearest. All her wounds are healed at last." Rachel assured her, and on Gervais's helping her to her feet, she brushed his cheek with her lips.